The Cemetery

The Cemetery

A Novel

Zeka Brü

Literary Works Specialist

Requests for permission to make copies in any form of any part of this publication in whole or in part should be mailed to:

Permissions
Literary Works Specialist, LLC
10001 Lake Forest Blvd, #507
New Orleans, LA 70127

Cover design by Cory Domio
@domiofactory

Published in the United States by
Literary Works Specialist, LLC.
10001 Lake Forest Blvd, #507
New Orleans, LA 70127
www.lwspublishing.com
Literary Works Specialist is a registered
tradename with the State of Louisiana.

Printed and bound in the United States of America
1 2 3 4 5 6 7 8 9 0

ISBN-13: 978-0-9746687-7-2
ISBN-10: 0-9746687-7-X

Acknowledgements

Thank you, God, for providing me with the energy to complete this work. Thank you to all of my supportive family and friends who provided me with constant motivation and encouragement. I thank my parents Joseph & Barbara Broussard for *always* showing me love and support. I thank my sister and brothers Pamela Blanche, Travis Arceneaux and James Arceneaux, my niece Brionne Blanche and my cousins Dana Arceneaux and Rayvin Chevalier for their positive vibes and input. A special thank you to my life-long friend Constance "Connie" Arceneaux who always bragged that I would finish this book.

And please know that I could not have completed this work without my personal "Dream Team" who always believed in me and who put up with months of my aggravation for them to provide feedback and complete a pre-read within a very short period of time. This team of amazing individuals pushed me to my limits and I know I could not have produced this book without them. They are none other than my cover artist on deck who helped to capture a deeper meaning of this novel with his talented and amazing book cover work, my son, Cory Domio; my social butterfly mini-me and social network guru, my daughter, Alana Broussard; my super smart (in my bias opinion) four-year-old son, Jadon Broussard, who allowed me to work on this novel and sacrificed months of baby and me time; my sweet and honest friend, Tyra Smith; my ride or die, ace in the hole, more like a sister than a cousin, actress in her own right, Tiffany McZeal; my niece who, in my opinion, can give the best commentary on the events in the book (I'm sure you'll get to meet her in a blog or somewhere) Tranise Arceneaux; and of course the man who has been my emotional backbone, my loving dear friend and beyond, Franklin Thomas.

... *"Blame it on my mind, not my heart"*

"When the characters take over, the only thing you can do is let them live."

Zeka   Brü

Chapter 1

Two more hours left on the road. It felt like the drive to Mintly, Texas would never end. It's a good thing I invested in one of those car seat massages. I used it mostly to help me stay awake than for back pain. Every time I filled up the gas tank, I also purchased a hot French Vanilla Cappuccino. It wasn't my usual custom coffee since it poured out from an automatic machine, but it made do. I didn't like drinking it while it was hot because it burned my tongue, so I first held onto the drink for about 30 minutes. My method involved gently blowing it to cool it off before I tasted the smooth creamy filler. This process helped me stay awake during my drive because I despised the thought of hot coffee spilling all over me. I purposely held it instead of placing the cup in the cup-holder as part of my strategy to stay awake while on the road.

Besides the coffee strategy, I had a little help staying awake with the phone ringing a million times. My mother devotedly called me 13 times since I had left home. Before I left, she did warn me about the calls she would make. She claimed she would ring my phone every hour on the hour. She kept her promise and called twice as much. As nagging as the phone calls were with the same questions being asked, I did appreciate my mother making sure I was up and safe. Each conversation started off with, "Hey baby. How's it going? Are you making it ok?" I answered her, "Yes Ma," each time.

The past few years in New Orleans had been a never-ending nightmare. The most disheartening struggle I dealt with was the break-up of my three-year engagement to the guy I knew was the man of my dreams. We had planned out our whole life together. We knew where we were getting married, the colors of our wedding, our kids names, house plan dreams and even where we wanted to be buried. Naively, I believed every story he delivered. The only smart move I made during that relationship was not giving up my home to move in with him.

It still feels like yesterday when I made the mistake of showing up at his house unannounced. I never had the need to announce my visits but I usually gave him the courtesy of asking if he needed anything before I stopped by and he treated me with the same respect. It was mid-morning on a Saturday and I had just freshened up after leaving the gym. I baked his favorite peach cobbler, wrapped it in a cute wicker picnic basket accompanied with white wine and drove over to his house. There was nothing unusual about the visit when I drove up. His car was home parked in its dedicated location and I could see the television showing a sports commercial. I held the basket with one arm and rang the doorbell waiting to see his handsome smile greet me and seal it with a kiss.

I saw a shadow approach the door and instead of Ralph, who was it? It was a little girl around five-years old who opened the door to greet me.

My inner emotions stood out like a surprised crowd watching a magic trick. "Hello, what's your name precious," thinking this was his niece whom he mentioned to me before.

"My name is Darla. Are you here to see my dad?"

"You said your dad?"

"Well, his name is Raphael but everybody calls him Ralph. I call him dad."

"I see. And where is your dad?"

"He's here. Him and my mom are in the kitchen putting up the groceries. We just got back from the grocery store. Me and my mom just got back from her tour in Europe and dad didn't have any snacks over here. Hey, are you the lady in the pictures on my dad's phone?"

I didn't know how to answer her question because I wasn't sure which pictures she was referencing.

"I guess I am." I heard Ralph come to the door and the expression on his face was even more surprised than the one I had when his daughter introduced herself.

He grabbed the basket from my arms and quickly placed it on the floor next to the door. "Come in Gretchen and have a seat. I see you've met my daughter." His actions were calm yet jittery. This was the first time in two years that I heard him call me by my birth name. He had conditioned me into answering only to 'Lovely'. As I watched him and his daughter interact on the sofa, I noticed a blurred figure come visible in my peripheral vision.

She was a slim ill-figured woman. "Hello," she spoke with a British accent. "I'm Ralph's wife, Mrs. Cooper." She awkwardly stretched out her left hand to greet me. When I responded with my left hand, she immediately turned it over, pointed to my ring and said, "I see that someone has made you a lucky woman."

Quickly pulling my hand back and maintaining my composure I replied, "No, not really. Unfortunately, he is already married."

"Married?" She looked perplexed about my response to her comment.

"Married." I motioned my eyes to the ring on her finger noticing that she also followed the same path and looked at her hand.

The house became intensely quiet. I don't think the volume from the television was even heard. I walked over to the door, picked up the basket and Darla was following me hoping that I would leave her a surprise. I felt her innocence and decided to leave her with the basket. I removed the wine and placed the handle of the picnic basket onto Darla's small arms. "Here you go sweetie."

"Thank you so much," she excitedly exclaimed running towards her parents. I closed the door behind me to the house while Ralph and his wife sat motionless on the sofa. I politely drove off numb to my true feelings. Ralph tried calling me a few hours later. I didn't answer any of his calls. The last message I listened to was the one telling me to keep the engagement ring. I had already stopped at the post office and put it in the mail shipping it straight to his house. After I went home and cried for hours, I called my mother to tell her everything that happened.

"I knew I didn't trust that bastard." My mother's tone sounded as if she was ready to proclaim every single horrible deed she knew about Ralph. "Listen baby, that man will get what is coming to him. Think of it as a direct blessing from Jesus Christ himself that you didn't go as far as to marry that worthless piece of shit."

It took me a couple of cases of bottles of wine each month to get over the pain but eventually it got to a point where Ralph no longer crossed my mind. I had deleted every picture of us from social media and from my phone. Aside from my personal relationship going downhill, I got bypassed at my job for two promotions to people who didn't have any experience at all. Lucky for them, their parents golfed with the president of the company. After I found out that they were making six figures and I was still making half their salary despite the fact that I was bringing in more clients than any other sports agent, I knew I needed a fresh start from everything. So, I put all my trust in

God and made a move to a whole new city where I could re-do my life so to speak.

I had spent all day tidying up personal business and closing on the sale of my home in New Orleans before I got on the road. I was glad that it actually took place before I left town because it had already been pushed back three times. I was initially going to let my mother take care of everything for me. I had given her power of attorney to handle my business but then she fell sick. She hated that she had to back out on helping me but I understood. Since I didn't have anyone else I could count on, I was going to have to make a special flight back just for the closing. It wasn't until 10:30 at night when I finally decided that anything not handled yet would have to wait until I came back to visit. Of course, my mother didn't agree with me leaving at such a late hour, but she knew how important this new job interview was for me the next day. Needless to say, we were both up all night. I drove all night and my mother called me all night. By the time I pulled up in front of my new home I only had about 45 minutes left to get dressed and rush to the interview.

It was past time for a change in my life and I was more than ready. I loved New Orleans, but it was time to move on where I could become more successful without all of the political limitations. I had visited numerous cities before finally deciding on Mintly, Texas. I was determined to either land a position at a sports agent firm or open an office and work independently. This was one of the most progressive cities I had found. The real estate was also affordably priced, so I was able to secure a deal on a cute brownstone looking home which had a garage to the side. The realtor had arranged for me to complete the entire closing through a live feed online. I had already assigned someone to represent me at the sale during my last visit, so everything flowed smoothly. The neighborhood homeowner's association included lawn service. The property did not have much of a yard but there was room for landscaped flowers in the front including built-in flower pots lining the stairs to the entrance. I parked in front and grabbed my bag from the front passenger seat which I had prepared ahead of time. I didn't bother parking in the garage first because I didn't have any time to spare. I anticipated this would happen, so I made sure I had packed exactly what I needed to change quickly. I took a deep breath which was the result of a mixture of relief from being off the road and taking in the thought of having an interview with the Koperneil Firm. This firm was always listed on the Forbes top list of successful sports agent firms.

After getting the keys out of the lockbox, I took a quick look around and I was even more in love with the place than the time I had flown to Mintly for a personal walk-through. The realtor who worked with me was the absolute best. She made sure the home was picture perfect when I arrived. She hired an interior decorator to have everything in order. Natalie, the interior decorator, met all of my needs and then some. When I walked in, I was greeted with sweet Jasmine incense. Natalie made sure the smooth gray microfiber sectional was positioned to provide comfort while watching television and it didn't interfere with the walk space. A fluffy faux cobalt throw draped the corner of the sectional and it was complimented by a vase set on the coffee table adorned with fresh blue orchids. The kitchen counter was clear of cluttered lagniappe appliances. The counter displayed only a stainless-steel toaster with four slots, a knife set with powdered blue handles and a set of oven mittens next to a displayed cake decorating book set on a book holder. I didn't have time to do a complete walk-through and absorb the whole set-up, but I was in love with the master bathroom when I walked in. The place was welcoming clean and complimented with fresh towels and toiletries. Natalie left everything I needed to pamper myself. As I rushed to get ready, my thoughts were in disbelief that I took a chance on life and made the move to Mintly.

Mintly is a mid-sized city with a mix of bustling businesses in the central business district filled with top class brokers and live country bands at local restaurants. I preferred rhythm and blues so when visiting Mintly before making the decision to move I frequently found myself at a place called Jazzes. I enjoyed the live mellow music because it reminded me of home. It is a modern styled restaurant with a cozy downhome feel to it. Nothing too fancy. If you want to find some real good soul food, this is the place to be. I learned it was the happening spot for business professionals to mingle and unwind on Friday nights. It is where I met my close friend Carl.

Carl is a free spirit. He doesn't take life seriously, yet he is a serious person. Carl knew just about everyone in town because a lot of people used his services.

One thing about the people of Mintly, they believed in going to the psychiatrist. They didn't look at it as a service for someone with a problem. They treated going to the psychiatrist like a necessary health check up with a doctor. Carl was a well-known psychiatrist in town with clients from high social statuses. There were still some people who refused to go to Carl simply because he was homosexual.

Since I was in a rush to get ready for this interview, I decided to put some of my military training to use. I took one of those quick, but thorough, military showers. My skin soaked up the moisture from the lemon-scented lotion which Natalie had in a cute welcome home gift box. I continued to rush, dressed, touched up my face with a little make-up, pinned up my locks in a bun and dashed out the door. I managed to have a few extra minutes, so I decided to stop by Han's Café for a quick pick-me-up latte. After drinking all those French Vanilla Cappuccinos, my caffeine sugar rush was starting to come down. I parked at a meter across the street and ran in hoping I wouldn't get a ticket. I kept all of my loose change at the bottom of my purse and I knew I didn't have time to dig in the clutter to find a few dimes. On my way back to the car, I noticed a young boy putting some change in my meter. He looked like he was only nine or ten years old. I remember thinking to myself, "*What a kind young boy.*"

"Good morning young man. Thank you for putting money in the meter for me."

"My name is Miles." He rushed to stretch out his little hand to greet me. I graciously accepted his handshake and while pulling my hand back, I noticed he was wearing a stringed bracelet with a black rugged glistening piece of rock clamped inside of crossed wiring. "I'm working on this project right here." Miles pointed to the vacant land right beyond where my car was parked across the street from Han's. It was filled with tall trees. He could see my confusion by the look on my face.

He quickly explained, "Oh, it's not what it looks like. You'll see."

I didn't quite know how to respond. I wanted to ask more questions, but I knew I had to get to this interview. "It was nice meeting you Miles. My name is Gretchen. I hope to see you around, so I can repay you for your kindness with the meter."

"Oh, you will, Ms. Gretchen. You will." Miles rode off on his bike in the opposite direction of where I was going. His large curls bounced freely as he pumped the pedals of his squeaky bicycle. I got in my car, turned to glance at the forested piece of land and peered through my rearview mirror adjusting it up and down but Miles was nowhere in sight.

I arrived and parked in front of the Koperneil Firm, turned off the ignition, took a deep breath, bowed my head and said a quick prayer for God to bless me with this position. Nervous butterflies made attempts to flutter their wings in the pit of my gut but my well-defined confidence won the battle. I walked through the lobby and found my way straight to the receptionist. She greeted me by name. It was odd because I hadn't introduced myself yet. The secretary directed me to the conference room where the interview was to be held.

The chair was oddly positioned low to the floor where my knees were cramped at a slant. I felt for the levers and adjusted it to a comfortable height. Seeing the reflection of my own appearance through the windows, I straightened up my posture in the chair waiting for someone to walk in. I heard the door open from behind me and there he was, Mr. Koperneil. He was dressed in a crisp button-down shirt with slacks. He walked to the other side of the table without saying a single word, placed both of his hands on the table, leaned forward without even sitting down and said in a solid voice, "Gretchen Hall. There is no need in wasting either of our time here with the entire interview lingo. I have read great things about you in the sports world. My wife made it a point to share every article about your success with me. As a matter of fact, it was her idea to bring you aboard. She is one of your biggest fans. You have sealed some fundamentally impressive endorsement contracts. I especially appreciate how you quickly accepted the invitation to join our firm. I also like how you have been volunteering your time on your visits to Mintly with our youth at the Sports Community Center. With all that being said, let me just get to the point. We have already reached a decision here at Koperneil Firm and welcome you aboard." He lengthened his arm to extend his hand in congratulations across the highly glossed wood table with his head a tad tilted. "That's if you still want the position."

A chill of fright and thrill charged through my body all at the same time. I stood up, composed myself and reached back to firmly shake his hand and graciously accepted the job offer.

"Well done then. First, let me buzz in one of our top sports agents here at the firm." Mr. Koperneil pressed the intercom button. A guy's voice answered on the other end. "Lance here." Mr. Koperneil responded, "Hi there Lance, come on over to the conference room for a quick second so I can introduce you to Ms. Gretchen here." The guy walked in with a clean professional look and well-built arms. Mr. Koperneil introduced us. "Gretchen, this is Lance Davidson. He is a lead sports agent here and also a mentor to nearly every agent working here."

I stood up to shake his hand. "Gretchen Hall, it is a pleasure to meet you."

He had an attractive demeanor which was welcoming but I also noticed he sported a shiny diamond wedding band, so I maintained a professional face. "I am glad we have you aboard Gretchen," He projected a gentle smile. "I look forward to working with you. You won't regret joining this firm because we are on a progressive move towards the top. I hate to rush out like this, but I have an important meeting in a few minutes."

"No worries," Mr. Koperniel partly sang as he walked with Lance to the door. "You two will have plenty of time to catch up on everything later. You just sit tight Gretchen. My secretary, Ms. Bernette, will come in with the paperwork for you to fill out. You can complete it here or return it when you report for your first day on Monday. I know you have been traveling and I want you to have a few days to get acclimated."

"Wow. Mr. Koperneil. Thank you so much. I will not let you down."

"I know you won't Gretchen. See you Monday morning at 9 a.m. sharp."

"Yes sir. 9 a.m. sharp. I will be here."

Mr. Koperneil gave me a gentle smile as he walked out of the conference room and glanced at his watch before he quietly pulled the door behind him. A few minutes later, Ms. Bernette walked in with the paperwork. She was a middle-aged woman with a jazzed-up hairstyle with highlights. She had an interesting vintage preppy style of dress. She set the neatly packaged paperwork which was in a custom binder. With the binder staring back at me from the table I felt across its embossed cover. "Don't worry honey." Her movements were fidgety, and she never looked me in the face. She rambled to the air while she picked up the untouched glasses of water from the table with an intriguing Texas twang. "Everything here seems fancy but the people at the firm are simply plain downhome folks. We love to throw office parties and let me tell 'ya honey, those parties are always a hit and filled with everyone in town."

Her voice suddenly changed as if she were auditioning for an old Hollywood movie and she started prancing around the conference room twisting from side to side. "I reckon folks simply enjoy mingling with celebrities. Oh, and I'm not talking about these big shots from this firm. I'm talking about real live celebrities out there in the real world. The athletes we endorse normally attend but then there are also the famous singers and bands. I hope you like having fun Ms. Gretchen because although this firm has some of the hardest working agents, we also believe in celebrating equally as much."

She rattled this silly giggle and cleared her throat. "Maybe I shouldn't tell you this but what difference does it make, you'll hear about it anyway."

I was lost because I had no clue what kind of office activity she was going to spill now. She put the glasses back down on the table, pulled out the leather rolling chair right next to me, sat down, looked me straight in the eye and whispered, "Do you see how fit Mr. Koperneil is?" My head impulsively nodded yes. It was pretty obvious he loved to exercise. "Now as fine as that fifty-one-year-old man is do you know there is a rumor Mrs. Koperneil has the audacity to cheat on her husband with clients from companies doing contracts with this firm?" She shook her head in disappointment and continued on her whispering rampage. "Honestly, she is lucky he even married her. I had been working with Mr. Koperneil for a few years before they got married and let me tell you he was nowhere near the marrying type. Now, don't get me wrong, he wasn't a player or anything. (She turned and winked at me with a smirk). He made a conscious choice never to fall in love. That is until he met Ms. Gabriella Trent. That's her maiden name. Oh honey, she came in town and wooed him with her cooking. I guess a single man couldn't resist a good home-cooked meal. Now she is about five years younger than him, but you wouldn't know it by looking at them. Even today I don't think you can tell the age difference. They have been married for twenty-one years now and Mr. Koperneil feverishly adores that woman. He is always having me send her flowers and gifts. Plus, he is a great ...(ahem)...father. They have four extremely respectful children. The youngest is five and the oldest just made her sweet sixteen. I forget the ages of the two in the middle. I'm sure you'll meet them soon. They visit the office pretty often. As devoted a husband and father as he is, I never could understand why Mrs. Koperneil would stoop so low and degrade herself and her family. Some people think she does it to help her husband's firm seal contract deals, but others rumor she is transparently a pure slut who hides behind her church Sunday homemade apple pies she bakes for service every week. Any outsider who doesn't know better would judge from a first impression of her that she is a pillar of the church community. She keeps up with all the church meetings, volunteers for community service with the church, sings in the choir, and bakes those sweet apple pies every Sunday morning. (*mmm mmm*). But to be honest, it does not make any difference to me who she is in her own personal life because she always welcomes me to their home for holiday meals. I enjoy her cooking and hospitality."

Then she gets up, grabs the glasses of water again and delivered her disclaimer. "Ok honey. I know I gave you an ear full but secretly keep all this juicy information between me and you." She winks one eye and exits the conference room leaving me in awe with my mind slipping in and out of consciousness replaying everything that just happened.

I immediately pulled my phone out of my purse and sent a quick text to Carl. "Lunch on me. Meet me at Jazzes around one." I had so much to tell Carl already about my morning.

I left the firm with my new hire packet in hand, rushed in my car and called my mom. She answered on the first ring. I knew she would be waiting for my call. "Guess what mom?" I tried to make my voice sound like I was disappointed so she wouldn't be able to detect my excitement.

"Please tell me you got the job." I could hear the pain in my mother's voice. I could tell she was worried.

"Yep, I sure did." I glanced over to the hire packet on my front passenger seat and tapped it like I was comforting a good friend.

My mother let out a sigh of relief. "Child, you had me for a minute. I knew you would get the job baby. When do you start?"

"Monday."

"Well, that's good. Now you can settle in and get some rest. How is your new place?"

"Gorgeous. I admittedly love it. I can't wait until you visit. Your emotions will tempt you to stay here forever."

"Well now. You know me sugar. Momma is a New Orleans girl. I might visit you out there in Mintly but there is no place like home." Our laughter copied each other like a game of Simon Says.

"Mom. On my way to the interview I stopped by a coffee shop and I met this unusual kid."

"Really?" she questioned suspiciously. She did not like meeting new people. "When you say kid, exactly what do you mean?"

"Well, he looked like he was about 9 or 10. He seemed like a sweet kid because he was putting change in my meter so I wouldn't get a ticket."

"*Hmmm*. That was nice of him but be careful baby. You never know about people. He might seem nice, but he could be up to no good." My mother was always quick to think that if a person did something for you then they most likely had an angle.

"Mom. He is only a kid. But he did mention something about a project and pointed to some woods."

"You see what I mean?" laughing as though she knew she was right.

"Yeah, it was a little weird. Now that I've thought about it, I've seen that kid before around the sports community center. I never see him being active with the other kids. He is always off to the side by himself writing in a notebook."

We both got a little quiet on the phone. "Ok mom, I will call you later. I'm about to get ready to meet Carl for lunch."

"Ok baby, love you."

"Love you too mom."

The day was gorgeous. There was not a single cloud in the sky and there was a hint of breeze blowing. It was the perfect day to ride with the windows down and the sunroof opened. I had a little time to spare before my lunch date, so I drove around Mintly taking in the sites. It almost felt like I was in paradise. The only thing missing for me was a nice clear blue water beach with white sand to sink my toes in. There was Bluewater Lake on the east side of town which sort of made up for not having a beach. The water was perfect for sailing. It kind of reminded me of Lake Pontchartrain back home but here the water was crystal blue and clear. Standing on the walkways near the banks you could see straight through the sparkling reflections of the sun which bounced off the waves like diamonds.

Lunch was right on time because I hadn't eaten all day and I was starving for a good meal. I met Carl out front, we exchanged our greeting smooches, went in and sat at our usual booth.

Carl mocked, "Soooo, how did it go?" I could tell he already knew my response to the question because I was having a tough time hiding the broad smile from my face.

"You already know Carl. I got the job."

"Yes," Carl whispered excitingly as he gave me a quiet high five.

"But listen Carl. That secretary. She is something else. She was spilling all the tea about Mrs. Koperneil."

"Yea honey I bet she was. I hope you can see right through all of her craziness. Don't believe everything she says. I can tell you some unbelievable stories. I'm surprised she is still working there. But then again, I know why she is working there but that is a whole other conversation for a whole other time. Let's talk about you sweetheart. How do you feel? Are you excited?" I could see Carl was excited for me and it made my day even more special.

"I am elated. I just can't believe this is all happening. It's been a long time coming and I can't wait to get started Monday morning."

"I was about to ask you when you start. So that's good. Now you have a few days to relax and get your mind ready for those big clients I know you will attract."

I giggled. Carl could say some of the most encouraging things. Then I thought about the young boy. I whispered to Carl from across the booth so eavesdroppers wouldn't hear our conversation. "But Carl, there was this young kid this morning who showed up out of nowhere. I think I've seen him before at the center, but he was across the street from the café and he put money in my parking meter. Then when I approached him, he said something about a project and pointed to the piece of vacant land with all the trees. It was a little weird."

Carl knew exactly who I was talking about. "Is he the sort of white but tanned kid with large brown curls?"

"Yep, that sounds like him."

"Yeah," Carl continued. "He is a little on the weird side. I heard him tell another kid he was going to build this massive project. I'm like to myself, yeah right, that's a bunch of dookie."

"Dookie?" I laughed hysterically.

"Yeah, that's right? What's so funny?" Carl looked at me a little offended.

"I mean if you want to use a curse word why don't you just say it?"

"Shhh." Carl was hushing me with one hand and holding his head down in embarrassment. "People out here don't curse."

"What do you mean?" At this point I'm confused.

"I mean they never use vulgar language. I slipped and said the 's' word in the grocery store when I couldn't find the kitchen bouquet and the people on the same isle with me looked at me like I committed a crime."

"Are you serious? You can't be serious." I was in disbelief.

"I'm dead serious honey. You don't believe me? Then curse right now."

"No."

"Go ahead. What? Are you scared?" Carl had now entered my dare zone. I would never let someone win over a dare.

"No, I'm not scared one bit." I built up the confidence in my posture and tone. "As matter of fact," I started to speak a tad bit louder with a smirk on my face. "I'm not scared of shit."

The waitress passing by dropped a plate. For a split second everyone in the restaurant looked our way.

Carl motioned for me to look around. "Do you see what I mean? Everyone is looking at you now."

"No Carl, the only reason they looked in our direction is because the lady dropped the plate."

Carl thought about it for a second. "Maybe....maybe not."

We both laughed but honestly, I didn't know what to believe.

Chapter 2

A few weeks passed by and I reached a point of being consistent with my daily morning routine. Being an avid jogger was no longer an unreachable goal. I used a tracking app to determine the perfect route for completing a full five miles. Running was never a real issue for me but finding the time was the actual challenge. I started jogging when I was living back home in New Orleans. It took me a few years to get up to five miles, but I was finally comfortable with the distance. Participating in charity runs played a role in my five-mile success. When I first started, I was the last runner. After understanding that training was a necessary component in conditioning my body, I set a schedule for myself and drastically improved my time with each race. The early morning jogs were the best time for me to maintain my exercise routine because of my demanding work schedule and somewhat social life. As lovely as the weather conditions were in Mintly the majority of the time, there were times when the fog created horrible visibility issues. The jogging path was located close to the lake which explained some of the fog conditions. The fog didn't bother me one bit. It was welcoming since it meant fewer people would be out exercising. On clear days, things could get a little crowded in the outdoor exercise world. You could easily find enthusiastic looking moms vigorously pushing their babies in strollers with the oversized wheels. Some folks walked briskly swinging their arms from side to side with extra force and others jogged with their chest out and shoulders back looking like they were in competition with themselves. Lucky for me, today was one of the foggy days so I didn't have to be concerned about too many people on the path. I guess people didn't like the idea of not seeing where they were going.

My new sports shirt felt comfortable during my run. It had a snug fit but didn't keep rising like some of my other shirts. Sometimes I spent more time pulling down my shirt in the back than concentrating on my run. The mood was perfect. Not many people were out, the temperature was around sixty-eight degrees and I was in a relaxed state of mind. I was at a steady pace and absorbed in my own zone. I had reached a point where I didn't have to think about which turn was coming up next or how long I had left to go. I was on auto pilot. It left me with time to clear my mind and concentrate only on how I would convince Mr. Koperneil to let me handle the upcoming endorsement contract for one of the top hockey players. I was zoned out to the point where I was blinded by my fancy of how everything would play out at work. I undisputedly could not see. It was like I was daydreaming while running. My eyes were wide opened, but my sight was sheltered from reality. I could only see Mr. Koperneil shaking my hand congratulating me on landing the contract and telling me I qualified for the promotional bonus. Except, my vision didn't quite make it to the bonus part because right when Mr. Koperneil smiled and said you will now receive the bo- I tripped over this old man. I didn't get to hear the actual word bonus. I snapped out of my zone entirely confused until I realized what I had done. The poor old man was using his walking cane and I didn't see him or his cane. My foot hit his jagged wood apparatus knocking it from his steady grip. The cane jerked from the ground and the old man was going right along with it. At this point, the next few seconds seemed to move in slow motion. All I saw was the cane going up in the air and the old man trying to reach for it while he was losing his balance. Luckily for him, his caregiver caught him before he hit the solid pavement. She gave me a furious looking snare and rolled her eyes in disgust. It was an awful expression plus she scorned at me like she was my elder. "What kind of person are you? Why would you clumsily run into him like that?"

I tried to apologize but she wasn't having it. For a split second I almost told the little girl that she'd better watch her tone, but I felt horrible and ashamed about what I had done. She didn't look a day above 20 and she made me feel like I was some bad kid blindly running around being mischievous. I was turning thirty-three this year. I'm the true adult not her. A few other people passed by and angrily glared at me as if I purposely ran into the old man. Part of me couldn't understand why she had him out of the house so early with it being immeasurably foggy in the first place but who was I to judge.

I kept jogging and reached the vacant land across the street from Han's Café. I thought back to the brief conversation Miles and I first had on the day near the meter. I peered at the forested land and it seemed like it was pulling me in, but I was still on the sidewalk. I couldn't help but wonder what kind of project Miles was up to. I was determined to find out. My imagination ran wild about this project. Thoughts about what it was consumed my mind the entire time I got ready for work. However, my thoughts switched gears when I started thinking about the bonus again. Today was my day.

When I walked in my office at work the walls were lined with congratulations balloons and flowers. Before I could pick up the first card to read it Mr. Koperneil walked in. "Congrats Gretch! You did it. You have the contract and the bonus."

"Yes," quietly shouting giving myself a victorious pull-down fist jester. I needed the bonus. I had used all my savings to buy my new home when I moved to Mintly and there was a cruise I promised my mother to Brazil. My mother dreamed about going to Brazil all the time. She said that is where my great-grandmother was from, but she never visited.

"Ok Gretch, I'm headed to my doctor's appointment. You enjoy the rest of your day." Mr. Koperneil often talked about having a doctor's appointment. After hearing about these frequent doctor appointments, I mustered up the courage to ask Mr. Koperneil if he had any health problems because he always talked about going to the doctor, but he looked so healthy from the outside. He kindly explained that Dr. Carl Granger was their family psychiatrist. He said his family went to a psychiatrist on a routine basis. He compared going to the psychiatrist with getting a massage. It leaves you in a relaxed state of mind knowing you are able to relieve some stress. Mr. Koperneil believed that talking about what was going on in his life helped him to focus on growing as a person and he claimed it played a major role in his success. I asked him why he didn't just talk about things with his close friends or his wife. Mr. Koperneil looked at me as if I were some little naïve child who had a lot to learn and he said there are some things your close friends and even your wife will not have an unbiased opinion about and those are the things that will shape you into being your true self.

I spent the rest of the work day communicating with my client and setting up meetings with the producers and networks. After work, I stopped home and changed before heading to the Sports Community Center. I was now a full-time evening volunteer at the center. The kids were involved in all types of sports. I started mentoring at the community center shortly after I first moved to Mintly. I had an appreciation for sports and I felt that playing sports served as a useful tool in building character in individuals, especially children. I was assigned to a small group of kids who needed a little more motivation than others when it came time to physically playing sports. After seeing their natural abilities clearly were not enough for sports, I decided to help these kids in a different aspect of sports. I figured since I was an active sports agent who traveled to designated cities recruiting athletes for endorsements, I decided to initiate a journey for the kids in my group to focus more on understanding what makes a convincing representative for a product. We studied other kids during games and made mock recommendations for what products they should endorse and why.

One of the kids who ended up in my group was the young boy Miles. He always carried around a journal. He wrote in that journal the entire time he was at the center. It did not matter if we were attending a live game or sitting at a round table for group discussion. Miles was extremely gifted. The only time he put his journal aside was when it was time to eat. Miles had what some people called a healthy appetite. He loved well-seasoned tasty food. His parents could not figure out how he could eat so much and never gain any weight. They said all the food fed his brain hence the reason why he was advanced and smart.

At the community center, Miles enjoyed holding private conversations with me about his dreams and ideas, especially his plans for the project at the empty lot. I thought it was charming the way he delighted in these intelligent conversations and voiced his opinion about what he felt was wrong with the world. Some of the things he said made me think about choices I made in my own life. I never expressed to Miles the impact his conversations had on me, but it was amazing.

I knew exactly how I would help Miles get his project financed. Carl had informed me about a broker he heard about by the name of Spencer Langley. Although Carl didn't know him personally, he was confident he could help. Everyone called him by his last name because Spencer insisted on it. Langley was a tall slim guy who always talked business. He didn't hold casual conversations. Langley was a successful broker with deep pockets and a board member of a non-profit which focused on the development of inventions by kids.

Miles was a big dreamer. He was different from the other kids. He was obsessed with his project and mentioned it to me every chance he got. The only problem was he said the project would cost more than his allowance budget. I didn't know all the details about the project, but I figured introducing his idea to Langley would be helpful. That thought proved to be fruitful because Langley immediately helped to get the financial support Miles needed through the non-profit. Langley and Miles did not meet personally but a representative from the non-profit organization came to the center to interview Miles about his project. After the interview, the representative came up to me excitingly shaking my hand. "Miles' project will be outstanding." She shaped her hands like a camera lens and pointed it towards the vacant land diagonally across from the center. "Yes, I can already see the building." Building? I thought. What exactly was Miles' project.

After the lady left, I turned to Miles and he was smiling broadly. "Miles. Exactly what did you tell the lady you were trying to make."

"Patience Ms. Gretchen. You'll see it for the Technology Fair in a few months."

Chapter 3

I woke up this morning with this weird feeling. I hate when that happens because then I spend the whole day looking for something out of the ordinary to transpire. It doesn't necessarily mean something horrible will occur. It can be anything. My mind goes crazy then I have a hard time focusing. I didn't let the feeling stop me. I got up, slipped on my sweatpants and favorite t-shirt, tied my shoe strings in a double knot and headed out the door. Even when I started my jog, something just didn't feel right. The early morning dew was sluggish and refused to move. Usually, around this time, the fog is already lifted, and I can see far ahead of where I'm jogging. Today was different. The fog was thick, and it lazily hung in my way. The chill of each molecule from the still fog hit my face on purpose with every stride I took. It felt like I was crashing its sleep. I broke through the hovering clouds hoping I would reach a clear point where I could see far enough ahead without worrying about bumping into anyone. I remembered that unfortunate incident with the old man and the cane.

I checked my watch and it was quickly approaching 6:45 a.m. I figured I needed approximately 35 minutes to get cleaned up and dressed and 20 minutes to drive and be on time for work. The fog was not letting up, so I decided to turn around and finish my jog a little early. Some days I looked forward to jogging and other days, like today, I was mechanically doing it to stay on my routine.

I hummed my short-lived military chants in my mind to stay focused on days like this. I could faintly hear this one chant inside of my head.

One mile (one mile)
No sweat (no sweat)
Two miles (two miles)
Better yet (better yet)
Three miles (three miles)
Looking good (looking good)
Looking good (looking good)
Feeling good (feeling good)
Haa haa (haa haa)
Haa ha ha (haa ha ha)
Haa haa (haa haa)
Haa ha ha (haa ha ha)

Between each stance, my ears were deafened by the strong pressure of air my lungs pumped out as I tried not to lose my momentum. It brought me back to basic training every time. I could still see my Drill Sergeant's expression when he mimicked mine because I was intensely into the song. He was one of those "I live for the military kind of people" and he looked forward to leading those songs while we ran in formation all in step the entire time. It was like 50 boots sounding like one large loud boot each time we quick marched forward. It's something about unity that makes everything work out.

I had 3 more blocks to go and I was back in my zone. I was also paying attention to make sure I would not bump into anyone. No more daydream jogging for me. When I turned the corner, it looked like some sort of figure stumbling from side to side. I couldn't make out the figure from where I was, but I still kept on running. The closer I got I noticed the figure was a man who looked like he was struggling with something. I couldn't tell what was happening until I got right up on him. When I reached for the man, he was slumped over and clinching his chest. I leaned over and touched his shoulder asking if he was alright. He slowly tilted his head up and barely gasped, "Please help." I immediately panicked because I realized it was Mr. Koperneil. I nervously took out my phone and called 911. My hand was trembling profusely, and I could barely dial those 3 digits. Mr. Koperneil was having a heart attack and all of sudden no one else seemed to be around on this busy jogging path except for me and Mr. Koperneil.

The ambulance finally arrived. Only two minutes had passed by, but it seemed like an eternity. Luckily, an ambulance was in the area. The paramedics rushed to stabilize Mr. Koperneil, asked me a few questions, placed him in the back of the ambulance and sped off with the sirens echoing against the silent air. Everything happened so fast and I was still shaken up. I didn't know what to do with myself. The first thing I could think of was to call my good friend Carl. He answered on the first ring with his usual "Good morning darling." I immediately started crying when I heard his voice. I could barely talk. I told him everything that just happened, and he said don't move, ping me and I'll come and get you. I told him I was just around the corner from my house and he could meet me there.

Keeping his promise, Carl showed up at the same time I was turning the key to unlock my door. All I could do was run to him and cry in his arms. He was so gentle. He walked me inside, covered me with a blanket, fixed me some warm tea and sat on the floor next to me while I curled on the sofa. Carl treated me like a patient. "Sit up darling and have some tea. Tell me what's bothering you." I guess being in his profession he intuitively had a knack of knowing when something was bothering people. I slowly sat up, cupped the warm tea in my hands and blankly watched the steam rise from the tea. He gently lifted my chin and convinced me with his eyes that he was concerned about my feelings. "Come on baby please talk to me. It's me."

I hadn't spoken about this since it happened, but I felt compelled to tell Carl everything. "It was late spring, and I was only seven years old. We had just started seeing commercials advertised for people to use 911 for emergencies. My grandmother made sure I knew those numbers and asked me every day what the phone number was to call if something happened. I would answer her, "911 Grandma." Well, this particular day, I happened to get out of school early. My parents and I lived with my grandmother. So, I ran from the bus stop all the way home because I was thinking about hurrying and getting to my favorite bowl of cereal. I still love Fruit Loops to this day. This was a time when there were only red, orange and yellow fruit loops. Everything changes with time, even the colors of Fruit Loops."

Carl chuckled, "Girl you sure do love Fruit Loops. I've seen you eat two large bowls back to back." Carl always tried to lighten up a low-spirited conversation. "Go on Gretch. Tell me what else happened." Carl slowly rubbed my back in circles as I finished my story.

"Anyway, I rushed in the house and there was my grandmother, on the floor. She was gasping for air and she had that same look in her eyes Mr. Koperneil had today. All I could think about was calling 911. I ran to the phone and called 911. I didn't know how to help my grandmother. I was so scared. It took forever for the ambulance to show up. They started working on her right there on the kitchen floor. By this time the neighbor came over. She touched me gently on my shoulders and led me out of my grandmother's house. I sat at the breakfast table of my neighbor's house and had my eyes fixed on the window waiting for my parents to get back home from work. The time went by so slow. Those hours at that table felt like forever. As soon as I saw the headlights to my parents' car, I ran outside to meet them. It was late at night by this time. Everything was solemnly quiet.

I asked my mother where Grandma was. She couldn't talk. She motionless sat at the kitchen table posed as if she were a statue. She wasn't moving or talking. The only way I could tell she was breathing was because her shirt was moving slowly up and down with each long exhaustive breath she took. My dad took me by my hand and sat me down on the sofa. All he said was Grandma is in a better place. (My head hung is sorrow recalling the details about everything that happened). I was only seven Carl."

By the time I finished telling Carl about my grandmother, my eyes were filled with tears waiting to fall. I always felt like it was my fault and here it was happening to me all over again. All I kept wondering was did I do everything fast enough. Could I have ran a little faster when I saw the figure in the fog? Did I dial 911 fast enough? I didn't want to think the worst for Mr. Koperneil, but I couldn't help myself.

Carl got up from the floor and sat next to me on the sofa. He didn't say anything, but his touch said more than words. That was the thing about Carl, he could say so much without saying any words at all.

I finished my tea and regrouped. I had to get myself together. I was already running late for work. Carl waited for me while I quickly showered and dressed. When I walked out of the room Carl had this shocked look on his face. He looked at me with uneasiness in his eyes. My heart was so full. I hated to ask the question, but I did it anyway.

"What's wrong Carl? What happened? Why are you looking at me as if something is wrong?"

Carl kept trying to find the right words to say but each time he started a sentence he stopped and changed the first words he wanted to use.

"Darling." Carl stood up, hung his head and started to shake his head.

I already knew he was about to give me bad news about Mr. Koperneil.

"Just tell me Carl. What happened?" At this point, I'm nearly screaming.

He started to talk but he kept covering his mouth as if he was scared the words would accidently slip out and crush me. He didn't want to hurt my feelings.

"Baby. It is straining me to tell you this, but I wouldn't be a good friend if I didn't let you know."

"What is it Carl?"

"I have some good news and some bad news."

"Ok." My nerves were starting to calm down because at least he said there was some good news.

"The good news is Mrs. Koperneil just called and wanted to let you know that Mr. Koperneil is doing fine."

"Thank you, God! Well, what is the bad news Carl?"

"You can't go to work."

"What? Why not? Did Mrs. Koperneil tell you I was fired? I knew something didn't feel right about today when I woke up. I can't believe this."

Carl rushed over to me to calm me down because I was rambling on and on about how I loved my job and I didn't want to lose it. He started rubbing my arms up and down and kept saying my name.

"Gretchen. Gretchen. Gretch."

Then he released a burst of laughter. I stopped rambling and spitefully looked at him in awe. I couldn't believe he was getting a kick out of my pain. I was having a rough morning and all he could do was laugh hysterically.

Then Carl walked me over to my full-length mirror and when I saw myself all I could do was join him in the laughter. I laughed until I started to cry. My pants had obviously shrunk and were beyond highwaters. I managed to have on one black shoe and one blue shoe. Smack dab in my private area showed up this camel toe that looked like my "sweet sweet" needed to go vegan. Plus, my pretty button-down blouse looked like the left side was fighting with the right side and the right side was winning because I clearly missed a few buttons and the right side of the shirt had me in a chokehold.

Chapter 4

It's finally Saturday. It was a wild and crazy week at work. With Mr. Koperneil being out of the office, the finance manager called four meetings to discuss the stability of "potential" contracts. What? There are way too many personal opinions thrown around without any substantial statistical support. I wish Mr. Koperneil was feeling well enough to drop in the office from time to time purely to bring some of his positive energy to the environment. There was an exhausting amount of tension the entire week and it mentally wore me down.

The only thing that kept the office partially peaceful were the motivational pep talks from Lance. The last session I attended there were at least 13 other agents at the round table. There had been buzz around the office uttering ever since Mr. Koperneil had been out a majority of the agents had been trying what they called 'new age' representation. It dealt with a lot of collaborating relationships virtually instead of in person. I personally did not see the advantage in obtaining clients using the 'new age' method and obviously from the tone Lance brought to the table, he didn't either.

He led the pep meeting on a positive note. "Good afternoon, ladies and gentlemen. I wanted to call this meeting so we could re-group and get our mojo back. I know some of you may have ideas of how you believe you should seek out new clients. Now my main purpose here is to provide you with some motivation. The thing about this business is it is built on relationships. Real relationships are built on real connections. That means in person ladies and gentlemen. In person."

Some of the people around the table were nodding in agreement and others were shaking their heads in a difference of opinion.

"Now just hear me out," he continued as he noticed everyone was not on board with what he was presenting. "How did each of you get hired at this firm? Raise your hand if it was over the phone. (No one raised their hand.) Raise your hand if you were hired through a text message. (No hands.) Ok. Now raise your hand if you joined this firm by video chatting with Mr. Koperneil. (Still no one raised their hand.) Do you see where I'm going with this? I know these clients are busy. I also know getting clients via video is a fast and what seems like a cost-effective way to obtain contracts. However, if you take a close look at the numbers of the percentages on the statistic sheet in front of you, you will see those agents who made in person negotiations have much higher returns. And ladies and gentlemen, let me tell you something else. Those relationships last longer. I will present one last scenario for you to think about before I let you all get back to work. Let's say you're at a dating party to meet the man or woman of your dreams. I'm talking about that person who you want to seriously spend the rest of your life with. Before entering the party, you have to choose one of two lines. Line one is to enter the party and meet people by video chat only and line two is to enter the party and meet people in person. Which line will you choose?" Everyone in the room was silent. Lance smiled, stood up, threw up two fingers showing the peace sign and walked out the room.

The weekend was a welcoming refresher. I still arose at the crack of dawn but at least there was the peaceful quietness of the air. The birds were chirping their sweet morning conversations and a smile slid on my face as if I understood what they were saying. My body did its usual stretching routine before pushing out of bed. The soft cushiony slippers were properly positioned so all I had to do was slide my feet in without having to get out of bed first and turning them the right way for me to put on. I washed up and went straight to the kitchen.

Hmmm. Is it too early for wine? Nope. I poured a quick glass of my favorite Moscato and took a sip. *Mmmm.* Now that's good. I grabbed two eggs out of the fridge, sautéed some chopped onions in butter and set the temperature just right for me to evenly divide my eggs in the pan and lightly scorch each side for the perfect eggs over hard. I already had the salt and cayenne pepper ready to dash a few sprinkles half-way through.

The doorbell rang. I glanced over at the door and looked at my clock on the wall. Shoot. Not again. I opened the door and there was Carl tapping his watch.

"Darling, we are going to be late. You did remember we volunteered to help set up for the annual Technology Fair at the community center, right?" Carl's New Orleans accent jumped out so hard it tickled me. It reminded me of home. He was such a cutie. Always clean, sharp and ready for anything. I'm sure it was apparent that it slipped my mind.

"But wait. Is that breakfast I smell?" Carl dashed over to the stove only to find a pan filled with onions. The eggs were lying in wait on the counter next to my glass of wine. Carl picked up the glass, turned to me and said, "What is this?"

"What does it look like?" I grabbed it from him and took a huge gulp from my glass. He responded with a happy jealous smirk. I poured him a glass and took out two extra eggs. After breakfast, we headed out the door to get to the community center.

Before I moved to Mintly, Texas, I had never heard of a Technology Fair. I remembered participating in Social Studies Fairs and Science Fairs when I was in elementary school, but this was my first-time hearing about kids at a community center participating in a Technology Fair.

Noon time quickly approached, and it was time to open the doors for participants to set up their presentations. Kids from surrounding cities of Mintly participated although they were members of other community centers. Miles appeared exceptionally excited. I went over to his display and surprisingly it was a blank board with a large titanium antique shaped key which had the words "The Cemetery" deeply engraved on its side. Miles pleasantly stood there looking confident that his project would win. I was concerned and confused. I cared about Miles and did not want to offend him in any way about his project. I especially did not want to hurt his feelings. He had enough recent disappointments from his parents. No one knew what was happening inside of the home of the Sinclairs except for me, Miles and Mr. and Mrs. Sinclair. Miles told me everything. It was heart-breaking, and I knew I had to do something to help Miles overcome the emotional pain.

Each day, Miles became more withdrawn and distant. He didn't talk much and had little input at the round table discussions with the other kids. One day I stayed late to wait for Mrs. Sinclair to pick up Miles from the center. We sat on those front steps of the building and it seemed like the longest 10-minute wait in history. I started the conversation with telling Miles a story about how my mother would pick me up late from track practice. Sometimes, I was the only kid left at school and no one waited with me. I told Miles I did not want to leave him because I knew how it felt to be left alone.

Miles followed up with a story of his own. "Ms. Gretchen. A week after my 7th birthday, my parents had another baby. You've seen my parents before, right?" I nodded yes, and he continued. "My parents always commented on my large loose ashy brown curls when they combed my hair because they both have straight blonde hair. They even slid in remarks about my large brown eyes. My dad's eyes are gray and my mom's eyes are baby blue. When my baby brother Zach came along, his features closely resembled those of my parents. Do you see my skin?" Miles rolled up his sleeves and showed me his arms. They were slightly tinted in color. Miles paused a lot during his story and held his head down winding the stringed bracelet with the black rugged rock around and around his wrist. When he was ready to continue, he lifted his head with pride and kept talking. I did not interrupt him at all. I just listened. The more Miles spoke about his baby brother Zach, the more I realized his parents clearly treated them different.

It was heart-breaking to hear this kid's pain. We saw the headlights of his mom's car heading our way and before she pulled up Miles started talking as if he was trying to beat the sand in an hour glass, "My parents think I don't factually belong to them. I asked if I was adopted and they say no every time. I overheard my mom talking on the phone with someone at the hospital one day and she kept saying she wanted an investigation opened about what happened when I was born. That is all I know and it is the main reason why I developed my project. The truth will be unburied once and for all. I think they love Zach more than me. But it's ok. I'll make them proud with this project and they will notice me." I vowed to myself from that day forward I would personally give Miles all the love and attention he needed when we met at the center.

"I wish you were here last year Ms. Gretchen because you could have introduced me to Mr. Langley and maybe The Cemetery would already be opened."

"The Cemetery?" I did not understand what Miles was saying.

"Yes, The Cemetery," he snickered. "That's the name of my project. Don't worry. It's not what you think. I can't wait to show it to everyone."

I looked at the key again on Miles' blank board. It seemed to glisten from the reflection of the sun peeping through the skylights of the center.

"Miles," I whispered. "What is the deal with the titanium key?"

He motioned for me to bend down and whispered in my ear, "It's a healing metal and The Cemetery is a place for healing. If you bury your burdens, then you can heal."

I stood back up and tried to study what Miles meant by staring straight into his eyes.

Ding, ding ding. Mr. Koperneil chimed the small bell and announced it was time for the presentation of the projects. The projects made by the kids were somewhat out of the ordinary. Instructions for the presentation allowed for three questions from the audience to be answered by the presenter. There was one project which attached to a training basketball like a patch and it served the specific purpose of rebounding to a single player if that person were to practice alone.

A few hands rose in the audience to ask questions about this technology.

"What happens if the person practicing misses the goal and the ball does not bounce off the backboard for the rebound?" I knew the kid asking the question and he was known to miss shots during basketball games.

The young girl who presented this project did not hesitate to answer. "The patch has a sensor which is wirelessly linked to a wristband you would wear. The sensors work almost like a magnet."

Another boy chimed in, "Well, if it works like a magnet won't it prevent you from shooting since the sensor would be pulling the basketball towards the wristband as soon as it's released?"

"Good question," the girl answered. "The sensor can determine when a ball is being released and deactivates until contact is made. Once the basketball makes contact with either the goal or the ground, the sensor re-activates, and the basketball bounces back to the person with the wristband."

"What happens if more than one person is practicing at the same goal and they both have on one of these gadgets?" This question came from the back of the room and after the question everyone in the audience turned back to the girl waiting to hear her response.

"I'm still working on that part but so far I have it working only for a single person. I am missing a part which matches frequency levels with a particular wristband to a particular patch when there is other interference."

Mr. Koperneil rang the bell which signaled it was time to move on to the next presenter. There were only five presentations at the fair. Two of the presentations were developed by single members and the other three presentations were developed by teams of members consisting of four team members. The second project was presented by a team of kids who developed a portable arena for wheelchair bound athletes to participate in an obstacle course of track and field activities. The project presented was only a model of the actual portable field. It was equipped with special wheelchairs that transformed into mechanisms with functional mechanical legs instead of using the wheels. A video presentation showed how the four legs of the wheelchair unfolded from the sides with the push of a button. The wheels of the wheelchair controlled the speed and direction of the legs. There was a leap and jump function attached to the controls.

"What happens if the person loses their balance?" This was the first of three questions coming from an elder man who was in a wheelchair on the front row.

The team captain answered, "The chair is equipped with an automatically balancing mechanism that prevents falls."

"Can the wheelchair be used outside of the arena," questioned a curious boy wearing a beige suede backpack.

"Not yet. We still have to get the chair approved by the health board to provide access for public use."

"Did you make it have four legs because you only have a pet dog as a best friend?" A kid yelled out and a group of kids around him broke out in laughter.

Mr. Koperneil rang the bell to calm everyone down. "It's ok Mr. Koperneil," the team captain professionally exclaimed. "Since you must know, the four legs are presented because currently it is the safest method to provide the most balance. We focus on safety along with trying to help the disabled have the chance to participate in sports."

The crowd clapped extra loud after the response and the kid who made the obnoxious comment along with his group of friends sunk with embarrassment in their chairs.

Another project was a helmet designed to measure the shock waves from any hit. It also contained an inner cushion protective shield that was firm enough to reduce the shock waves from a hit while simultaneously adjusting to prevent head injury to the player. A few doctors asked the team questions for this project.

There was one more project before it was Miles' turn to present. I slid over to Miles while the fourth project was being presented. "Miles, are you sure about this project?"

"I sure am Ms. Gretchen."

The other projects seemed pretty amazing and I was concerned about this cemetery Miles kept talking about. Mr. and Mrs. Sinclair walked in with baby Zach. Miles' eyes lit up when he saw his parents show up. He wanted their approval. During our many talks, Miles expressed how eager he yearned to be loved and accepted by his parents. He knew he looked different from them, but he was their son and could not understand why they did not give him as much affection as they gave to Zach.

They quickly sat down while the last question was being asked about the fourth project. "How exactly do these glasses work for referees to wear?"

"It's quite simple," one of the team members confidently boasted as she took her place in front of the team. "The glasses trigger the pupils to the object to be judged. Once locked in, there is a faithfully safe transmission that sends signals to the pupil to create a hologram of what the referee saw."

A slew of other questions was shouted out, but Mr. Koperneil rang the bell. The three questions were already asked.

You could hear the murmuring of some of the guests saying there is no way they would put on those glasses if they were refereeing a game.

Miles had covered his presentation with a dark blue velvet piece of material. He had the whole audience's full attention. Everyone knew Miles was a genius and could not wait to see what type of technology he developed. Miles stood up on the stage and walked up to the mic rolling his covered project on a table. He began.

"Good afternoon everyone. As you may or may not know my name is Miles Sinclair. This year, I have completed a project I have been working on for several years. I could not financially complete the project on my own, so I would first like to thank the Living Edge Non-Profit for funding this project for me." Miles pointed to the representative from the non-profit organization and signaled for her to stand. She nervously yet proudly stood up and everyone gave a soft round of applause.

Miles continued, "I call this project The Cemetery." His parents looked at each other in confusion and there were moans of discernment from the crowd. Miles knew how his parents felt about toying with religion, so he figured he should explain himself.

"Hold on. Let me finish. Most people think a cemetery is a place to bury the dead. Well, in my case, and I'm sure in a lot of other people's cases, there are some issues or problems we would like buried so we can move on with our lives." People in the audience nodded in agreement and with keen looks of curiosity for more explanation. "I know for certain athletes suffer from psychological self-disappointment in not being able to achieve whatever goal they desire to achieve with their particular sport. Sadly, the same concept holds true for other people and their personal lives. It's so easy, or sometimes it's not so easy, to just talk your problems over with your best friend, if you have one, with your family, with your social worker or professional psychiatrist. Well, today all of that will change. I present to you..." Miles raised the velvet material from his board. "...The Cemetery." Miles removed the key attached to the board and raised it high up in the air and shouted confidently, "Follow me!"

Miles did not bring his arm down. He held the shiny key high and straight above his head and walked briskly across the room out of the door of the center. The rock from his bracelet glistened with reflected rays from the sun. The crowd surprisingly orderly followed him. I didn't know what to think at this point. Miles walked over to the vacant land which was located diagonally across the street. I looked over at the café next door to the center and I saw Langley standing there expressionless with both hands in his pockets. I was hoping and praying Miles would not embarrass me, himself or Langley.

Miles shouted at the top of his voice, "Everything is not what it seems!" There was a loud clang and the realistic mural forest painted curtain fell to the ground exposing this immaculate structure made of steel. The structure had been hidden behind the curtain. Miles had an artist paint the mural on a curtain which camouflaged the building. The mural was so convincing no wonder it felt like it was pulling me in that day I was jogging nearby. The building was sharply architected with layered angles. The immense engravement centered above the door read "The Cemetery."

The crowd stood in an awkward silence. No one knew what to think of this structure. The representative from the nonprofit was the only person excitingly clapping. Miles lowered his arm when he reached the door, placed the engraved key into the lock and turned the doorknob. Through the silence of the crowd we could clearly hear the clicks of the door hinges. The building was constructed using natural unmanufactured materials. The walls, floors, doors and ceiling were all from natural materials. The hundreds of feet from the guest who walked in echoed against the cold appearance of the walls.

Miles swiped his hand over a wall and a touchscreen appeared. Miles looked across the faces of the crowd. When he reached the faces of his parents he continued with his presentation. He pressed different buttons on the touchscreen as he explained its function.

"Ladies and gentlemen. This building contains soundproof rooms each measuring 12' x 12'. Each room has four stone chairs and a wall equipped with a touchscreen like this one. The purpose of this place is to communicate freely with the subconscious mind. Communication is done through digital reading of oppressed telepathic messages. I have constructed the walls of the entire building with magnetite. This is a mineral with natural magnetizing capabilities. The force of the magnetic walls collaborates with oppressed messages in your brain and your thoughts are read telepathically through the digital screen.

Anyone can use this technology to help them overcome different problems. For example, if a kicker in a football game misses the winning field goal for the season, this may haunt him for months. He has to mentally overcome this issue. This place, The Cemetery, is a place where he can come and totally release the guilt he may be feeling so he can move forward. When I say totally release, what I mean is the feeling he has is broken down by the magnetite in the walls to the point where those thoughts are altered to a positive state. I named this place The Cemetery because it is a place where you can come to bury your problems. Negative energy oppressed in your mind is changed into positive energy. This technology not only can be used for athletes, but it can also be used for anyone who wants to overcome a problem they are struggling with.

Also, another highlight of this place is in addition to having the capability of communicating with yourself you can also communicate with others. In order to communicate with someone else each participant must be registered in the system. Once a person registers, they can set their preferences to be private to only themselves or to other named registered participants. A person can come to The Cemetery and discover awareness of issues and solve problems. The system is programmed to reject negative and untruthful communication."

Hands flew in the air with questions.

The first question came from a well-known attorney. "If this cemetery can help to get the truth out of people can it be useful information in a court of law?"

"The idea of The Cemetery is to come here and bury your burdens. Please keep in mind there is an agreement of privacy when meeting with someone else. While in the secured room, all telepathy conversations are kept confidential including those held with yourself. Once you leave the room, this information should be used only as an emotional form of relief.

As I specified earlier, many people are suffering psychologically from issues they cannot resolve. This technology is designed to serve as an enhancement, not a replacement, to other types of therapy."

"So, is your memory erased after you leave a room?" A medical doctor expressed his question with uncertainty in his voice.

"No, your memory is not erased. The program detects what negatively emotionally affects each person based on thermal measurements of disturbance in the heart and other vital organs. Once a negative emotion is detected, the thought attached to that emotion is dismantled to the point where it no longer poses a health risk physically or emotionally."

Miles did not hesitate with his answers and he was prepared to answer any question.

Mr. Koperneil announced only one more question could be asked during the presentation. A young girl who looked no older than six years old blurted out, "What about the dead? Can we come to The Cemetery and talk with the dead?"

Miles knew this question would come up and he was prepared to answer it. He knew his mother was an active member of the church and he wanted to make sure he didn't offend her beliefs.

"The system programed does not allow a person to directly communicate with the dead. Remember, you can only communicate with another person who is registered. However, there is the chance while communicating with your own subconscious, which some believe has the ability to hear other voices besides its own, you may tap into communication with others in that manner."

"So, are you saying there may be a chance to communicate with others who are not registered if you can find a way to communicate with them spiritually?"

Mr. Koperneil noisily rang the bell. "No more questions. No more questions. We must move on to the judging of the projects. Remember this year's winner will receive a $20,000 reward towards the enhancement of their project."

The crowd dispersed. Some of the people went back to the center across the street and others stayed behind to take a tour of The Cemetery.

I ran over to Miles and gave him a tremendous hug. "Miles, this is magnificent. I had no idea this is what you were up to. We have to talk about this place later when not so many people are around."

"Sure thing Ms. Gretchen. I have so much more to tell you now." Miles' excitement was partially mature mixed with the jitters of a child's behavior. I could see he was trying to compose himself. His parents walked up, and Miles' face changed to that withdrawn look I had seen so many times. It was like their presence sucked the thrilled spirit right out of him. His father wasn't much of a talker, but his face showed a reaction of disappointment. I stood aside not to interfere with their conversation, but I could still hear his mother's stern whisper even amongst the chitter chatter from the folks who lagged behind.

"Miles Christopher Sinclair. Your father and I are extremely disappointed in you. We asked you every day about your plans for the technology fair, and you never uttered a single clue. And today we show up only to be embarrassed by this spectacle of a building. What is the meaning of this Miles? I mean honestly. The Cemetery? What are you trying to do?"

Miles hung his head low. I wanted to run over and rescue him, but Carl walked up and pulled me by the arm signaling not now. I wanted to save Miles. He stood there motionless.

"We will stick around until the end, but you are coming straight home so we can talk about this," scorned his mother. They walked away with his father holding baby Zach in his arms. Miles blankly observed as they exited the door of the lobby.

Carl and I rushed over to Miles. I could tell he was holding back tears. "It's ok Miles." I held him around the shoulders and tapped him on the back. Carl chimed in with his timely cheerfulness, "Good job Miles. For a minute I thought you made this big old building for the sole purpose of getting rid of me and my business. I was like, hold up...but then you said it should be used as an enhancement and not a replacement of other therapy. I was like ok, I get it."

Miles couldn't help but laugh at Carl. His actions were so comical.

"Come on Miles." I led the way. "Let's go back to the center and wait for you to win that prize because I know your project was the best."

Miles straightened up his posture showing he was still proud and confident about his project and we walked back to the center. I glanced over at Han's Café and Langley was sipping on a cup of tea still standing in that same spot. I couldn't exactly see his expression, but I could tell he could not keep his eyes off the building.

"Alright everyone," Mr. Koperneil announced on the microphone. "Let's take our seats and prepare for the awards." The crowd respectfully took their seats. The panel of judges gathered their voting cards and passed them down to the lead judge. While Mr. Koperneil continued with his praises to all participants, I focused on the head judge who was quickly tallying up the scores. She handed over her final sheet to Mr. Koperneil who made the announcements.

"And the moment we have been waiting for...Third place goes to Melissa Young with the "Rebounding Basketball."" The young girl stood up and ran to the stage to receive her award. She was emotionally excited, and her parents ran up to the stage and took pictures of her as she received her award.

"Second place goes to...Team Explore with the "Protective Shield Helmet."" The team and a crowd of supporters cheered loudly. I looked down at Miles who sat upright next to me politely applauding each winner. My heart was thumping so loud in anticipation for the final winner I was sure you could see my pulse moving on my neck. Mr. Koperneil looked at the final card and glanced over to the panel of judges. I was getting nervous. I prepared an apology speech to Miles in my mind in the event he didn't win. I reached over for Miles' hand and although my hand was shaking his was calm, Miles also cupped his other hand on top of mine as if he was the one doing the consoling.

"Ladies and gentlemen. I am extremely proud to announce this year's first place winner for the Technology Fair. This project exemplifies thoughtfulness beyond the physical challenges of sports." At this point I knew Mr. Koperneil was speaking of the wheelchair project. I felt my leg tapping up and down as I waited for the final announcement. Mr. Koperneil continued, "It is with honor and curiosity for the progress and future of this project that I present the first-place winner.... Miles Sinclair!" The whole place cheered and clapped as Miles took proud steps to the stage to accept his award. I looked for his parents to go up and take his picture as he accepted the award but when I looked to the back of the room, they were exiting the door. Miles also noticed their exit, but he was quickly distracted by the excited representative from the non-profit who was snapping picture after picture of Miles while he held his oversized $20,000.00 check with Mr. Koperneil by his side.

I was so proud of Miles, but I also felt an awkward sense of pity for his success because it still did not seem to please his parents. Carl and I dashed over to the stage to support Miles during this electrifying time and in that moment our support seemed to content his heart. At the back of the room it looked like Langley was standing there in his usual emotionless posture with dark shades. Miles shrugged at my arm to pose for a picture and when I looked back up Langley was nowhere in sight.

Chapter 5

The next day at the office started normal. Mr. Koperneil was finally back at work and the atmosphere at the office immediately changed from its uptight and uncomfortable feel to a relaxed yet productive air. As soon as I sat my things down on my desk and got my pen and paper ready to jot down notes from my phone messages, Mr. Koperneil called me into his office. I didn't know if he heard anything negative about me since he was out, so I was a little nervous. Voices were rushing in my head trying to convince me to calm down, but my facial expressions were not cooperating with the same level of confidence. I was sweating profusely and tried waving the wet spots under my arms dry before I walked into his office. When I sat down, I could tell Mr. Koperneil was reading my expressions.

"Gretchen." He always said my name with the kindest tone in his voice. It was especially calming this time, so I finally relaxed. He continued, "Did you know about Miles' project all along?" His eyes were excited, and his posture was hungry to know more about the project.

"Honestly Mr. Koperneil, I only knew the simple basics. Miles never even told me the name of the project. I am as anxious and curious about the whole thing myself. As a matter of fact, I'm going to meet Miles at the building after work today. It's the grand opening. I'm hoping I can learn more about what The Cemetery can do for people. It seems so interesting."

"Oh, and Gretchen, I never did get a chance to personally thank you for saving me that day. I have to let you know that if it wasn't for your quick response with calling for help, I wouldn't be here today." Mr. Koperneil reached out and gave me a gentle hug. "Thank you so much Gretchen. You are a true gem and a life saver. I won't ever forget it."

Mr. Koperneil's words were so touching I fought to hold back my emotions as I still struggled with what happened with my grandmother. I had a lump in my throat, but I managed to reply to Mr. Koperneil's gratitude, "I'm glad I was there and able to help."

I left work and headed straight to the grand opening of The Cemetery. The representative from Living Edge had a team of volunteers helping people register. Miles led a brief orientation and explained the panels in more detail. Miles spoke to the group with ease. "If you notice (pointing to the panels) the panels open up with sensors when you wave your hand over the area. Registration is pretty simple. You just give some basic information about yourself and list, if you want, your profile to be private or public. If it is private, then only those people who you list can also go to a session with you. You must have their name and birthdate to list them. If you set your profile to public, you can include an alert so you can give permission to the participant. If you are not physically present during a session, your thoughts which are recorded in your profile are accessible to whoever requests you. You will not know what thoughts were revealed unless that person tells you. The experience you have with each session should leave you feeling relieved of whatever mental issue you are having. The sessions do not have any effect on your physical body. This has all to do with the mind. The entire building was run using solar energy to avoid static interruptions in the therapy produced from the natural material of the walls. I hope you all enjoy your experience at The Cemetery."

It sounded a bit chilling the way he said it, but I signed up and listed my mother, Carl, and Miles as automatic accepted participants and made myself available to the public with alert permission.

Carl walked up right when I was finishing my registration process.

"Hey Gretchen. Did you sign up already?" He looked uneasy about the whole experience.

"I did, and I listed you as an automatically accepted participant."

Carl looked at me with a suspicious attitude. "What does that mean?"

"Well after you sign up, you can make yourself private or public. If you are public then anyone can find you and include you on one of their sessions. The thing is you wouldn't know what happened in the session. Your thoughts are recorded when you register, and they can communicate with your thoughts without you knowing what was revealed." After I finished my explanation, Carl appeared overwhelmed.

"Oh, now that is scary. I wouldn't want to do that. No telling who would know what about me," he joked.

I also thought about different scenarios that could happen. "Yeah, that's true. I think I better change mine back to only private."

"So, what happens when you automatically list people?"

"You fundamentally allow those particular people to have access to include you in their session without an alert. I listed you, my mom and Miles. I don't think I have anything to hide from any of you."

"Honey, I have a lot to hide. I need everyone to get my permission first." Carl smartly rolled his eyes at the thought of everyone getting in his personal business.

I started laughing. "Well, do you want to take a chance and try a session with me right now?"

He thought about it for a second. "I guess so. Just stop the session if you think it's getting too personal."

"Agreed. You too." I smiled to myself out of nervousness not knowing what to expect.

We walked into our assigned room and it was uncannily empty except for the stone chairs Miles mentioned at the fair. When the solid door closed behind us there was a hollow silence in the room. Carl and I both looked at each other wondering exactly what would happen next. Without either one of us moving the digital screen lit up. I remembered Miles said the screen was designed to detect our mental energy levels. A sentence appeared on the screen saying the exact same thing simultaneously with my thoughts. Carl quickly looked at me and the screen typed, "Who typed that?" Carl then realized his thoughts were being displayed on the screen. Both of our eyes widened in astonishment.

"Oh boy Carl, this is scary." My thoughts typed again across the screen.

"It sure is," typed Carl's thoughts.

"How is this happening?"

"It's from the mineral, remember? It is processing our thoughts."

"Wow. Well, I better be careful what I think about."

"Yes Gretch, you better."

"I guess I'll start thinking about something that has been bothering me the most lately. My grandmother's passing."

"Yes, think about the story you told me and how you felt and let's see what happens."

I closed my eyes for a moment and thought back to that day. I could see my grandmother's face as clear as day. I did everything she told me without stalling. I called 911 and I waited. I opened my eyes and saw a sentence.

"I did everything, and I remember my grandmother panting that I did good. She told me she loved me, and I kissed her on the face and said I love you too Grandma. I stood by the door and waited for the ambulance. I kept looking back at my grandmother, but I screamed for them to hurry because she wasn't moving."

"So, Gretchen, there was more to the story than you had told me. This is good information because it means you shouldn't question your actions anymore. Your grandmother loved you and you were there for her."

"You're right Carl. I guess I held on to the thought of wondering what I could have done differently. I couldn't see everything which I had wholly done. I've been living with this since I was seven and now I feel like I finally have closure and peace."

A smile glowed across Carl's face. I could feel that he was genuinely relieved for me.

"What about you Carl? Is there anything that has been bothering you?"

"I'm almost ashamed to admit it Gretch but since we started the session this overwhelming feeling has built up in me. I have been fighting the thoughts so you wouldn't see it on the screen."

"It's ok Carl. Whatever it is, we are here to get help. We agreed to come here together because we are best friends and we trust and care for each other. Just let your feelings come through."

Carl let out a sigh that nearly took on a human form. "Ok. I've been feeling defeated by not being accepted by some people in this community because of my sexual preference. I don't feel like it's fair and it makes me feel bad about my own self-worth. It's like regardless of my education and reputation in this field, I am still not accepted or respected by some people."

I attentively read the screen and felt Carl's feelings come through with each word. I glanced over at Carl and he had tears streaming from his eyes.

"Honestly Gretchen, this feeling didn't just start from the people in this community. This is a problem that began a long time ago. It initiated way back when I was in high school. I hadn't come out yet, but everyone could tell I was gay judging my mannerisms. I couldn't hide it. I was determined to prove to the world that the way I acted didn't mean I was less of a person. So, I worked hard in school and I made sure I did well in college. Even after college I had a hard time getting a job because companies would say their clients wouldn't feel comfortable seeking psychological help from a gay guy. After that last rejection I decided to move to Mintly and try to open my own practice. It worked out well. I kept my gay mannerisms to a minimum so I wouldn't discourage new clients."

Carl was in a full cry by this time, but the typing continued.

"Eventually, word got out that I was gay, and it tarnished my reputation with some of my clients. Now that I think about it, I have been struggling all of this time to be accepted by people when I should have mainly concentrated on those clients who remained loyal to my professionalism despite my personal sexual preferences. It is funny, but I am a psychiatrist and I couldn't even figure out how to deal with my own problems. I guess it's something like a hairdresser who never combs their hair."

"There you go Carl, always making light of a situation." I had a slight smirk on my face.

"Well you know me darling. I can't help myself."

"I know. And that's what's so wonderful about you. You are a positive person."

"Yes. I need to humbly use positive thinking for myself."

The panel shut down and the door opened. Carl and I walked out of the building and I felt this enormous sense of relief. The energy from the room refreshed my spirit. It was a warm feeling and I wished other people had a chance to experience it too.

"So how do you feel Carl?"

Carl thought about it for a second, "I feel light."

"I know what you mean. I feel the same way. It's like my spirit has been recharged with this new energy making me feel warm."

"Exactly."

"Do you have time to grab a cup of coffee with me?"

"Yep, I don't have any evening clients today, so I have all the time in the world."

We walked into the café and Paisley was at the counter as usual. "Well hello my two favorite patrons." Paisley greeted us as we sat down at the coffee bar. "I didn't expect to see you two in here at this time of the evening. Hey, do you want to try some hot tea with a blend of my secret herbs?" Paisley kept raising her eyebrows up and down as if she was trying to convince us with her facial expressions.

Carl and I both looked at each other as if to say *she's crazy*. "Uhm, no thanks Paisley. We'll just each have a plain cup of decaf." I explained as I took out the money to pay for our order.

"Ok. Well, if you insist but I know you would both like it." Paisley reached for the pot of decaf and poured us each a cup.

"Maybe next time," Carl said being his usual positive self.

I blew the steam from my cup of coffee and took a tiny sip to check its temperature. Carl chuckled at me, "You always do that."

"I know. I can't stand burning my tongue."

"Oh, I know what you mean. Maybe you should seriously think about ordering an iced coffee next time."

"Well, what's the point in that? The idea for me is to enjoy the warm feeling."

"But it looks like you take the warm feeling away because you spend so much time blowing the steam off your coffee before you even start to drink it. I guess that just goes to show you two people can like the same thing but also like it to be different at the same time."

"Wow Carl, sometimes you go way out with your analogies. I just don't like to burn my tongue. You are so funny."

The bell chimed to the café signaling that someone opened the door. I looked over and it was Langley. He didn't say a single word. He walked over and tapped twice on the counter. Paisley immediately reached for an unmarked jar and pulled out what looked like a tea bag with a purple string. She settled it in an empty oversized coffee cup and poured steaming hot water into the cup. She handed the cup to Langley and he took the bag by the purple string and started to dip it up and down in the cup. After several dips he placed the bag in a big spoon over the cup and took another big spoon and pressed the two spoons together. The solution from the bag drained into the cup. Langley placed the used bag onto a napkin and began to sip the tea.

Carl hunched me with his elbow and whispered, "Gretchen, you are staring." I immediately turned around. Paisley saw my reaction and winked one eye as she wiped down the counter. Carl and I finished our coffee and exited. I didn't get to see when Langley left the café because he had disappeared without me noticing. I wanted to know what he thought about The Cemetery.

As Carl and I walked down the sidewalk I couldn't help but to keep looking at The Cemetery. It felt like it was calling me back. I didn't want to tell Carl how it made me feel because I didn't want him to use his psychology tricks on me and dig deeper into my past.

"Ok Carl. I guess I'll turn it in early today."

"What? No dinner date tonight. All this new feeling inside me has stirred up an appetite." Carl put on a pouting face I usually couldn't resist.

"Aww. Not this time my love. Besides, I have a left-over dish of shrimp and chicken pasta from Jazzes I am craving to finish."

"Well I do understand that. I would hate for you to let such good food go to waste. I'll call and check on you later." Carl made it a point to always make sure I was home safe.

"I know you will Carl. You always do." I gave him a quick hug and we went our separate ways.

When I got home, I flicked off my shoes and lazily flopped down on the sofa and started flipping through the channels. The six o'clock news was almost over. I didn't like watching the news because it often focused on tragedies. There were reports about tragic accidents, tragic weather, tragic sports injuries, and on and on. That kind of negative information would without compassion extract all of the joy right out of me, so I seldom watched the news. For some reason, I didn't change the channel. It could have been that the commercial highlighted one of my clients for its product, but I kept watching. When the news came back on, the newsman in the field was shooting in front of The Cemetery. I had to hear this story. I turned up the volume and scooted to the edge of my sofa as if I all of a sudden was hard of hearing.

"Good evening. I am Byran Zanders and I am standing here today in front of this new building called The Cemetery. Don't be alarmed by the name because the developer explained the name merely represents the purpose of the services of the building. It was described to me as a place to come and bury your burdens. Believe it or not folks but this building was orchestrated by a young boy who is only ten years old and who many in the community are referring to as a pure genius. I spoke with his parents earlier today and

they didn't exactly approve of the project, so they chose not to allow me to release his name for this report. Despite that, I must say I have been getting positive reviews from people who have already registered and are using the services of The Cemetery. One lady reported she suffered from depression for over a year after losing her job. She stated after leaving The Cemetery, she finally felt closure about that situation and is ready to move on with her life. There were at least a dozen similar stories and only time will tell what will come of The Cemetery. Back to you Tamron. "

I couldn't believe it. Miles had made the news. I wanted to call him and congratulate him, but I knew his parents wouldn't approve. I'm more than sure he didn't even know about the news report on The Cemetery. I couldn't wait to tell him about it the next day at the center. I warmed up my pasta and enjoyed every ounce of flavor. I topped my dinner off with a slice of homemade cheesecake Mrs. Koperneil had delivered to me as a token of her appreciation. I must say, Ms. Bernette was right. Mrs. Koperneil knows her way around the kitchen. This cheesecake was the absolute best I had ever eaten. Ms. Bernette told me the only time Mrs. Koperneil made cheesecake was for their anniversary. She was surprised to hear Mrs. Koperneil had made one for me and had it special delivered to my house. Needless to say, it was creamy and smooth with the perfect texture of crumbly crust at the bottom. I almost fixed me a second slice but then I figured I would pay for it later, so I chose not to be gluttonous.

Carl called faithfully as promised. "I see you made it in safely. So, how was the pasta?"

"Delicious."

"I'm jealous now. All I could find in this place was a dried-up piece of chicken and burnt scrapings of corn."

"Carl. I know you didn't eat that."

"Of course not. I threw it straight in the garbage. I settled for a hot bowl of oatmeal with a little butter, sugar and milk."

"That sounds good. Hey Carl, did you watch the news?"

"No way. You know I don't like that negative stuff."

"I know, me either. But I watched it tonight and guess who was on."

"Who?"

"Miles."

"Wait, what?" Carl was surprised, and I could hear him fumbling to find his remote. "Just in case I'm sleeping later I want to record the news at ten. So, our little Miles made the news, huh?"

"Yep. Well, they couldn't legally mention his name, but they filmed in front of The Cemetery and gave a respectable report about how it was relieving people from anxiety."

"That is freaking amazing Gretchen. His parents have to be proud of him now."

"You would think they are, but the news reported they disapproved of the project and that is why Miles' name was not released."

"I just don't get it."

"Neither do I Carl. I honestly can't wait to see Miles tomorrow afternoon at the center."

"I'll be there for extra support." Carl reassured me.

As soon as I hung up with Carl my mom called.

"Hey baby. How's it going?" She never changed. I loved when she would call because it made it feel like I wasn't far away from home.

"It's going pretty good momma. Do you remember the kid I told you about?"

"Is he the strange one who was secretly stalking you and supposedly put money in your meter?"

I couldn't help but laugh. "No momma, he was not stalking me. But yes, that kid. Anyway, his project made the news today."

"Wait a minute child. Is it called The Cemetery?"

"Yes, how do you know?"

"Because it was on the news over here too. People are talking about it all over the place. What kind of weird name is The Cemetery? It sounds like some kind of voodoo shit if you ask me."

My momma didn't hold her tongue for nothing. She freely said whatever came to her mind. "No ma, it's not voodoo. In all reality, it is a building made out of natural materials and it produces positive energy to help people deal with issues they are struggling with."

"Well if that's the case, then maybe I should send your Uncle Charles over there to help him deal with the issue of not paying people back because I sure could use that twenty dollars I loaned him last week for groceries."

"Momma," I said with a begging sound in my voice. "Don't be like that. You know Uncle Charles can't work because of his disability. At least he used the money to buy groceries this time and not to go sit at the penny slots at the casino all day."

"You're right baby," momma laughed. "You are always taking up for your uncle. So, have you been to this cemetery place?"

"I did go there today. It was the grand opening, so Carl and I went together. It was impressive, to say the least."

"Well baby, I'm glad it turned out good for you. I'm still not too keen on this strange kid. Just be careful with that one. You never know about people."

"I love you momma. Good night."

"I love you too baby."

As much as I love my mother, sometimes the negative energy she pushed off was brutally too much for me to deal with. I know she always meant well but sometimes I just couldn't take it. I tidied up in the kitchen and laid out my work clothes for the next day. I relaxed and took a long hot bath and went to bed. I was tired, but I couldn't fall asleep because I was anxious to tell Miles about the news and about my experience. My thoughts were all over the place. I thought back to the way Mr. Koperneil acknowledged I played a part in saving his life. I thought about how I felt after leaving The Cemetery. I also thought about Langley. I had to make sure I made time to visit him at his office to get his opinion about The Cemetery. I hoped he would be proud of its success and its exposure, especially since my mother said it was on the news all the way in New Orleans. Mostly, I couldn't stop thinking about Miles. He demonstrated a lot of courage proceeding with his project despite how his parents felt. Miles's determination was motivating. I wished that his parents could see what everyone else could see in Miles. It was heartbreaking and I was stuck in a situation that was beyond my control. There were so many conversations I held in my mind that I wanted to relay to the Sinclairs so they could realize just how selfish they were acting. I never acted on my thoughts because I didn't want to interfere and cause even more problems for Miles. I said a prayer for Miles that night and I eventually dozed off.

Chapter 6

When I arrived at work, everyone was exceptionally quiet. There was no usual chitter-chatter going on between workers in their cubicles. Everyone had an intense look on their face. It felt like I had walked into a twilight zone. I tried to tell the communal secretary good morning, but she quickly turned her back towards me when I passed by her desk.

I couldn't figure out what was going on. I glanced back at everyone on the floor before I opened the door to my office to see if anyone was staring and not a single person was looking my way. When I opened the door to my office and turned to walk in, the Sinclairs were sitting there waiting for me with Miles. I surely didn't expect to see them, and I had no idea why they were here so early or what they could possibly want with me.

I quickly shut the door behind me and I could hear everyone on the office floor starting to make their usual morning conversations. I shook my head in confusion and walked over to my desk, set my purse inside of my desk drawer and greeted the Sinclairs.

"Well, good morning everyone. This is an unexpected surprise." My greeting spirit was unsettling while I focused mostly on Miles' expression. Miles was sitting in between his mother and father as if he was punished. "What brings you all here this morning?"

"Ms. Gretchen, I told them not to come here. I told them not to do this." Miles blurted out before his father firmly grabbed him by the arm pushing him to the back of his chair.

My concern for Miles intensified. "What is going on here Mr. & Mrs. Sinclair?"

"Oh, I'll tell you what's going on," snapped Mrs. Sinclair. "Miles here has chosen to embarrass our family with this ridiculous cemetery project."

"It's not ridiculous," Miles muttered underneath his breath.

"Miles. Mind your manners." His father's voice was sternly strict.

Mrs. Sinclair continued, "Miles has been secretly working on this project for years and he refused to tell us anything about it. We have tried to get him to open up to us, but he plainly refuses. Now, the only thing he tells us is that he only trusts you."

I looked back and forth at Mr. & Mrs. Sinclair and their facial expressions were more of disgust than that of concern. I was at a loss for words and almost stuttering, "Uh well, I don't know why Miles would say such a thing. He talks about you guys all the time. He loves you and honestly..."

"Honestly what Gretchen?" yelped Mr. Sinclair. "Don't you dare tell us we don't love Miles."

"You don't!" Miles yelled. "All you both do is ignore me. You ignore me and only give Zach all the attention."

"Oh, I see." His mother seemed even more agitated. "You are jealous of your baby brother."

I had to jump in then because Miles' eyes were filling up with tears and he was holding his chest and shoulders up high to prevent from crying. I knew I had to try to keep the situation calm so I was talking slow to choose my words wisely. "Now Mr. & Mrs. Sinclair. Let's see if we can get to the bottom of this. I was not going to say you don't love Miles. I'm sure you do love your son. At this point, all I know is Miles has grown close to me at the center. I have conversations with Miles all the time and he loves his baby brother so there is no way he is jealous of him. I think maybe, perhaps sometimes, he feels a little left out. I don't think he is asking for all of your attention. He is only asking for *some* of your attention. Now grant it I don't have any kids of my own, but I do know children since I have been volunteering at different centers back home and here in Mintly. Do you think there is any way you can fit just a little time to spend with Miles?"

"Oh, so now you are an expert on kids, right?" Mrs. Sinclair was clearly upset. Her eyes were wide, and her lips were tight. "Since you are such an expert, let's see how well you do giving *a little* time to spend with Miles."

"What are you talking about Mrs. Sinclair? I'm not following you."

"What I am saying Gretchen is we came here to leave Miles in *your* custody for a few weeks while we travel out of the country. At first, we were going to take Miles along, but he keeps placing himself in a corner of the sofa, or at the lonely end of the dinner table instead of moving in closer to eat with the rest of the family, or he just stares out of the damn window when we go places. He never talks to us and like I said, he said he only trusts *you*. So, since *you* and Miles have this 'perfect' relationship, my husband and I feel it is best for you to watch after him while we are away."

His father made it a point to add salt to the injury. "Plus, Miles decided single-handedly to embarrass the family by coming up with this cemetery which I know will become a spectacle for the whole town of Mintly and honestly we don't want to be a part of it."

All three of them intensely scrutinized me waiting for a response. Truthfully, I wasn't ready to be a parent even if it was only for a temporary time. But when I looked at Miles' face, I couldn't bear the thought of letting him down.

"I'll do it." I firmly glared at Mr. & Mrs. Sinclair dead in the eyes. "I'll do it."

Mr. & Mrs. Sinclair stood up and extended their hands to give me a handshake to seal the deal as if we had arranged some formal agreement. I immediately stood up and shook their hands with confidence. Mr. Sinclair handed me an envelope and afterwards they quickly left the office. Everyone got quiet again as they left out. I watched them until the elevator doors opened. As they entered the elevator Mr. Koperneil was getting off. He didn't say a word. I guess he didn't know the Sinclairs had left my office a moment ago. I closed the door and sat at my desk in awe. I was almost afraid to open the envelope, but I did anyway. There was a neatly folded paper which gave me full custody of Miles until such designated time of revocation by the Sinclairs. There was also a letter from Mr. Sinclair instructing me to pick up Miles from the center that afternoon to begin the arrangement. He also stated, in the meantime, they were having Miles' belongings delivered to my home along with his school schedule. The Thanksgiving holiday was approaching so Miles would soon have at least a full week off of school. I had to quickly think of how I would deal with coming to work and making sure Miles was taken care of during that time.

Mr. Koperneil knocked on my office door before opening it. "Good morning Gretch. Did Mr. & Mrs. Sinclair come by to meet with you?" he asked with a perplexed look on his face.

"Yes, Mr. Koperneil," I answered with an apologetic tone.

"Was it something about the project?"

"I guess you can say that," I said as I looked at the floor while I answered his question but made my way to Mr. Koperneil to signal for him to come all the way in. I shut the door behind him and I sat next to Mr. Koperneil in one of the chairs intended for guests.

"Talk to me Gretch. What happened?" Mr. Koperneil was sounding more like a father than a boss.

"Long story short, the Sinclairs without warning gave me full custody over Miles because they are leaving the country."

"Are you serious?"

"Incredibly serious." I reached across my desk to show Mr. Koperneil the paperwork.

Mr. Koperneil leaned back after reading the document and rubbed his hand over his mouth. "What kind of parents would do this? I'm sure you're a good and trustworthy person but I know for sure they barely know you because you recently moved in town."

"I know Mr. Koperneil. This is all a surprise to me too. They kept saying Miles said he only trusts me. I'm at a complete loss for words right now."

"Oh dear. Don't worry about it. You know I owe you in a big way, so I will let my wife know we have to help you in every way possible. Did they say when they would return?"

"I think they said a week or two. My memory can't keep up Mr. Koperneil. Everything was happening so fast."

"Wow. Ok Gretch," he expounded benevolently with his voice as he arose from the chair. "Everything will work out. You and Miles will be well taken care of. Just focus on your clients for now and let me figure out the logistics about the arrangements for Miles while you are at work. I have four kids at home, so I think I am pretty qualified in this area." Mr. Koperneil gave me a wink as he walked out of my office.

God, I don't know what you have planned for me, but I know you will show me and guide me on the right path. I had a quick conversation with God then I re-focused and got back to work.

The secretary buzzed in, "Ms. Gretchen."

I pressed the button on my office phone to answer, "Yes Stephanie."

"Your ten o'clock is here."

"Ok, can you please set them up in the Beta Conference Room and start the commercial video."

"Sure thing."

I quickly gathered my presentation material for this client. This was a pitch for a charcoal commercial. I walked into the conference room and there were two ladies and one guy from the company. The commercial was timely ending when I walked in.

"Good morning everyone. I'm Gretchen Hall." I went around the table and shook each person's hand as they introduced themselves.

"Good morning. I'm Leslie Steinhalt, head of marketing at Kings Coal."

"Welcome Leslie."

"And I'm Julie Ford, creative sound director."

"Welcome Julie."

"And I'm Dale Sturgess, research statistics advisor."

"Great. Welcome Dale." I walked over to the still picture of the commercial ending, let out a short sigh and said, "So what are your thoughts? Did you find the commercial appealing for your product?"

Leslie took the lead with answering the questions. "I must say Gretchen, it was rather amusing. I especially like the part where the football player runs out the sliding door and his wife grabs the bag of charcoal and passes it to their son who looks like he is around eight and he passes it to his sister who looks like she is around twelve and she passes it to her dad. That whole part right there shows how the whole idea of a bar-b-que is to bring the family together. I like the idea of the commercial being more family oriented and not purely centered around the concept of bar-b-que celebrations being a "man's" thing."

"Exactly," Dale jumped in to add his knowledge. "Research has shown commercials which show the male either doing all the work or enjoying most of the benefits mainly produce the sale of male buyers. With the commercial the way it is structured, the results should produce a wider range of buyers from all genders and all ages. It is almost like a family game."

"Why did you choose Larry Hitzman?" Julie asked.

"Good question Julie." I changed the clip to one of Larry's football pictures. "For starters, he has great hands and shouldn't have a problem catching the bag of charcoal. Secondly, he has the kind of character and style that can fit a family man in the backyard on the grill. Lastly, and most importantly, I needed for the person in this commercial to be old enough to have kids. There were other prospects I had in mind, but they didn't fit all of my needs for this product."

Leslie took back over. "I fanatically love the pitch Gretchen. The only thing I would change is the size of the charcoal bag. I would use the smaller bag for the commercial so it's not a physical strain on anyone and plus the whole bag can be poured in the grill without a problem."

I added, "That is a great suggestion and I passionately agree. We strive for a consideration of people and don't want them getting injured from using the product. The idea is to make it fun and family friendly."

"Exactly Gretchen. Now that we are all in agreement and this project looks like it's a go, I will immediately meet with other key personnel at our company to discuss the logistics of the production costs and send you an endorsement package proposal by the end of the week."

I was all smiles as I thanked each of them for attending the meeting this morning and I provided them each with a lunch voucher at Jazzes. Dale said he loved their food and he would not let the voucher go to waste. I walked them all out to the elevator and I headed back to my office.

Mr. Koperneil came back with his usual double knock and entrance. "So how did it go Gretch?" I gave him a simple thumbs up and he gave me one in return then closed the door.

I checked my schedule and I didn't have any other appointments until three o'clock. I called Larry to give him the news about the commercial and he was thrilled. He said he knew they would like it. I just laughed at his humorous confidence. I told him I would call him back at the end of the week after they sent me the endorsement proposal. He said he looked forward to the call.

I spent the next few hours concentrating on regular office tasks like checking and returning emails, reading over contracts and checking on clients courteously to see how they were doing. I enjoyed speaking with my clients often even if it wasn't about business. I felt we also needed a solid relationship on a personal level so I understood all of their needs for their career when promoting them as their agent.

My cellphone chimed with a text message from Carl. I had so much to tell him. I didn't want a big lunch, so I told him to meet me at Fresh Garden, so I could quickly grab a light salad.

Carl met me for lunch at our usual time. As soon as we sat down at our table, I immediately handed him the envelope with the documents from Mr. & Mrs. Sinclair. Carl gave me a clueless look and slowly opened the envelope. He read a few lines and chokingly said, "What is this Gretchen?" Carl was in the middle of taking his first sip of water when he started reading the document.

I gave him a quick tap on the back to help him clear his throat. "It's exactly what it looks like," I answered with clinched teeth and barely moving my lips.

"Have those people gone bitterly mad?"

"Yes, they have Carl. They were waiting for me in my office, with Miles, early this morning."

"What? And you weren't even expecting them?"

"No, not at all. I mean I barely speak to those people. The most I've said to them was hello and good-bye. Poor Miles looked so distraught."

"So, what are you going to do?"

"I mean, what else can I do. I have to take care of him. I can't easily abandon him like his parents. Miles trusts me, and I care a great deal about that kid. Seriously Carl, he is not just some ordinary kid. Look at his project. Plus, he has such a sweet and tender heart. I could never hurt him."

"So how are you going to juggle 'parenting' and work?"

"I haven't figured that whole part out yet. But I did tell Mr. Koperneil what happened."

"Wow, what did he say?"

"He was so comforting. He said he and his wife would help out in any way they could."

"I must say Gretchen. You are one lucky lady to have such a caring boss."

"As my mother says, 'blessed.' I am one blessed lady."

Carl gave me an Amen to that. We finished our lunch a little early because Carl had a client. "I have to head back to the office darling because I have a one o'clock who always shows up fifteen minutes early."

"Ok. I should get back too so I can regroup before my three o'clock meeting."

Carl gave me a tight hug and said, "Don't worry about anything. You are not in this alone. We are in this together."

Those words were so comforting I hurried and waved him off before my emotions got the best of me. When I returned to the office the secretary handed me a note stating my three o'clock needed to meet at one instead because they had an emergency flight departing sooner than originally planned. Stephanie said she knew I would agree because there weren't any other appointments on my schedule. The excitement was almost overwhelming because the thought of landing a free agent contract with this client was only moments away. I had only fifteen minutes to prep everything, but it worked out well. I met with the client and he agreed to my terms of representation. The meeting only lasted ten minutes because he was in a rush. He said he heard great things about me, so it was a no brainer for him. His complement flattered my ego.

Since I didn't have any other appointments, I spent some time researching more prospects. Surprisingly, the time flew by. I rushed out of the office to head to the center because I heartily wanted to hug Miles. When I walked in, he was already there with his head down between his folded arms on the table. I sat next to him and placed my arms around his shoulders. He raised up and recognized it was me, then calmed himself by embracing in my arms. I rocked him back and forth for a few seconds and whispered, "We will get through this Miles. You don't have anything to worry about."

Chapter 7

I woke up the next morning ready for my usual morning jog. I was about to head out the door and I noticed a smaller pair of shoes next to mine at the door entrance. "*Oh boy, this is going to take some getting used to,*" I thought to myself. For a moment I had forgotten Miles was now living with me. I knew he was mature enough to stay home alone but I wasn't at peace with leaving him in the house by himself. To my surprise, when I turned to head towards the guest bedroom, Miles was already sitting on the sofa fully dressed.

"Ouu, good morning Miles. You scared me." I had clinched my chest at first but smiled immediately afterwards so Miles wouldn't feel guilty.

"Sorry Ms. Gretchen, I just couldn't sleep anymore. I've been up since five o'clock thinking about The Cemetery. I wonder if it can help me to get over this feeling of missing my family." Miles was clinching his fingers together so hard I could see the imprints of the pressure on his skin. "Ms. Gretchen, I know I should understand why they left me like this, but I don't. I tried to talk to them, but they kept yelling and saying I didn't care about them. I need them to know I care about them. I need them to know that I love them, and I love my baby brother. And I miss him so much and I know he misses me."

I went over to Miles and knelt next to him while he sat on the sofa. "Miles, deep in their hearts, they know you love them. It's possible they may be having a hard time dealing with how smart you are." I tickled Miles at the end of my pep talk to try to get him to cheer up. It seemed to be working because he started to chuckle a little. I combed through his hair with my fingers to get a good look at his face. "Hey, I have an idea." I stood up and latched onto him by his hand.

"What?" His face held a definition of curiosity.

"Why don't you come with me on my jog this morning?"

"Uh, do you mean your full-blown run? I heard about you Ms. Gretchen. You are fast."

I blushed at his comment, "Well, you don't have to run. I have an extra bike in the garage and you should be tall enough to ride it."

"Perfect." Miles lightened up his mood and followed me to the garage. "Whoa! Now that's a bright yellow bike!" Miles said with excitement in his voice.

"Do you like it?"

"Do I like it? I love it!" Miles sprouted a huge smile on his face as he walked slowly around the bike admiring its every feature. "Cool cushiony seat, soft handle grips and a not one but two water bottle holders. This is the best Ms. Gretchen. And as they say in the old western movies 'Let's ride'." Then he looked at me and said, "Oh well, I'll ride, and you jog." Miles burst out laughing. He was laughing at his own joke. It was so cute.

"Alright now Miles. There you go. Let me grab us some water to place in those holders." I went to the kitchen and grabbed two bottles of cold water I had in the freezer. "These should be thawed to perfect temperature after we reach one mile."

"One mile?" Miles' screech of concern broke through like horses in the gates of a horse race at the sound of a gun. "Exactly how many miles are we going Ms. Gretchen?"

"Don't you worry your little heart about the distance Miles. You'd better just keep up."

We headed out and started on my usual path. It was nice having Miles with me because watching him enjoy himself while riding the bike gave me motivation. I wanted to keep running so he could keep having that happy feeling. It felt good knowing at least in that moment, Miles was enjoying being a normal kid filled with excitement and joy. This was a different side of Miles from the kid at the community center. We went all the way to the edge of the lake and turned around.

"Let's go this way Ms. Gretchen. I know a short-cut back."

I didn't like going off my path, but I followed Miles anyway because I didn't want to disappoint him. He seemed so proud of this short-cut. Miles made two left turns on a few side streets and he stopped at a corner house then froze gazing at the door. I caught up with Miles and asked, "Do you know who lives here?" The house was in immaculate condition. It was a colorful wood house with southern charm. The front wood slates were all different colors. It looked like no two slates were the same color. The windows were trimmed with carved shutters. The carvings had the appearance of embossed wings. "Miles," I whispered loudly to get his attention.

He shook his head breaking his staring spell. "I'm sorry Ms. Gretchen. Did you say something?"

"Yes." My annoyance was clear. I know he had to hear me, but I repeated my question anyway, "Do you know who lives here?"

"No, but it's weird because this house is always in my dreams. The crazy part about it is I don't remember if I dreamed about the house first or saw it first when I was riding my bike."

"So, what happened in the house in your dreams?"

"Well," Miles paused and hunched his shoulders as if he had said more words during his pause. His lips started moving but words were not coming out. Miles finally spoke, "I keep waiting to see who is going to come out of the house. In my dream the door opens, and someone walks out backwards but then I always wake up before they turn around."

I didn't know what to think at this point. I could hear my mother's voice in my head, *"Child, you better be careful around that lil' boy. Something's not right about that one."* Miles was still in a trance staring at the house. "Miles, we have to go. You have to lead the way because I'm not familiar with this shortcut."

"Ok Ms. Gretchen. We should just be right around the corner and one street over." I didn't think we were around the corner for one second because on my regular path we would still have about eight more blocks to go. Miles hopped back on the bike and I followed close behind. He made a right turn and 'voila' I could see my house. I couldn't understand how we were so close. I guess my sense of direction wasn't as good as I thought or there was something strange about the city of Mintly.

I showered and dressed for work. When I went to the kitchen to whip up a quick breakfast for Miles, he was already dressed and sitting at the table with an already half-eaten sandwich. "You move fast huh Miles?"

"Yes ma'am." He managed to speak with a mouth full of food.

My cell phone rang. It was the Sinclairs. "Good morning." I had to force out the words.

"Morning Gretchen," Mrs. Sinclair plainly responded. "Is Miles around?"

"Yes, he's right here. I'll give him the phone."

I handed the phone to Miles and whispered, "It's your mom."

Miles looked excited and quickly grabbed the phone, "Hi Mom." He was smiling for a few seconds then his smile faded. I couldn't hear what she was telling him. "Yes ma'am," was all he said before handing me the phone.

I looked at the phone and the call had ended. "Is everything ok Miles?"

"Yes, she just wanted me to know she was about to lose service and she didn't know when she would be calling back."

"Ok." I glanced at my watch. "Your van will soon be here to pick you up for school so try to finish your sandwich."

"This is my favorite sandwich. I will put it in my pocket if I'm not finished."

I laughed, "You can't do that Miles. It will be all squished up."

"I ate squished sandwiches before and they taste just as good."

"You're so silly Miles." After a few minutes the van sounded the horn. Miles got up and went to the door. I was following him to see him off. After Miles got to the bottom step he turned around and ran back up the steps quickly to me and gave me a tight hug and said, "I love you Ms. Gretchen. You're the best." I stood there in shock not knowing how to respond. He looked once before he closed the door to the van and I raised my hand to wave and sounded 'I love you too' with my lips. I know he understood because a smile came on his face as he closed the door.

I thought about Miles all day at work, but I kept busy. At least I knew I would see him at the center and at home. We would have plenty of time to talk. I was thinking of ways I could get him to open up more and something he said kept resonating. Miles had mentioned going to The Cemetery for help with his own personal issues. I met Carl for lunch and talked it over with him.

Jazzes was packed for lunch, so we decided to go to Han's Café and have brunch. Paisley was there with her usual casual cheerful greeting offering us her special secret herb tea.

"No thanks," Carl politely declined. "But what is that delicious smell?"

Paisley pointed to the other end of the bar where a chef had a portable flat grill set up with an assortment of choices for fresh omelets. "Jeff from the brunch food truck asked if he could use my spot to serve custom omelets. I was like, why not. That will save me a lot of time in the kitchen." Paisley was moving one arm and had the other hand on her hip.

"I know what you mean Paisley. Why bother in the kitchen if someone else is willing to do it?" Carl conversed.

"Ok Carl," I said. "Let's get our order in before this place gets crowded too."

I ordered an omelet filled with sautéed spinach, onions, bell peppers, mushrooms, shrimp and pepper jack cheese. It was lightly topped with a crabmeat flavored sauce. I'm not sure what Carl had but it looked plain.

"So Gretch?" Carl put on a slick voice. "Any more comments from that secretary Ms. Bernette?"

I wasn't sure what he meant. "Well, she has been pretty quiet lately. I think something is happening at home because every time I pass by her desk, she is checking the messages on her cell phone. Why?"

"Well, our conversation about how she was blabbing on your first day at the firm dawned on me and I wanted to see if she was still chattering. You know she is on her third marriage, right?"

"No. What in the world happened?"

"The word is that hubby number one caught her cheating."

"Cheating? What?" I couldn't imagine Ms. Bernette cheating on her husband. She liked looking at attractive men and making comments, but I don't think she would ever go as far as having an affair with any of them.

"Yes, honey. But in her defense, it surprisingly wasn't her fault."

"Now how in the world was it not her fault?"

"Funny story, I can't make this stuff up Gretch. They were only married for two years. They went on a trip with some social club they were a part of. The trip was in Vegas and you know how things can get in Vegas. She got wasted, it was late, she went into the room next to hers thinking it was her room and fell asleep in the bed. She claims the door was cracked open. When her husband went up to the room, he didn't see her in there, so he left out to go look for her. He heard some moaning coming from the room next door which sounded striking similar to his wife. Again, the door was cracked so he walked in and low and behold there she was saying oh baby to someone who wasn't her baby. Her husband turned on the lights and that's when she saw the man on top of her was not her husband. The rest of that story is history."

"You have got to be kidding me. That didn't happen in real life."

"It did. Then hubby number two was an up and coming sports agent. He was selfishly looking for a come-up. He selfishly married Ms. Bernette to get on at the Koperneil firm. The day after he got fired for falsifying documents, he filed for a divorce from Bernette."

"Oh no. That is horrible. She must have felt so used."

"She did and that's when she started to come see me. I would tell you more, but all the other parts are confidential. Everything I just told you was merely common knowledge everyone else in Mintly already knows."

"So, what's the deal with this hubby number three?"

"Oh, nothing major. He is almost the perfect guy."

"What do you mean almost?"

"I can't tell you anything else. It's confidential. Remember?"

"Huh? Well then, why did you bring all this up?"

Carl hunched his shoulders and said, "I don't know. I guess this mimosa got me talking."

"Really Carl? Mimosa?"

"Yes. And you know when I get alcohol in me, I can hit those high notes." Carl tried to sing, but his tune was off key.

"Stop it," I tittered. "First of all, who told you that you could sing? Second of all, you are just being plain old messy."

Carl laughed. We finished brunch and left out to go our separate ways. On my way to my car I couldn't help but stare over at The Cemetery. It always felt like it was speaking to me or calling me or something. I shook off the feeling and went back to work. When I passed by Ms. Bernette's desk I couldn't help but think about everything Carl had recently told me.

"Good afternoon," I told Ms. Bernette.

"Good afternoon dear. How was your lunch?" She had such a pleasant mood whenever she held a conversation, I could see why she worked so long for Mr. Koperneil.

"It was delicious. I had this yummy omelet. Something not too heavy yet satisfying."

"I know what you mean. I messed around and had a plate delivered from Jazzes and now I feel stuffed and getting a little sleepy." She rubbed her stomach to exaggerate her full feeling and yawned.

"You'd better go to the break room and fix yourself a quick picker upper."

"Good idea." Ms. Bernette walked towards the break room.

I finished my day at the office and headed to the center. When I arrived, the first thing I did was look for Miles. I checked the meeting room where my group usually met, and he wasn't there. I walked outside to see if I could see his van coming down the street and I checked my watch to make sure I wasn't too early. There was no van in sight. I went back in to get my phone to call the van service. I picked up my phone to dial the number and I heard Miles' voice coming down the hall talking with one of the other kids. The kid was asking him about The Cemetery. Miles didn't usually talk but he had plenty to say about his project. It was pleasant seeing Miles socializing with other kids.

"Hi Ms. Gretchen." Miles always greeted me when he walked in the room.

"Hi Miles. How was your day at school?"

"Pretty good. We had three tests today and I think I aced all three."

"I'm sure you did Miles."

"Ms. Gretchen?"

"Yes Miles."

"Do you think we can go over to The Cemetery today?"

"Of course, we can. What kind of question is that? It's your creation. Why wouldn't we be able to go?"

"Well, my parents always tell me no whenever I ask them to take me."

I was beginning to feel a tad bit of hatred for his parents, but I couldn't say it out loud to Miles. Even though I didn't appreciate how they treated him, they were still his parents. I had to put on a fake face like his response didn't bother me.

"After we leave the center today, we will walk over there and stay as long as you want."

"Yes!" Miles was stuffed with excitement.

I had the kids in my group play a few games and everyone had a great time. The time at the center went by fast. Afterwards, Miles and I headed to The Cemetery.

Miles went straight to the registration room and found a free panel to register a session. "Will you come in the session with me?" Miles looked straight into my eyes with a pleading look on his face. My heart sunk at the thought of going into the session because there was a risky chance of the panel reading my thoughts. The thoughts in my mind would display the intense dislike I had developed towards his parents.

"Of course, I will." I forced the words out of my mouth and clinched my lips as I followed Miles to the room. We entered the room and the door closed behind us. The panel instantly came on and the typing started.

"Mom and dad, why did you leave me?" Miles thoughts ran quickly across the screen. I tried my best not to think about anything, but my thoughts came out anyway.

"Miles, they are not in here to answer you."

"They don't have to be here. They both came and registered the day after this place opened. They don't know I saw them come and they didn't put any restrictions on access to their accounts, so I included them on this session."

Now my heart was starting to beat faster. I could feel the pulse in my neck. Miles repeated his question.

"Mom and dad, why did you leave me?"

Some words typed slowly across the screen and it wasn't coming from me.

"Miles, we are worried that something might be wrong with you." The message came from his mother. The screen ended the quote with her name in parenthesis. I guess it indicated those were the thoughts of a person who was not physically present in the session. Me and Miles' thoughts did not have our names at the end.

"What do you mean something is wrong with me? I feel normal." I could see Miles hands stiffening as his thoughts scrolled across the screen.

"Something happened to you when you were born, and it didn't bother us at first but now we have to figure out what happened." This was his mother speaking again.

"Something like what?" Miles asked.

"We are not sure Miles, and that is why we have to do some research and find out." His father's thoughts displayed this time.

"I don't care about any research and I know nothing is wrong with me. I love both of you, but you keep treating me like I'm an outsider. Do you even love me?"

My nerves were bad. I had to control my thoughts so I wouldn't curse these people out if something crazy came across the screen. I almost couldn't look.

"Miles, we know you are too young to understand this, but love has different levels. To answer your question, yes, we love you," his mother replied.

"What do you mean love has levels? If that's what you think about love, then do you love me at a low level or at a high level?"

"We love you enough Miles," his father's thoughts displayed.

"Enough?" My thoughts jumped on the screen without me even able to hold them back. "I apologize but both of you are being ridiculous. I'm sorry Miles but I can't let this go on."

"It's ok Ms. Gretchen. I have to hear what they feel. I need to know for myself even if it's something I don't want to hear." Miles had a determined look on his face. A chill came through my body calming my spirit. My pulse immediately dropped to its normal beat and I sat back attentively observing the panel.

"Miles, when we say we love you enough what we are saying is we love you enough to accept you with whatever may be wrong with you. We planned for you and when you finally arrived, we were overexcited. Then, as time went on, we noticed your skin and hair looked different than ours. It's not a big deal but it did raise questions in our mind. I called the hospital for answers and they have refused to cooperate."

His father's thoughts added, "Things will change soon. We are tremendously close to figuring everything out. Maybe with the information we discover we will be able to spend more time working on our relationship with you."

"I'd positively like that," Miles shared.

The session ended, and the doors opened.

Miles got up and walked out. I remained sitting staring at the wall as if I was paralyzed. "Ms. Gretchen, let's go," Miles whispered. I got up and followed Miles out of the building. I bumped into Ms. Bernette on the sidewalk outside and she looked embarrassed that I had seen her there.

"Oh, hi Gretchen, I didn't expect to see you here." Ms. Bernette looked around as if she was being followed.

"I've been here a few times."

"So how is it?" She whispered as if she was asking me a secret.

"It's fine. Are you going in alone?"

"Yes. Have you ever gone in alone?"

"No. I haven't but I'm sure it will be a good experience for you."

Ms. Bernette seemed unsure about the whole thing, but she still headed towards the door. I was about to get into my car before I heard someone screaming my name, "Gretchen! Gretchen!" I looked up and it was Ms. Bernette running my way. She startled Miles too because he was looking at her strangely. "Gretchen, can you please come in with me?" Ms. Bernette begged. I gave a long sigh because I was sort of drained from this last session with Miles but then I thought about all of the things Carl told me about Ms. Bernette and I did not want to let her down.

I motioned for Miles to come to my side of the car. "Miles, go across the street to Han's and wait for me there. I shouldn't be too long."

Miles happily went across the street into the café. After I made sure he was inside I turned to Ms. Bernette and went in The Cemetery and joined her in a session. I focused with a strong level of intensity so my thoughts would not jump out on the panel. Ms. Bernette's thoughts started.

"Bernette, do you think something is wrong with you?" Ms. Bernette looked at me in shock because she wasn't expecting her thoughts to immediately show up in a panel on the wall, but it continued. "Your first husband left you, your second husband used you and now this husband doesn't even want to touch you."

My eyes were stretched wide and I leaned my head back in shame for Ms. Bernette. I couldn't believe what I was seeing. First, she was talking in third person. Then she was filling in all the blanks that Carl didn't tell me. I kept quiet and allowed her thoughts to flow.

She started reasoning and answering herself, "There is nothing wrong with you. You have a great heart and a kind spirit. Your first husband was a complete fool. He should have forgiven you. I guess he forgot the way you forgave him when you walked in on him getting pleasured orally from the maid in your own house. As for that second 'thing', you are way better off without him. He never loved you in the first place. He disgustingly wanted to use you for a job. And this one now does try. He is just on a lot of medication because of his health. You do remember how it was when you first got married and before he got sick. He couldn't keep his hands off you. Oh, I know. I'll get him to come here with me next time and maybe we can think it through together."

I looked over at Ms. Bernette and she was shaking her head in agreement with the words on the screen. The session ended, and the door opened. Ms. Bernette got up, gave me a hug and thanked me for going with her then she left out. I could see that she was embarrassed about everything that came out concerning her past relationships and even her current relationship.

After those two uncomfortable sessions I needed a break. I walked across the street to get Miles. He was sitting at the counter and sipping on something. "Look at this Ms. Gretchen." He raised his cup up to my face. "Paisley let me try this secret herb tea. It tastes so good. You should try it."

I looked at Paisley with slight disapproval and she must have read my mind. "I'm sorry," she apologized. "Do you want me to take it from him?"

I looked back at Miles and he started to sip it like he was in a sipping race afraid that he wouldn't finish before the time ran out. "Take your time Miles," I subdued. "You can have it. I doubt Paisley would give you something you shouldn't have."

"Now you know I would never do that," Paisley enlightened.

The door to the café chimed and Langley walked in. He stopped at the counter and did the same thing he did last time. He tapped twice on the counter and Paisley reached for the unmarked jar and served Langley the same drink he had before. While Langley was dipping the purple stringed tea bag in the cup Miles slid over next to him, "Mr. Langley, thank you so much for helping me with The Cemetery."

"You're welcome," Langley spoke in an expressionless manner. Langley then glanced over my way and said in the same tone, "Good evening Gretchen."

"Good evening." I was shocked and partially blushing because I didn't expect for him to acknowledge me.

Miles finished his tea, we left the café and picked up our to-go order from Jazzes before we went home.

Chapter 8

At work the next morning, as soon as I placed my purse in my desk Ms. Bernette walked in out of breath and closed the door behind her.

"Good morning dear." She seemed frazzled. "About yesterday evening."

I stopped her before she kept on her rampage. "My lips are sealed," I promised. She looked relieved to hear this. "You don't ever have to worry about me telling any of your business Ms. Bernette. I take information shared at The Cemetery as ever so personal and confidential. That was the whole point of the place anyway. Right?"

"Exactly," she expressed out of breath from holding in all the words she wanted to let escape. "I'm sure that kid didn't choose to call it The Cemetery for nothing." She hummed a sweet giggle afterwards.

"He sure didn't," I proudly proclaimed as if I was his parent. In a sense, I was his parent at that moment because of the official paperwork.

Ms. Bernette seemed to have calmed down when she went back to her desk. A few hours later Mr. Koperneil stopped by my office. *Knock knock.* "Hey there Gretch."

"Hello Mr. Koperneil. How are you feeling?"

"I'm well Gretchen. Hey, I've been meaning to ask you. Have you tried The Cemetery out yet?" I could almost predict his next question before I even answered this one.

"As a matter of fact, I did. I have been there several times." I peeped over, and Ms. Bernette looked as if she was staring straight at my lips to read every word I would say.

"So, what do you think?"

Bingo. There's the predicted question. "It was a unique experience. Are you thinking about trying it?"

"I am."

"Good, you should entertain the idea of going at least once."

"My wife and I are planning on going together around noon today."

I froze. All I could think about is how much dirt Mrs. Koperneil might not be able to keep in about herself.

"Do you think she will like it?" Mr. Koperneil asked me this as if I were the expert at The Cemetery.

I didn't want to lie to Mr. Koperneil, but I had to because I didn't want to discourage him from going. "Honestly, it depends. But she will most likely find the experience interesting."

"Ok then. That settles it for sure. We will head out there, have our session and go to lunch. I'll let you know how it goes." Mr. Koperneil gave me a slanted salute and walked out.

I had no idea why Mr. Koperneil thought it would be necessary to give me an update on his session at The Cemetery, but I was not looking forward to it. I caught Ms. Bernette peaking over her desk to eavesdrop. She was shaking her head no then she quickly pretended to be doing work on her computer when Mr. Koperneil passed by her desk.

I started pacing the floor in my office shaking my hands trying to think of ways I could stop Mr. Koperneil from going to The Cemetery. I almost went to his office twice but then I kept turning around because I had talked myself out of following through with that strategy. I mean, I didn't know what kind of excuse I would give him in the first place. If I told him the truth, then he would know someone told me all the dirt about his wife. I couldn't let that happen. He likely mistakenly thought I only looked at Mrs. Koperneil as his sweet innocent wife. I'm more than sure he didn't know my opinion about her had been tainted by his very own dear secretary.

I had to shake this off. I had too much work to do. I was glad when my phone chirped letting me know I had a text message. At least it interrupted all those crazy thoughts I was having. I felt in my purse and couldn't find my phone. I knew it was in there because I hadn't taken it out yet. I spent the next two minutes emptying everything from my purse and still couldn't find it. I checked my pockets and it wasn't there either. My day was not going so well. This was crazy. I knew I had it because it just chirped so it had to be in my office somewhere. I checked under paperwork on my desk and plowed through every drawer of my desk. No phone. It couldn't be far. I picked up my desk phone and called my number. I heard it ringing. I rushed to figure out where the ringing was coming from. It felt like I was playing a game of hide and seek with the phone and it was giving me hints of where it was. I had to call it a second time before I found it on the floor underneath the curtain. I was on my knees by this time. I checked my text message and it was from Mrs. Sinclair. Seeing it was Mrs. Sinclair aggravated me even more. She is the last person I wanted to hear from this morning. I was hoping it was one of my clients with good news about an endorsement deal. Not even close. It was the witch mother letting me know she would try to video chat Miles this afternoon on my phone. I got up off my knees with the help of the edge of my desk and slumped down in my chair. I stared at her message and all kinds of thoughts ran through my mind. I especially kept thinking about the visit with Miles at The Cemetery. I now knew how they truly felt about Miles because of the session and it made me tremendously angry. I responded "ok." I wanted to add some other choice words to the text, but I knew I would regret it, so I stopped typing and left it at "ok."

I closed the door to my office and called Carl.

"Morning darling." His voice always ushered me to a place of conciliation. "How's everything going with Miles?"

"It's going good," I certified. "But listen Carl. That's not why I called you. Mr. & Mrs. Koperneil are going to The Cemetery today around noon."

"Noon today?" He sounded like he was looking at a calendar to see if it was even possible.

"Yes, noon today."

"Are they going together?"

"Yes, together."

"Ohhhh, this is not good Gretch."

"I know, that's why I'm calling you. Do you think you can stop them from going? Or at least stop them from going there together?"

"Now how do you propose I do that when I'm not even supposed to know they are going?"

"I don't know." I rushed to think of ways he could stop them. "Maybe you can happen to bump into them there by coincidence."

"Bump into them and then what?"

"Pull Mr. Koperneil off aside and let him know how thoughts impulsively flow freely on the panel."

"Uhm. I don't know Gretchen. That will be somewhat intrusive. I mean, I have a pretty good relationship with both of them but it's strictly professional. I don't think I should go because I could jeopardize their trust with me and they are some of my most devoted clients."

"Dang it Carl. Are you pulling some of your psychology tricks on me right now?"

He babbled, "No darling, but you know I have to remain professional. I have an image to uphold."

"Yeah. I know. I guess you're right," I reluctantly admitted. "I guess I'll patiently wait to see what he says when he gets back from the visit."

"Yes Gretchen. That will be the best thing to do. He might even bring up some of their conversation in one of our sessions, so I can address it at that time."

"Alright then. Let me get back to work and stop worrying about things out of my control."

"Yes, you do that. Will I see you at lunch today?"

"Yes, can you go around one?" I knew if I had a late lunch, I wouldn't have to face Mr. Koperneil for at least an extra hour.

"Let me see." I could hear Carl flipping through the pages of his appointment book to check his schedule. "How about 12:30 because I have an appointment for 1:45?"

"Ok," I puffed. "That's fine. Do you want to go to the Chinese buffet on Grand Boulevard? They have a variety to choose from plus I am in the mood for some of that tasty egg drop soup they serve."

"We can go there. I haven't been there in a while, so it will be a nice change."

"Good. See you at 12:30."

"Yep, see you then." I heard Carl repeating the time to himself so he wouldn't forget before hanging up.

I put all my junk back in my purse and read through a few contracts. The time was moving so fast. When I looked up again it was time for lunch. I met with Carl for lunch and he could tell something more was bothering me.

"What's going on Gretchen? You are not yourself today." I almost hated that Carl could damn near read my thoughts.

"I'm fine," I said unconvincingly. "I just have a lot on my mind."

"Are you worried that much about what will happen between Mr. & Mrs. Koperneil?"

"Yes, that and this Miles situation and my mother..."

"What's going on with your mother?"

"She hasn't been feeling well. You know she has been sick for a few years now, but it is starting to get worst. Her treatments are taking a toll on her and I am way over here. I feel like I'm neglecting her, and she has always been there for me no matter what."

"Well, from what you've told me about your mother, she is a profoundly strong woman. And she knows your heart. I'm sure she doesn't feel neglected. She knows what you are doing with your life and I can only imagine how supportive she is and only wants the best for you."

"I suppose you're right. I feel like I should be doing more for her. I don't have any brothers or sisters like you who can help out. It's just me."

"Why don't you just ask her to come here and live with you?"

"I've mentioned it and she is stuck on New Orleans." We were both quiet for a moment. "I don't blame her though. There is no place like New Orleans."

"There sure isn't honey. I guess we will have to make it a point to visit home more often, right?" Carl cheerfully suggested.

"Yes, it undeniably sounds like a great plan. We don't have anything stopping us. Plus, I know we would have a blast every time."

"Yep," Carl agreed.

We finished our lunch and I headed back to work. I dreaded going back because I didn't want to face Mr. Koperneil. I was hoping he changed his mind about telling me how the visit to The Cemetery went. I stopped by Ms. Bernette's desk on my way to my office. "Did Mr. Koperneil make it back yet?" I whispered.

She whispered back, "Yes, and he didn't look so good. He didn't say a word to anyone. He went straight to his office and shut the door."

Not being able to see Mr. Koperneil didn't help to sooth my nerves. I walked to my office and pretended to be busy, but I kept waiting for Mr. Koperneil's knock on my door. The rest of the day seemed to drag. Every time I checked the clock only fifteen minutes had passed but it felt like it should have been an hour. It was getting close to five o'clock and I still had not seen Mr. Koperneil. I called Ms. Bernette's desk phone, "Are you sure he is in there?"

"Yes dear. I saw him come in myself and I haven't moved from my desk. He never left his office yet."

"Ok, if he doesn't come out before I leave, I'm going to knock on his door."

"Ok. I'll stick around just in case," Ms. Bernette added.

The time rolled on and Mr. Koperneil never left his office. It was now five minutes to five and all I could do was stare at his office door hoping I didn't have to go knock on it because I had no idea what I was going to say and still sound normal. Two more minutes passed and other people in the office were packing up to leave out. Some people had already left with the hopes of beating five o'clock traffic. There was still no sign of Mr. Koperneil. Ms. Bernette signaled for me to go over and knock but I was still hesitant. Another minute passed and I built up the nerve to walk over to his office and knock on the door. I slowly paced towards the door glancing back and forth at the time. I went to knock on the door and I changed my mind. I turned around to rush back to my office. As soon as I reached halfway to my office, I heard his office door open. I turned around and there he was. I didn't know if I should come out and ask him what happened or think of something else to say.

"Oh, hi there Gretchen." He was acting as if nothing was wrong. "Are you about to head out?"

I didn't know how to answer his question. "Yes, I am. I'm going straight to the center after this. The school van dropped Miles there and I have to make sure I go straight there."

"Yes, that's right," he recalled. "Why don't you two come over for dinner tonight around seven-thirty? I know Miles appreciates good food and it is something that will surely be at the table." He winks one eye.

Mr. Koperneil was so convincing, so I couldn't refuse the offer. "Of course, we will come over and I know Miles will also enjoy meeting your kids." I smiled with approval.

"Great, we'll see you both tonight." Mr. Koperneil got on the elevator and I was still standing in the same spot as if I was seeing him off. As soon as the elevator doors shut, Ms. Bernette and I both looked at each other wondering what that was all about.

I went to the center after work and let the kids have a free day. I was mentally drained and now I had to get ready for dinner with the Koperneils. I told Miles about our dinner invitation and he started rubbing his stomach. "Oh boy." Miles gazed in the air as if he were seeing a whole layout of food right before him. "I've tasted Mrs. Koperneil's food before at church and it is fantastic. Way better than my mom's, but you know I would never tell that to my mom."

I remembered his mom said she would try to video chat, so I checked my phone. There were no missed calls yet so I made sure the ringer was turned up so I wouldn't miss the call. I didn't tell Miles about the text in case she wouldn't call. I guess by Miles mentioning her he thought her up because she called a few minutes after I checked my phone. When I saw it was her, I handed the phone to Miles for him to answer. We were the only ones left in the room, so I sat nearby in case they needed to talk to me.

"Hey mom." Miles was excited to hear her voice.

"Hi Miles." His mom's tone was as dry as a judge announcing a sentence for his closest relative.

"Where's Zach?" Miles pretended not to catch on to her unenthusiastic demeanor.

"We had to leave him with Grammy in New York. He came down with a bad virus and they wouldn't let him board the plane. Miles, we just wanted to see you before we lost service. Since your dad and I had time to deal with some things we wanted you to know we love you."

"I know." Miles turned so that I wouldn't hear what he was saying. "You love me enough."

His mother looked confused, but she didn't correct him. I could hear his father whispering in the background, "Do you see what I mean honey? He always acts like this." She pretended like he wasn't saying anything and kept talking. "Miles, your Grammy has Ms. Gretchen's number and is supposed to call you tomorrow."

"Will you be back before Thanksgiving? I'm off of school all next week. Maybe you can send for me if you aren't back yet." Miles was nearly begging for them to say yes but he was having no luck.

His dad came on the screen. "Hi Miles."

"Hi dad. I miss you."

"I hope you're being good for Ms. Gretchen." He ignored Miles' 'I miss you' comment. "We won't be back until the Saturday after Thanksgiving. It's too dangerous for you to fly overseas by yourself. We will see you when we get back."

"Ok." Miles strained to keep a positive temperament. "I hope you don't lose service so you can call me back tomorrow."

His mother responded, "Yes, baby, we will try to call back tomorrow if the phones are working." This was my first time ever hearing his mother call him an endearing name. I was happy for Miles because when she called him 'baby' an appreciative smile slid on Miles' face.

"Ok, mom and dad. Talk to you tomorrow." Miles spoke with satisfaction in his voice.

"Talk to you tomorrow," they expressionlessly spoke in unison.

They ended the video chat conversation and I watched as Miles appeared to be focused on the floor but he had a smile on his face so I knew he was rethinking about the call with his parents.

"Hey Miles," I interrupted his daydreaming. "Let's go home and change before we go to the Koperneils for dinner. We left the center and went home and changed into comfortable clothes. When we arrived at the Koperneils, their children were waiting near the door. We could hear them fighting to open the door first when we rang the doorbell.

Mrs. Koperneil opened the door. "Come on in Gretchen and Miles." She welcomed us in with hugs and kisses. She pointed to each of her kids starting with the youngest. "This is the last of the bunch, little miss Ainsleigh. She was our surprise baby and turned five-years-old last month." Ainsleigh reached up and gave me a hug. She also hugged Miles and he stiffly kept his arms straight because he was afraid to move. "And this is Michael," she continued. Michael immediately stuck out his hand to introduce himself and he said his name at the same time his mother said his name. "Michael," he said as he shook my hand. "I am the big brother of the family. I know this one next to me looks older, but he is spoiled." He looked over at his brother and gave him a smile that said *'ha'* as if he won some kind of bragging competition.

"And how old are you?" I asked Michael.

"I'm ten." He turned to Miles, "I think I've seen you around school. You're the one who made the cemetery building huh?"

Miles shook his head yes without making a sound.

Michael continued, "That is amazing."

His older brother added, "Yeah, you are like a mini-genius."

Miles looked surprised they were sincerely saying good things about him and not calling him weird names like some of the other students did in his class. Judging by their manners, these kids were exactly as described by Ms. Bernette when we first met, respectful.

"Tell them your name," Mrs. Koperneil tapped her oldest son.

"My name is Charles. I'm named after my dad."

"Yeah," his little brother chimed in. "He's a junior," exaggerating it like it was something he despised.

"Michael always does that." His mother felt the need to give a more in-depth explanation. "We did at least give you your dad's middle name," she reasoned as she tapped him on his head.

The oldest daughter was waiting patiently for her introduction. She politely stood there quietly smiling the whole time. She was beautiful but plain. "And this is our first born. Nalia. She made sixteen this summer and this is her senior year in high school."

"Yes," Nalia added shyly with her hands behind her back as she slowly rocked her shoulders back and forth. "I'm so looking forward to college."

"Oh, that's great." I gave her an impressed smile. "Where do you plan on going?"

"I'm thinking about either The Julliard School in New York or Berklee College of Music in Boston."

"Oh, so you like music?" I asked Nalia.

"Yes ma'am." She was tenderly polite. "I play the piano and the saxophone."

"Ok, I took a few piano lessons when I was young. Maybe you can play something for me later."

"I would love that." Nalia's eyes sparkled. I was surprised she wasn't shy about agreeing to play a song because she was extremely shy while talking.

"Ok, enough with the introductions." Mrs. Koperneil brought the meeting to a conclusion. "Good thing we stopped at four kids or we would be standing at this door forever," she said jokingly.

The oldest son guided Miles to the living room where they were watching a movie and I followed Mrs. Koperneil to the kitchen. "Why don't you help me put everything out on the table Gretchen," she said as I followed her lead of washing my hands at the kitchen sink. She politely instructed me where to place everything on the table. "If you think this is special, wait until you come over for Thanksgiving next week. You will be here, right?" she waited optimistically for me to answer her question.

"I'm not sure yet. I may have to fly home to be with my mother. I have to see if she will come here or if I will go there."

"Well, try to convince her to come here because you are all welcome and there will be plenty of food, and desserts, and drinks, and different kinds of breads, and..."

Mr. Koperneil walked in the dining room right when Mrs. Koperneil was listing everything they had for Thanksgiving. "Oh Gabriella, don't scare the poor girl. She might think we are some kind of strange people if you tell her every single dish we have for Thanksgiving." Mr. Koperneil walked over to me and gave me a gentle peck on the cheek then grabbed the dish I was about to place down and placed it on the table himself.

The table was set, and Mr. Koperneil called the kids over to come and say grace. Mr. Koperneil prayed over the food and his kids begged to eat in the living room so they could finish watching their movie. Mr. Koperneil didn't hesitate to allow them to go. "Just take out the tv trays so you don't drop food all over the floor," he spoke to the kids gently as they walked away with plates served. Miles simply followed along staring at his plate of food the whole time it was being served and while walking back towards the living room. He loved food.

I took a bite of the stewed chicken and it melted in my mouth. I almost moaned because it was so good, but I kept my composure. "This is delicious Mrs. Koperneil," I said after my first bite.

"Thank you dear," she politely responded.

"Gabriella here stole my heart with this cooking," Mr. Koperneil bragged as he chomped down on his plate of food. "I barely like to eat out because no other food tastes as good as my Gab's food." They were both smiling at each other as if they were so in love. It made me want to have love like the Koperneils with a house filled with kids. The only problem is that I hadn't even found a decent man to marry yet plus my biological clock was ticking on the family part. But, looking at these two gave me hope. Ms. Bernette told me the Koperneils had been married for twenty-one years and by the calculation in my head from the age of their oldest kid, Mrs. Koperneil had to be around my age, give or take a few years, when she had Nalia.

Miles walked back in the living room with an empty plate. "Ms. Gretchen, may I have seconds please?"

I was glad Mrs. Koperneil responded for me because I wanted to say yes but I didn't want to sound intrusive, especially with it being my first time visiting. Mrs. Koperneil reached for his plate and gently smiled saying, "You sure can baby. You can eat until your little heart is full." She served him more food on his plate and Miles went back to the living room smiling and staring at his food the whole time all over again.

After I finished my plate I got up and took their plates to the kitchen too. They thanked me and I rinsed off the dishes. When I got back to the dining room, they were awkwardly quiet. I could feel there was a little tension in the room. I quietly sat down and tried to break the ice. "I am stuffed. I am so glad we were invited over for dinner."

"And I'm glad you came Gretch," Mr. Koperneil hypothesized in an almost here comes the bad news voice. I looked over at Mrs. Koperneil and she was shaking her head no and I could read her lips saying, '*not now.*' Mr. Koperneil kept talking anyway. "Gretch you know where we went before lunch today, right?"

I shook my head yes and kept quiet hoping he wasn't about to tell me a whole bunch of things he learned about his wife.

"Well Gretch," he continued. "I have to be honest with you here and I know all of this might seem strange and you might be feeling like we shouldn't be telling you all of our personal business but hell, I know most people talk about this stuff anyway. I have been trying to ignore it all of these years."

Mrs. Koperneil was beginning to turn red and I was feeling extremely uncomfortable about where this conversation was going. "Mr. Koperneil, you don't have to tell me about your visit. Whatever happened is personally between you and your wife. Please know that regardless of what people might gossip and say, your personal business is private."

"Oh, I know they gossip about me." Mrs. Koperneil let out a deep sigh and quietly slammed her napkin on the table. She reached over and held her husband's hand. "Charlie, I hope you forgive me for all of that infidelity stuff but all of it is in the past baby." Mr. Koperneil looked like he had lost his best friend.

"Maybe we should just leave," I tried to recommend so they could change the subject.

"No Gretchen," Mr. Koperneil insisted. "You stay. We want you to know everything. I need you to know everything." I kept thinking to myself, what does any of this have to do with me. He continued, "You see Gretchen, the thing about marriage is sometimes it is not always perfect. As a matter of fact, a lot of times it is not always perfect. And yes, I know my Gab made some mistakes during our marriage but as a man of God I have to forgive her. Look at my family. We have four beautiful children and I wouldn't want to mess up their lives just because of things I can't deal with at times." Mr. Koperneil shook his head as if he was trying to get all of the negative things about their marriage pumped out of his mind. Mrs. Koperneil couldn't look at him anymore. She kept her head down propped in her hand with her elbow on the table. He sat up straight, poked out his chest and cleared his throat. "She is not the only one with secrets Gretch. I have secrets of my own."

"Mr. Koperneil," I pleaded trying to stop him again.

"No, let me finish. Before I was married to Gab, and I didn't know she knew this, but she told me at The Cemetery, I was married to someone else. It was a long time ago. It is such a strong distance in time I sometimes forget that part of my life ever happened until Labor Day rolls around. I can't ever forget that Labor Day when I was eighteen years old. I was just a kid now that I think about it. But I was a kid with responsibilities. Me and my high school sweetheart at the time messed up. She ended up getting pregnant and both of our families insisted for us to get married. They were old school and didn't believe in having babies out of wedlock. Anyway, we rushed and got married before she had the baby. The baby was due mid-September. Being the young free-minded kids we were, we decided to take a trip to Pensacola for Labor Day weekend. It was only a three-hour drive from New Orleans. I bet you didn't know we were from the same city," he commented while still keeping the pace of his story. "We figured it would be alright to take the short drive, so we went for it with our young hearts leading the way. We had a *great* time. She couldn't drink of course but I did. I was so hung over the next day, but we had to get back because she had a doctor's appointment that afternoon. She couldn't drive because it was a stick shift and she didn't know how to drive my car. As soon as I made the curve after the Morrison exit, I hit a water puddle and hydroplaned. The last thing I remember is the car flipping over. By the time I woke up, I was in the hospital. My parents were both by my side crying. They said I had been in a coma for two weeks and it was a miracle I made it out alive."

This was a lot of information. I looked over at Miles and instead of watching the movie with the rest of the kids, he was leaned backwards on the sofa holding on to every word of our conversation. I used my hands by my lap to signal for him to turn around and watch television. He turned but I could tell he was still listening.

Mr. Koperneil went on with tears built up in his eyes but not falling, "My parents told me my wife and unborn child didn't make it. They brought me to the graveyard site and told me they were buried together. Like I said Gretchen, I was still a kid. This was all so much for me. I didn't know what to do with myself after that. Well, my parents sent me away to try to forget about everything. After college, I ended up here in Mintly and started my own firm. It was just a one man show at the time but eventually my business flourished."

The room felt tense and we were distressingly silent. Mr. Koperneil shook his head as though the thoughts were too much to bare so he got up and walked away. Mrs. Koperneil got up and sat in the dining chair right next to mine. She took me by both of my hands and placed both of her hands on top of mine. She spoke softly and said, "He didn't tell you everything. Before I met Charlie, I did some research on him. I knew all about his first marriage. I didn't let him know I found out until we went to The Cemetery earlier today. It wasn't done on purpose or with ill intent. It all came out on its own. I guess it had been bothering me. Well, I know it had been bothering me. You see Gretchen, when I researched that accident the newspaper reported that the baby survived. I didn't know that Charlie didn't know this until today. I foolishly always thought he was keeping this unknown child a secret from me all these years. That's partly why I did some of the stuff I did even though it is no excuse. We never talked about any of that stuff. Anyway, the thing is I traced the records of that baby."

Mrs. Koperneil had my full attention at this point. Now I wanted to know what happened to the baby. Mrs. Koperneil suddenly stopped talking and stalked my past as if she was possessed.

"It's you," she whispered.

I quickly moved my hands from hers and pulled myself back. "I'm sorry Mrs. Koperneil. What are you talking about?" I was getting nervous and positively wanted to scurry out of the house. I was stuck between wanting to hear more and wanting to leave.

She hesitated before continuing, "You are that baby. You are Charlie's daughter. I knew the whole time we were married. That's why I knew so much about you and I was able to convince him to hire you. I still didn't know he didn't know about you at that time. I thought once he hired you, he would tell me the truth about his past. Now I know why he didn't tell me. He didn't even know himself."

I felt Mr. Koperneil walk back in the dining room. I turned and looked at him. He was looking at me as if he had seen a ghost. His wife made him sit down. "Gretchen, I'm so sorry." He could no longer hold in his tears. "I didn't know. I promise you I didn't know. After lunch, I called my aunt to see if she knew if any of this information was true because both of my parents passed away years ago. She did confirm my parents lied to me when I came out of the coma. She said everyone was worried I couldn't raise a little girl by myself. I thought you died in that accident. All of these years and I sincerely didn't know. I'm so deeply sorry."

I immediately got up and grabbed my purse from the table by the door. "Let's go Miles," I firmly called out without even looking back at the Koperneils. Miles got up quickly and we left out without saying good-bye. It was a quiet ride home and I could feel Miles looking at me.

"What's wrong Ms. Gretchen?" Miles' soft voice of concern was hard to resist.

"Nothing Miles." I gave him a fake smile trying to hide all of the emotions I was feeling.

Miles was persistent. "Ms. Gretchen, you know if something is bothering you that you can just go to The Cemetery. I think it can help you."

Help me? I thought to myself. It seems like that place was bringing out more harm than help the way I was feeling. I didn't answer Miles. I stayed focused and kept driving. I quietly went to my room when we got home and barely told Miles good night.

So many questions were going through my head. I didn't know what to think. Was all that stuff true? Did my real mother die in a car accident? Why didn't I know about this? Was I adopted or something? None of this made sense. I looked strikingly similar like my mother. Everyone always told me that since I could remember. The Koperneils had to be wrong. I started to pick up the phone to call my mother and ask her some questions, but I looked at the clock and knew it was too late to call her with that kind of foolishness. I thought about what Miles had said about The Cemetery. He was right. Maybe I should go there to get some answers. Maybe the answers are all in my own mind and I apparently need to dig them out.

Chapter 9

The next few days at the office were extremely awkward. I couldn't look at Mr. Koperneil in the eyes. I avoided him every chance I got. I made it a point to leave out early for lunch to avoid seeing Mr. Koperneil. On my way out, I was in such a rush to get on the elevator I never looked up. Lance was getting off the elevator and I bumped into him as soon as the doors opened. Lance caught a glimpse of my face when he was exiting the elevator and could tell something was bothering me. He had walked in with one of the top football players, Leon Charvette, but Lance kept his focus on making sure I was fine.

"Are you ok Gretchen?" his actions of concern took over.

I gloomily shook my head no. At this point I knew that if I spoke even as much as a single syllable the tears would frantically start pouring out. He was already out of the elevator but held the doors opened so he could get me to look up. I avoided eye contact while I waited anxiously for him to compassionately let me leave. The pressure was eating me alive. Lance finally let the doors go. I pressed the close door button and stood at the back of the elevator waiting for the doors to shut. The tears immediately dropped and I quickly dried my face before I reached the bottom floor. I rushed to my car before anyone else could see me and drove off as fast as I could. As soon as I made it home, I sent Lance a text message apologizing and asked him to please let Mr. Koperneil know I needed some time off. He responded stating I should take as much time as I needed and not to worry about any of my clients because he would meet with them on my behalf. I was relieved to know I didn't have to think about work at the moment.

The next morning after I saw Miles off to school I went back in the house and shut myself in my room. After about an hour of complete silence I decided to get up and go for a walk. I walked over a few blocks and found myself in front of the colorful house with the carved shutters. There was a calm breeze blowing and the wind chimes on the porch gently sounded. As the wind blew the chime softly, the sun shone through the stone in the center. I squinted from the distance and the stone looked similar to the one on Miles' bracelet. I started to walk closer to the house to get a better look. When I reached the edge of the porch, the door opened. A lady walked out backwards just like in Miles' dream. I was already in her yard, so it was too late for me to turn around without speaking. "Hello." I spoke at a low pitch not to startle her. She didn't answer so I guess my pitch was too low and it was drowned out by the sounds of the wind chime. "Hello miss," I said a little louder with a touch of crackled nervousness in my voice.

She immediately turned around and her face had a soft smooth glow to it. Although she didn't display a single wrinkle, she was partially slouched in posture, so I figured she was advanced in years. "Oh, hello there. I wasn't expecting anyone. Can I help you with anything dear?" She was irresistibly kind in her gestures and didn't seem to mind at all that I had invited myself onto her property.

"Uh, no not really." I was unsure of what to say. "I was just admiring your wind chime."

She stopped and looked at it herself as if it held a dear place in her heart. "Oh yes, this wind chime was handmade by my great-great-grandmother. I found it full of dust in the attic of this house."

"Oh, so you grew up here," I asked the lady.

"Well, yes and no," she curiously replied. "This is my home. I did go away for a little while but now I'm back to stay."

"I understand. No place like home, right?"

"That's perfectly right my dear. No place like home. And what may I ask is your name dear?" She gave me a strong yet soft look right in the face and patiently waited for my response.

"I'm sorry. My name is Gretchen." My voice cracked because of the butterflies in my stomach. I was too afraid to ask for her name, so I kept quiet.

"Gretchen," she repeated while she pondered on the name as if it rang a bell. "I'm not sure I've ever met a Gretchen before in my lifetime but it sure is a pretty name."

"Oh, thank you very much." I was still afraid to ask for her name.

"My great-aunt on my mother's side gave me my name," she volunteered to give me more information about herself. She looked back at the wind chime and said, "Hannah. My great-aunt named me Hannah because she said my birth was a sign of grace to her because she could not bear children. She was like my second mom. I spent more time with her than I did with my own mother. She taught me the secret to living."

I wasn't sure about the meaning of everything she was talking about, but her story had me in a trance. I listened and watched her as she made sure her door was securely locked and I headed back home. I called into the office to check my messages on my desk phone. Surprisingly, I had a message from Langley. The message was from yesterday and he asked if I could possibly have lunch with him tomorrow, which was today. I looked at the time on my watch and it was approaching eleven-thirty. I wasn't in the mood for any company being I was continuing my sulking fast, but I called him anyway on the number he left on the message. It must have been his cell phone or a direct line because it didn't go through the secretary. After about four rings he answered, "Hello," with a mild alto voice.

"Hello," I echoed. "I'm trying to reach Langley."

"Speaking," he replied.

"Oh, hi Langley. This is Gretchen. I know its last minute about the lunch request, but I just checked my office messages."

"I understand. If you still have time, the offer still stands." He caught me off guard.

"Sure. I have time. Where do you want me to meet you?"

"How does Carmen's sound? Have you ever been there?"

"No, I haven't," I answered. "What kind of food do they have?"

"It's mostly burgers but they do serve a platter with chicken fingers or fried seafood."

"Sounds good. I'm sure I can find something there. What time is good for you because I'm pretty much free all day?"

"Let's meet around one if it's ok with you," he suggested.

"One o'clock sounds good. Text the address and I'll be there."

As soon as we hung up, a text message came through with the address to Carmen's. I freshened up and changed three times before deciding to settle on wearing some plain jeans, a button-down blouse and heels. I felt like it was cute enough for lunch and not too casual for Langley because most likely he was wearing a suit. At least every time I saw him, he had on a suit.

I arrived a little early so I could have a chance to look over the menu before he got there. He snuck behind me at the bar and said, "Hello there," as he greeted me with a loose hug. I half leaned and hugged him back.

"I was sneaking to check out the menu so I could decide what to order before you got here but now, I'm busted," I admitted.

Surprisingly, he jokingly responded, "Yep, busted you are miss lady. Let's have a seat on the patio. It overlooks the lake and the breeze is nice today."

I followed Langley to our table and he was the perfect gentleman by pulling out my chair for me to sit first. "Two waters for now," he told the waiter.

I looked at the view and it was desirably stunning. The waters were calm and glistening with the sun and there was an extra breeze under the patio with the rotating ceiling fans. I caught Langley studying my appreciation of the scenery. "So, what do you think?" he inquired.

"I think it is lovely."

"Wait until you try the food. I know the work week doesn't end until five o'clock this afternoon, but do you want one glass of wine?"

I thought to myself, is this a trick question. I don't care what time it is, wine is always good. "I guess one glass won't hurt," I answered modestly.

When the waiter returned with the water, he requested the wine, "Two glasses of the McGuigan classic Merlot please." The waiter gave a positive nod and walked away. Langley held up his menu and gave me his personal recommendations. "Now Gretchen, two of my favorite things here are the cheeseburger and the grilled chicken sandwich. Both of those sandwiches have fluffy a bun and will blend easily with each bite of your sandwich. If you are not big on sandwiches, the catfish platter is pretty good too."

"Honestly, all three sound good to me. But since this place is famous for the burgers, I guess I'll try one of those."

"Good choice," he conceded.

The waiter came back with the glasses of wine and placed them on the table. "Are you ready to place your order," he asked.

"Yes," Langley answered and gestured for me to place my order first.

"I'll have the cheeseburger, well-done, with everything except the pickles."

"The pickles give it that extra flavor," Langley asserted before placing his order. "I'll have the same thing except I do want the pickles and make it medium-well."

The waiter walked away. Langley raised his glass and I joined him. "To a beautiful Thanksgiving week coming up and to a beautiful lady." We clanged glasses and both sang, "Cheers." I took my first sip of the wine slowly in case it was bitter. To my surprise it had a pleasant smooth texture.

"Good huh," he inquired about the wine.

"Yes, intensely smooth," I had to admit.

"I know you are wondering in your suspicious mind why I invited you to lunch but I couldn't figure out any other way to approach you for a conversation outside of discussing business."

I couldn't tell if Langley was hitting on me or not, so I came straight out asked him, "Spencer Langley, are you hitting on me?"

"Well, since you brought it up Ms. Gretchen. Yes, I am."

"Wow," I pondered. "That's different."

"What do you mean?"

"I mean people don't usually ask you to lunch before even getting to know you these days. They usually want to take you out to the club and get you wasted before you ever visit a restaurant together."

"Oh, well, I don't do clubs, so I guess I'm a little out of touch with the rest of society."

"No, it's ok. I like it."

"You like what? Me?"

"No, that's not what I meant. I mean, yes, I do like you, but I was trying to say I like your approach. Wait a minute? I'm not saying I like you, 'like you'. I'm saying I appreciate your kindness. That's what I mean."

He laughed, "Don't worry Gretchen. I'm not taking it the wrong way. I know what you mean. I was just kidding."

I laughed, "You're pretty funny. Besides today, I've only seen you being serious and hardly ever holding a conversation. This is nice."

"What's nice? Me?"

"Oh no, you're not getting any other words out of me this time. I'm simply saying I'm having a nice time...at lunch...with you...here."

Our food was placed on the table and everything looked and smelled delicious. I quietly bowed my head and said a private grace. When I looked up, Langley also had his head bowed and when he raised it, he said out loud, "Amen."

"Amen," I repeated.

I checked the burger to make sure it didn't have any pickles and I was pleased to see it was exactly how I ordered it. I took my first bite and the flavors of the meat burst into my taste buds. The bun was soft and sweet almost like Hawaiian rolls. "*Mmm mmm.* This is delightfully tasty," I expressed to Langley.

"I knew you would like it," he boasted. We kept eating and I was enjoying the moment. Above the conversations of the moderate crowd of people in the restaurant I could hear the birds chirping. Everything felt so peaceful. It was nice to get out and do something different and not think about work or any of the other things happening in my life lately.

"So, what do you think about Miles' project?" I was dying to know if he approved.

"I think," he paused. "I think it can help a person to get over obstacles they may have but I'm not one-hundred percent convinced the technology can work the way he says it does."

"What do you mean?" I pushed for him to give me more insight into his thoughts.

"Truthfully, the project is genius. I read up on the materials used to construct the building and I had to approve each phase of the building. I must admit it did take some convincing for the non-profit board to agree to disperse the funds."

"Were they giving you a hard time?"

"Somewhat. They couldn't understand how funding this project was in line with their mission. I had to use Miles' research material to explain how their mission of helping others get ahead in life could be enhanced by this project because it was an approach directly to the psyche of each person. I understood The Cemetery would be a place to 'bury your burdens' so to speak, but I had to take it a step further in my explanation to the board and inform them how the technology in collaboration with the natural materials worked."

"Wow. So, you had to almost do your own presentation?"

"Yes, pretty much. I'm still skeptical about the whole telepathic function. Thankfully, in the end, I was convincing enough for the board and they agreed to finance the project. I do hope it helps enough people practically so funding can continue for the upkeep of the building each year."

"Wait, are you saying there is a chance The Cemetery can be shut down if it not successful within one year?"

"Yes, that is a possibility. Hopefully, it won't become an issue to worry about."

This was news to me. I hadn't thought about the operation costs of The Cemetery and I wasn't so sure Miles had thought that far either. We finished our lunch and Langley walked me to my car.

"I had a great time Gretchen. I'm glad you checked your messages and called me back."

"I'm glad too. This was rather nice," I said as I looked back at the restaurant and thought about the view of the lake from the patio before getting in my car."

I allowed Langley to close the door for me. "Now that we have at least had a regular conversation and you see I'm not some weird uptight guy..." Langley teased.

"I don't remember calling you weird," I said as I tried to recall our conversation.

Langley laughed, "Maybe you didn't say it out loud, but I know how to read between the lines. Anyway, would it be ok if I gave you a call sometimes...just to talk?" Langley was partially leaning on the roof of my vehicle and down towards me by my window.

"I would for sure appreciate keeping it at innocently talking for now," I softly blushed.

"Good," Langley said. "I'll be talking with you soon."

"Sure thing." I adored Langley as he put his shades on, stood up straight, smiled and walked to his car.

I drove off and allowed my thoughts to drift about our lunch date. A feeling of calmness had entered my mind and I was in a good place compared to everything else. I drove off route to pass in front of The Cemetery. When I got closer, I noticed one of my clients was leaving out of the building. I couldn't help but wonder how his session went but I didn't want to pry. Across the street I spotted Carl's car parked in front of Han's. I quickly found somewhere to park and rushed in looking for Carl. I found him having lunch alone and reading an article at a table in the back corner. I sat down uninvited and tapped my hand on the table to get his attention.

Carl looked up surprised, "Well, well, well, look who the wind blew in. And where may I ask have you been all day long? I tried calling you, but I kept getting your voicemail. I knew I didn't do you anything, so I figured you'd come around once you came out of your shell."

All I could do was laugh. "Carl, why are you so dang funny? Listen I have some things I don't want to talk about and some things I do want to talk about."

Carl shook his head in confusion. "What exactly are you saying because that doesn't make any sense to me?" Carl looked at me wanting direct answers.

"I know," I confessed. "A lot of stuff is not making sense right now. But, guess what."

"What?"

"I went to lunch with Langley today."

"Lunch as in a business setting or lunch as in a date?"

"Lunch as in a date," I excitedly answered clinching my nails near my lips.

"Girl shut up. How in the world did that happen?"

"Generally, he left a message, I called him back and voila there we were having a nice quiet lunch and sipping on some smooth wine."

"Sounds to me like the wine was not the only smooth thing at the table," Carl slyly remarked.

"Hmm. I know what you mean."

"So, I'm guessing that's the thing you did want to talk about. Do you want to share that something you don't want to talk about?"

"All I can say is I have a lot of questions and I will get to the bottom of everything real soon."

"Does it have anything to do with those wacky Sinclairs?" Carl pried.

"No, not this time," I sighed. "It's some crazy stuff with the Koperneils but we have to wait until another time to talk about it because it is too much for me to even think about right now," I said not wanting to hurt Carl's feelings because I was sort of shutting him out.

"It's ok Gretch. I know that when you are ready to talk you will. So, tell me more about this sexy lunch date."

"I didn't say it was sexy," I laughed. "It was pleasant. It was at a place called Carmen's."

"Oh yes, Carmen's is nice. It sorts of brings back bad memories for me because that's where I saw my ex having an intimate dinner with someone else."

"Aww. I'm sorry Carl. I didn't know." Carl mostly listened to other people's problems rather than talk about his own. I only knew the happy cheerful Carl. I didn't know anything about personal relationship disappointments he may have had.

"It's ok. It was his lost anyway. I'm remarkably better now that he is out of my life. Now, tell me more about Mr. Suave."

"Well, he was particularly talkative. Not stuffy like he usually appears whenever we see him."

"Yeah, they say it's those quiet ones you have to watch," Carl joked.

"Anyway, lunch was a nice refresher. It was a much needed break from all the chaos thrown my way."

The door to the café chimed and my client walked in smiling. This was the first time I had ever seen him smiling. He is usually intensely serious. "Excuse me for a minute Carl. Let me go say hello to one of my clients."

Before I left the table, I recognized Carl seemed star struck when he saw Solan Elka standing there. "I take it you're a fan," I addressed Carl before I walked away. He kept a concrete stare on Solan and couldn't answer my question. I walked over to Solan and tapped him on his shoulder. He turned around and gave me a big hug which was odd. "How are you Solan? I didn't know you were in town."

"I'm better now Gretchen. I heard about The Cemetery and thought I would give it a try. You know I have been suffering emotionally from fan bashing for any little mistake I make. I figured if I tried out a session at The Cemetery to see if it would help." Solan was talking slightly above a whisper so people nearby couldn't hear what he was saying.

I wasn't sure if I would be crossing the line by asking how the session went so, I listened while he talked to see if he would volunteer the outcome of his experience. I put my head down wondering if he found out things he didn't want to know, the way Mr. Koperneil found out about me. It was at that point I realized Mr. Koperneil didn't try to hurt me and I shouldn't be angry with him. I also thought about Miles telling me I should try The Cemetery alone to help with my issues. I was hoping that Solan could give me some kind of comfort in his experience. He ordered a plain coffee and dropped two sugar cubes in the cup. "You know Gretchen, I flew all the way here not knowing what to expect but hoping to see if I could get some answers. I needed closure. I didn't want other people's opinion of me to control my happiness. While I was in my session, I found out I also felt the same way about myself that some of those people whom I despised felt. I believed in my mind they were right about me. I didn't feel that way on the surface but that is what I discovered I felt deep inside. It felt like I was arguing with myself while I was in there. But I must say, in the end I learned there is also a part of me that is spiritually above all of those negative feelings and that part told me I am still alive and still playing the sport I love despite how people may feel. I have a talent and I refuse to let it go to waste."

"So, it sounds like you had somewhat of a breakthrough," I commented.

"I did Gretchen. I truly did. I don't know how that building works, but I do know it is amazing and works miracles. I feel so much better and will recommend it to all of my teammates."

Great. I thought to myself because I now knew how important it was for The Cemetery to be successful. "I'm very happy for you," I expressed to Solan. I knew in that moment I would have to at least give The Cemetery a try by myself to help me figure out this whole situation with the Koperneils.

"I'm glad I ran into you here. I was planning on stopping by your office before I left town." Solan pulled out some cash to pay for his bill.

"Well, I'm glad too because I didn't even go into the office today. What time are you leaving?"

"My flight leaves at eight tonight. I found out a few of my teammates are also in Mintly visiting The Cemetery so we will meet up before I leave." Solan looked so relaxed.

"That is great Solan. I'm happy everything worked out for you on this trip."

"It did Gretchen. It really did." He gave me another hug before he left out.

I went back to Carl's table. "Did you get his autograph for me?" Carl jokingly asked.

"No Carl." I was amused at Carl's reaction to seeing Solan. "He was telling me about his session at The Cemetery. From what he says, he has no regrets."

"Good." Carl sounded as if he was speaking as a professional. "When are you going back?"

"Back where?"

"Back to The Cemetery."

I had to think about it. I didn't know if I was ready to face the truth about my entire life which I had no idea that something was even wrong in the first place. "I guess I'll go soon."

"Me too," Carl imitated.

Chapter 10

The next day at the community center I sat alone at a table scrolling through my phone. Carl popped up unexpectedly and surprised the hell out of me.

"What are you doing," he whisper shouted as he popped his hands on the table. I jumped because I wasn't expecting anyone to come to my table and he startled me.

"Carl," I responded a tad bit aggravated. "Why did you scare me like that?"

He laughed, "Girl I was trying to break this crazy ignoring spell you've been giving me all day. I mean no morning call. No lunch date. What's up baby girl? Are you ok? I'm seriously concerned about you Gretch." Carl ended on a more solemn note.

I couldn't deny any of the accusations. All I could do was hold my head down. "I know. I know. I haven't been myself. I guess I should go ahead and tell you now because I can see you won't stop pestering me."

"No, I surely will not."

"Ok, then. Do you remember how I told you I had a lot going on, but I only told you about the good things?"

"Oh yes honey. Good things like that sexy lunch date?"

"Stop Carl," I giggled.

"Ok, ok. I quit."

"When Miles and I went to eat at the Koperneils they ended up telling me about their visit to The Cemetery." I paused so I could think of how to explain the rest of what unexpectedly happened at the Koperneils.

"And..." Carl waited with anticipation.

"Awww, I don't know Carl. This is all too crazy to even talk about."

"Come on now Gretchen. Don't shut me out like this. It's me. You know I'm not going anywhere with whatever you tell me."

"I know you're not going to say anything Carl. That's not what's bothering me."

"Well, what is it? Are they some kind of freaks in the sheets and want you to participate?" I gave Carl a look that a grandmother gives their grandchild for saying something out of place in church. "Alright girl, I quit for real this time. Talk to me." Carl straightened up his posture in an attempt to prove he was being serious now and attentively ready to listen.

"I found out when Mr. Koperneil was a teenager, he was in a serious accident. It was a freak accident that depending on an individual's luck could have happened to anybody and it left him in a coma for two weeks."

"Whoa, I didn't know any of this," Carl reacted surprisingly.

"But that's not all. He was also married, and his wife died in the car crash."

"Oh no. I didn't even know he was married before. I thought you said he was a teenager. I wonder why he got married so young."

"Why do you think?"

"Oh snap, a freaking shotgun wedding. She was pregnant."

"Yep."

"Wow, that's deep. But wait, why did you feel you couldn't tell me that?"

"Because it's not the whole story."

Carl looked confused.

It strained me to talk about everything in that moment, but I figured it couldn't hurt anything at this point. "He was married to a black girl."

"Now that right there does not surprise me at all because for a white guy Mr. Koperneil has some pretty cool laid-back vibes. I can see him having that jungle fever being smooth as butter on hot glass."

"The black girl was my mother."

"Wait a minute. What?"

"You heard me. Mr. Koperneil was married to my mother."

"But I thought you said his wife died in the car crash?"

"She did. But I didn't."

"What do you mean, you didn't?"

I was clinching my teeth because I could barely speak the words, "I am the baby from the accident."

"Oh my God Gretchen. Are you saying Mr. Koperneil is in reality your...?"

"Biological father, yes. I know. It is a lot to take in. The crazy part is he didn't know either."

"Well, how in the world didn't he know? That doesn't make sense."

"He was in a coma for two weeks. Remember? And his family told him the baby died too."

"Oh no, that is so messed up. Why would they do make up a whole lie?"

"He said he only found out by going to The Cemetery with his wife. She knew everything way before they got married. She thought he was keeping secrets from her and wanted to get him to tell her the truth. But the truth was he had no I idea I even existed. Everyone thought it would be too hard for an 18-year-old kid to raise a baby by himself. And a white kid with a black baby at that."

Carl was at a lost for words. He hunched back in his chair and gaped at me.

"Now he wants to have this 'father-daughter' relationship and I seriously don't know how I feel about the whole situation. All these years I thought my father was already dead. And now, he is not. What am I supposed to do Carl?"

"This is extremely awkward but honestly Gretchen I would recommend for you to talk with someone. You know. A psychiatrist. This kind of thing can cause extreme issues if they are not dealt with. I mean, it can even get to the point where it can affect your health."

"My health?"

"Yes darling. Emotions play a huge part in how our bodies chemically react to different things. A positive clear mind does the body good. Trust me. I know."

"So, who do you recommend? Yourself?"

"Of course, I do. But if you are not comfortable with that, I will not be a bit offended if you see someone else. I have a colleague who I can set you up with right now if you like. All you have to do is say that you are ready."

"Let me think about it a few days and I'll let you know."

"Ok baby, just let me know. I'm here for you. You know that, right?"

"Yes, I know." I reached out to Carl for a hug.

Instead of playing with the kids, Miles was hiding in the hall listening to our entire conversation. I hadn't even noticed him. On the ride home, my eyes were open while I was driving, but honestly, I was partially daydreaming. Miles looked over and noticed I was exceptionally quiet. He tried to break the ice knowing all the while what was bothering me.

"So, Ms. Gretchen can I ask you a question?"

I wasn't in the mood to answer any questions, but I felt I should amuse Miles anyway. "Sure Miles, what is it?"

"Do you think you should try going to The Cemetery by yourself to get some answers?"

"Get some answers about what Miles?" I was beginning to have an attitude and I felt my blood pressure rise.

Miles whispered, "I don't know. I guess about everything Mrs. Koperneil told you."

"Now Miles, I know you might mean well but you should consider staying in a child's place."

He got quiet and muttered under his breath that people don't understand.

I couldn't contain myself any longer. I started yelling at him, "People? What do you mean people? What are you?" He glared at me piercing his innocence through my soul. "And stop looking at me with those large eyes," I shouted with an insulting tone. "My whole life is in question now. No one is who they say they are. I am not who I think I am. This is all too much and now I'm confiding in a ten-year-old or at least I think you are ten years old about grown up problems. What is it Miles? Are you in fact an adult stuck in a child's body? Are you some kind of ..." I had to stop myself because I saw my words were hurting his feelings. "I'm sorry Miles." I pulled over and hugged Miles extra tight while he was in his seat. "I am so sorry. I didn't mean to yell at you. None of this is your fault." All I could do was keep kissing him on the forehead.

Miles finally answered, "It's ok Ms. Gretchen. You're not the first person to yell at me but at least you apologized. My parents never apologize."

I felt horrible. "Hey, do you want some ice cream?"

"Sure," Miles rejoiced. "I never get dessert before dinner."

I drove to the ice cream parlor, ordered two sundaes topped with whipped cream and a cherry and we sat on the patio and enjoyed our ice cream with no talking. I studied Miles' reaction and every time he looked at me, I smiled at him. He smiled back then concentrated back on his ice cream.

When we got back in the car, I checked my phone. I had five missed calls from my mother. I had been avoiding calling her ever since I found out the truth. Or at least what I was told was the truth. I still didn't understand the whole thing. I didn't know what I would say to her. When we got back home, I sent Miles to get cleaned up and ready for dinner. I grudgingly picked up the phone and called my mother.

She picked up on the first ring, "Well now child, I was about to say. If this lil' girl doesn't call me in ten more minutes I will call the police out there in Mintly and put out a missing person's alert."

"Really mom," I answered knowing she was joking. "It's only been a few days."

"Well it feels like fifty-five days."

"Fifty-five days?" I couldn't help but laugh. "You come up some off the wall stuff."

"Oh, I'm gonna show you off the wall if you keep playing with me. I better hear from my baby every single day. Do you understand me?"

"Yes ma'am." I laughed. I kept thinking to myself, how could I even be mad with this woman. I love her to pieces no matter what.

"Hey mom."

"Yes baby."

"You are coming here for Thanksgiving, right?"

"Well, I guess I can. That will at least give me a break from your sorry ass uncle coming around here asking me for change to buy him a fried turkey."

"There you go."

"What? I'm just saying. It's only the truth baby."

I cleared my throat to try and build up an ounce of courage. "Speaking of truth mom. I have to ask you a question."

"Go ahead baby. You can ask me anything. You know that."

"Ok then." I was trying to think of how to ask about my real mom, *if there was any truth to what the Koperneils said,* without hurting her feelings. "Do you know anything about an accident when I was born?"

The phone line was silent. At that moment I knew there was some truth to the story. My mother's tone dropped down to an almost whisper. "Yes, I do. Why do you ask baby? Did you hear something from somebody?"

"Well, maybe it's not a good idea to talk about all of this over the phone. Let's get back to our Thanksgiving plans. Let me check the flights right quick."

I quickly opened up my computer on the kitchen table and luckily found a cheap last-minute flight. "Here's one mom. It leaves out on Tuesday at 3:15."

"Tuesday as in three days from now?"

"Yes, why is it too soon. Do you want me to check for Wednesday?

"No dear, Tuesday is fine. I have a doctor's appointment early that morning, but I should be out in plenty enough time."

"Ok then mom. I'm booking it right now. I will email you the confirmation number."

"No, text it to my phone because you know I might forget to check my email. I don't know why you think I'm into all that fancy email stuff."

"You are so funny woman. Anyway, I'll text it to you. I can't wait to see you."

"I can't wait to see you too baby. It sounds like we will have a lot to talk about."

"Ok then, let me go get this food ready for Miles so he doesn't go to bed hungry."

"I had forgotten that child was staying with you. And when did you say his parents are coming back? Will he be there for Thanksgiving too?"

"Don't start mom."

"Ok, I won't. But you best believe I will be having both of my eyes on him the whole entire time...just in case."

I laughed, "Ok mom. Love you. I'll talk to you tomorrow."

"You'd better. Love you too baby."

After I got off the phone, I prepared a quick spaghetti meal for me and Miles. He walked in the kitchen in his pajamas rubbing his stomach.

"Mmmm mmm. Something smells de-li-cious."

"Thanks Miles," I acknowledged as I strained the spaghetti noodles in the strainer. "Everything is almost done. Why don't you get us each a glass and put some ice in it?"

"Okie dokie. I can do that. This is so much fun. I had ice cream plus I get to help out in the kitchen."

I smiled as I finished preparing dinner. It was something about this 'playing mom' thing that filled my void. I served us each a plate, sat down and Miles led the grace.

"Thank you, God, for this food we are about to receive from your bounty. And thank you God so much for Ms. Gretchen. Amen."

"Amen," I seconded as I admired the prayer from Miles.

The doorbell rang and Miles and I both looked at each other in curiosity.

"Hmmm, I wonder who that could be?" I walked over to the door and peeped through the peephole.

It was Carl. I opened up the door in pure astonishment.

"Surprise!" Carl blurted as he pulled a single rose from behind his back and cupped a bottle of wine in his arms.

"Come on in Carl. We were just sitting down for dinner. Would you like a plate?"

"Now you know I won't refuse your cooking Gretch." Carl walked over to the cabinet and poured he and I a glass of wine. "And how is everything going with you young man," Carl addressed Miles as he pulled out a chair to sit at the table.

Miles was in the middle of chewing, but he still managed to answer, "Everything is good. Especially this food."

"I bet it is," Carl added.

"So, what brings you by Carl?"

"Well, I figured you could use some more company plus a gentle conversation over wine."

"You know me terribly well my friend. Not to say that Miles isn't good company."

"Don't worry about me Ms. Gretchen. I'm not offended at all." Miles said as he finished up the last bite on his plate.

"Do you want seconds Miles?"

"No ma'am. I'm pretty stuffed right now so I will excuse myself to bed if that's ok."

"Of course it is. Before you go to bed, rinse off your plate and leave it in the kitchen sink."

"Yes ma'am." Miles rinsed off his plate and told us goodnight before he left the kitchen.

Carl and I finished eating and he helped me wash the dishes. Carl poured us each a re-fill and walked over to the couch with both glasses. I grabbed the bottle from the counter and followed behind him.

"What a last couple of days huh Gretch?" Carl reminisced.

"You said it Carl. I am mentally exhausted."

"I know baby. But I was thinking on the way here...Do you think you should try a session at The Cemetery by yourself? Do you remember how your client said it made him feel? Maybe it can help you too."

"Maybe so. But I'm incredibly scared. Well, I take that back. I'm not scared. I was already comfortable with my life the way it was and now *everything* has changed. I think I'm mostly freaked out about the whole situation. It's making me question who I am."

"Oh no Gretchen. It should not make you question who you are. None of those things change who you are. Look at it as more life."

"More life?"

"Yes, sometimes changes come with a life lesson which if used correctly can help you grow into a better you."

"I guess I see what you mean. I think I need more answers. I wonder why my mother never told me the truth. Why did I have to find out like this?"

"I'm not sure about that but I'm guessing she has her own reasons."

"Yeah, I guess you're right."

"Is your mom coming for Thanksgiving?"

"Yes, I booked her flight today."

"I'm shocked. Did you ask her about the whole Mr. Koperneil situation?"

"No, but I did hint I knew something about an accident when I was a baby. She seemed ready to answer any question I had but I told her I'd rather talk about everything in person."

"That's a good idea. Well, I'm glad she is coming here so I can meet her. Will the Sinclairs be back by then?"

"No, those crazy people are talking about coming back *after* Thanksgiving," I whispered in case Miles was listening from the room. "So enough about me. What about you? What's been going on in Carl's world?"

"Well, I think I met a new friend." Carl blushed waiting for my reaction.

"Oh really, and how did you meet?"

"Child, on the internet of course. I'm not about to go out and meet someone from Mintly. This place is way too small. Someone is bound to know a person if I meet them here."

"So, did you talk to him yet? Like, on the phone and not through the internet."

"I did. I did. I even have a picture I took while we were video chatting."

"Let me see." I squealed excitedly as if we were in high-school.

Carl pulled out his phone and scrolled to the screen shot. "Tell me what you think." Carl held his phone with the picture waiting for me to respond.

"Ouuuuweee, he is a cutie."

"I know. And he has great conversation. He is looking for a serious relationship and saw my profile and reached out to me."

"Wow, this is great news Carl. Do you think you would be ok with having a serious relationship?"

"I think if the timing is right and we are compatible then it should be great."

"You're in every respect correct."

Carl and I finished the bottle of wine and he left for the evening. I thought about our conversations the entire night. Listening to Carl's excitement gave me hope in myself.

Chapter 11

My mom arrived at the airport on time. I met her at the gate and went with her to the baggage claim area.

"How was your flight mom?" I kissed her on the cheek before taking over pushing the courtesy wheelchair.

"Baby, they treated me like a queen?"

"Oh, they did?"

"Yes, they sure did. I sat in the front row and was served a full sandwich and not one, but two, glasses of wine," my mother said proudly while clinching her purse on her lap.

"You're joking right."

"Nope. And the flight attendant was a tall, handsome and fine young fellow. I got his name and phone number so you can give him a call."

"Mom, I don't need any help with finding a man. And, you have to know I don't want some flight attendant."

"You could have fooled me child. And what's wrong with a flight attendant. You see, that's your whole problem now. You are too picky. Anyway, grab my luggage before we miss it."

I laughed at her and reached for the bags on the baggage carousel and picked up the two suitcases marked with yellow ribbon tied on the handle.

"You've been tying yellow ribbons on your suitcases as long as I can remember."

"Yes, it was my sister's favorite color."

We pull up to my house and my mother is amazed.

"Baby, this is much bigger than the pictures you sent me. I love it."

"Thanks mom. I'm loving it too. I can't believe this is all mine."

"Well you worked hard for it sugar so you deserve every inch of this place."

"Thanks mom." I showed her the room where she would be sleeping. I had it set up with a neatly wrapped gift basket on the bed.

My mother zealously loved gifts. "Look at this gorgeous basket. It has my favorite lemongrass bodywash. Thanks baby."

"You're welcome mom. Now you know we have a lot of preparing to do for our Thanksgiving meal, right?"

"But it's only the two of us so why do we have to fix so much food."

"I invited a few friends over plus you know Miles is here."

"Oh yes. Where is this special kid anyway?"

"He is at the community center. I will pick him up a little later."

"When are his parents coming back?"

"I don't have any idea."

I sat on the couch with my mother and she continued to admire my place. I felt proud of her enjoying and admiring everything.

"So how is work going?" my mother asked me with a touch of unsureness in her quest for an honest answer.

I hadn't mentioned that I had taken off since last week because I didn't want to deal with facing Mr. Koperneil yet. "It's been going well," I pushed the words out to sound as convincing as I could. "One of my clients recently visited The Cemetery and he said it helped him immensely."

"So how does that place work in all reality? What exactly does it help people with?"

"It's unexplainable mom. But in essence, you go into a room and your thoughts are typed out on a panel on the wall."

"That's interesting. I would like to bring a few people in there myself so I can know what they are thinking."

"Do you want to go with me because I've been thinking about this a whole lot lately?"

"I don't know baby. I mean, I might be thinking about some man and I might frighten you with the details about those thoughts."

I laughed, "No mom. I don't think it works like that. It only brings out feelings having to do with issues. I'll start off the panel discussion with my thoughts and you can follow my lead by thinking about what I bring up."

"Ok, and what exactly do you plan on bringing up *if* I decide to go. You know I'm not about all that freak shit," my mom explained with an attitude.

"I was thinking you could tell me what you know about the accident that happened when I was a baby."

My mom was quiet and looked like she had sort of lost her cheerful spirit. "Look baby, if you genuinely want to know we can talk about everything now."

"No, I'd rather learn about everything at The Cemetery. I think the atmosphere will be better because there won't be any tension."

"Ok, I'll give it some serious thought. I'm only considering doing this for you. You know that, right?"

"I know mom. I know." I was still struggling with the thought about everything because this is the woman I knew as my mother. Deep in my heart I didn't want it any other way. A part of me did not even want to worry about it anymore but than a small part of me needed to know. I looked at the time, "Come on mom, ride with me to pick up Miles from the center."

"Ok, let me get my purse. You know I don't go anywhere without my purse."

We left out and headed to the center. I passed in front of the colorful house to show my mom. She was amazed at all of the colors. She took out her phone and snapped a picture. "That house reminds me of the colorful houses back home in New Orleans." She gazed at the picture she had captured with her phone. I stared at the wind chime as I drove by.

We arrived at the center and my mother waited in the car. I went in and got Miles. Miles came out holding my hand but hiding behind me as if he were embarrassed when we got closer to the car.

"What's wrong Miles? Don't be shy. It's just my mother."

My mother was staring out the window expressionless with her eyes straight at Miles. I tried to give her a look to soften up but she didn't budge. Miles got in the back seat behind her. "Good evening," Miles greeted my mother in a mild tone.

"Good evening to you," she resounded as she turned around to get a closer look at Miles. "Why don't you scoot over behind Gretchen so I can get a better look at you?"

"He can't do that mom. I have the seat too far back. Miles this is my mother."

"You can call me Ms. Hall," she instructed.

"Yes ma'am," Miles responded trying not to make eye contact.

"That's a peculiar bracelet you have there." My mom noticed everything. When she made the comment, she said it in a tone to hint to me that it seemed strange. I pretended to ignore the hint.

"I've had it ever since I was a baby."

"Ohhh," she voiced. "I see. So what kind of stone is it?"

Miles didn't answer. He hung his head and started rubbing his bracelet. I whispered for my mother to be nice. I turned up the radio and my mother started snapping her fingers singing along to a soulful hit song. I joined in and watched her mood start to soften. I sort of zoned out mesmerized by the lyrics. By the time we reached my house, my mother had learned more about Miles than I even thought about. She knew his favorite color, what size shoes he wore, his favorite television show and even what kind of toothpaste he used.

"I'm hungry Ms. Gretchen," Miles expressed as he was getting out of the car.

I had not even thought about what we would eat. I decided to order in from Jazzes. The food was delivered in less than thirty minutes. Miles took out 3 glasses, filled them with ice and placed the glasses on the table. I could tell my mom seemed stunned. She watched as Miles took his time and helped me serve the food. She gave me a sign of approval. I beamed with pride.

"I guess you're not so strange after all," my mom slyly remarked not able to control her thoughts.

"Mother," I aired as if I was secretly scolding her.

"What?" she whispered in disgust at the thought of me trying to correct her.

"It's ok Ms. Gretchen," Miles spoke with confidence. "I'm used of it. I knew you would warm up to me sooner or later Ms. Hall." He grinned as he addressed my mother.

"Oh, you did?" she queried.

"Yes ma'am," he kindly replied.

"And exactly how did you know that," she questioned Miles as if she were talking to an adult.

"It's simple. I'm lovable and eventually people can't help themselves."

Me and my mom laughed hysterically. Miles joined in with an awkward laugh making us laugh uncontrollably as if we had been stung with a burst of laughing gas. Miles felt like it was the perfect opportunity to tell a joke.

"Knock, knock."

"Who's there?" Me and my mom responded in unison.

"Donkey."

"Donkey who?"

"Donkey t-t-teasing me."

The laughter continued. I chimed in, "Knock, knock."

"Who's there?" my mother and Miles sang.

"Rat."

"Rat who?" they asked.

"Rat-a tat tat," I ended while laughing harder at my own joke than anyone else.

"Ok, ok." my mother sneered. "I have one. Knock, knock."

"Who's there?" Me and Miles strained between our laughter because she was making comical gestures with her face.

"July."

"July who?"

My mom screamed out in a humorous expressive tone, "July all the time!"

Miles started slapping his leg while trying to catch his breath from laughing so hard. Miles repeated the punch line, "July all the time. That is so funny Ms. Hall."

"I bet you didn't think I had it in me huh," she bragged to me and Miles.

"We sure didn't," I disclosed. "But you fooled me and Miles both."

We finished eating dinner and Miles helped me clean up in the kitchen. "Are you always this helpful in the kitchen?"

"I wish I could be, but my parents don't let me help."

"What in the world kind of parents are those?" my mom muttered under her breathe. I gave her another look as if to give her a subtle warning to watch what she says about his parents. I knew Miles loved his parents immensely although they treated him like an outsider. Although I agreed beyond doubt with what my mother was saying I still wanted to be considerate towards Miles and spare his feelings every chance I got.

My mom had a big heart even though she seemed cold at times. "Come over here young man and let me ask you a question."

Miles walked over to my mom and stood by her while she sat in the chair. She looked him lovingly in the face recognizing the innocent child in him and rubbed the side of his arms up and down while she talked to him. "Do you know the project you made was on the news where I live?"

"No ma'am." Miles answered not sure how to feel about where the questions were going.

"Well, it was, and I must say I am pleasantly impressed by your talents. You have a true gift and it is a blessing you are sharing it with the world. With that being said, do you think it is a good idea for me and my daughter to go to this cemetery place together?"

Miles instantly froze observing her afraid to answer the question. I recognized Miles felt a little uneasy so I jumped in, "It's ok Miles. You can tell her how you feel about it. I promise you she won't bite."

This sort of eased some of the tension from Miles' shoulders and he relaxed a little bit, "Yes ma'am. I do think it's a good idea. If I ever get a chance to go with my parents I will not hesitate to go. I made it a place to help people and I know it can help ..." Miles paused.

"Help what baby." My mom's anticipation was a declaration of concern.

"Help them love me," Miles whispered. My mom immediately pulled him closer to her and held him extra tight and said, "Oh baby, I'm more than sure your parents love you. Some people just have a different way of showing it."

"Mom is right Miles." I knelt next to Miles and rubbed him on his back. Miles' eyes were filled with tears waiting to fall. I gently wiped his eyes dry and sent him off to bathe and get dressed for bed. When he was out of sight, I took a deep sigh. "Mom, I honestly don't know what I'm going to do. Those people literary dropped Miles in my lap out of the clear blue sky and I am no where near ready to deal with all of this."

My mom sat there and listened to everything I was saying. "You know what baby? Maybe you're right. Maybe we should go to The Cemetery. It looks like there are some deeper issues we need to resolve and I'm willing to help in any way I can."

"I'm so relieved to hear that mom. We can go in the morning after I drop Miles off at the center."

"Sounds good."

When we arrived at The Cemetery the next morning, I parked in the parking lot of the community center since it was right across the street. All the spots right in front of The Cemetery were taken. More people than usual were visiting The Cemetery that morning. I was surprised at the crowd since it was the day before Thanksgiving.

"Gretchen," my mother announced when she stepped out of the car.

"Yes mom."

She held her hands on her hips gazing at The Cemetery from the distance. "You mean to tell me we were this close to that cemetery building when we picked up that little boy and you didn't bother to even show it to me?"

I laughed, "I know mom. It was a little late and I knew you were over exhausted from the flight so I didn't want to bombard you with everything about Mintly at once."

"Ok, I understand that. But seriously. It's like literally right here. All you had to do was say momma, turn around. There's The Cemetery."

"You are something else lady." I shook my head and led the way. "Come on let's go so I can show you 'The Cemetery'."

As we walked up to the building, I had that same feeling about the place I had when I first looked at the forested mural. I felt like it was drawing me in. It is that same feeling I used to get as a child when I would spin in circles super-fast and lie on the grass staring at the sky. It felt like it was moving towards me. Although I had frequented The Cemetery several times already, I still couldn't get over the massiveness of the structure and the details of the material.

"This is amazing." My mother gazed in awe as we got closer. "It is way bigger than what it looked like on the news. Look at the quality of it all. Do they wipe down the exterior of this thing or something?"

"No mom. It's made out of pure unmanufactured materials."

We walk in and I register our session. The guide walks us over to our room. We enter and I can feel the hesitation from my mother. Her eyes roam curiously at the walls as she rubs her hands back and forth on the cold stone chairs in anticipation. She looks over at me and I give her a sign to just relax. She takes heed to my advice and takes a deep breath to relax. I start to focus on my thoughts.

"Hi mom." My thoughts appeared on the screen and it startles her. I knew it would so that's why I thought of something easy to say so she could get comfortable.

"Hi." This was the only word that appeared on the panel.

"Are you ok?"

"Yes, but this is some freaky shit. I mean I understood what you said would happen but I guess I didn't believe you."

"It's ok. We can take it a little slow if you like."

"No. Let's jump right into it so we can get out of here before my thoughts start rambling all over the place."

"Ok then. Do you remember the phone conversation we had the other night?"

"Yes, about the accident when you were a baby."

"Yes. So, is it true that I wasn't born yet and my real mother died?"

My mother's thoughts took some time to show up across the screen. She was squinting her eyes extra tight. I waited patiently for her to respond. I didn't want to push her. I wanted answers but I was prepared not to get any if she didn't want to talk about it.

"It was one of the scariest nights of my life."

"Wait, so you didn't die in the accident? Why did Mr. Koperneil and his wife say that you died? That is so cruel and evil. I was paralyzed with distraught all of these days thinking you were not my real mother. I have been so confused. I just don't understand why they would even make up a whole story. None of it makes sense."

"It will in a minute baby. Hold on. Stop thinking for a second and let me concentrate."

"Ok mom. Take your time." I waited patiently again while my mom sat there and shut her eyes extra tight and shaking her head no.

"It was my sister who was in the accident. My closest sister to me in age and my dearest best friend. That night was the worst night of my life."

"So, in all actuality, you are my aunt?" I questioned with a pinch of sadness in my heart because she was not my real mother but still satisfied that she was at least a close relative.

"Yes baby. But I have loved you since you were born as if you were my own. Your grandmother was already too sick to be able to handle a baby. Plus, my husband and I knew it was the best thing to do for everyone."

"But what about Mr. Koperneil? What was wrong with him? He was alive. Why didn't he take me and raise me like a real father should? He walks around here like he is father of the year but yet he abandoned me."

"No baby, he didn't abandon you at all. From what I understand, Charlie was in a coma for about two weeks. They said the first person he asked about was his baby. His parents told him that both you and my sister didn't make it from the accident. You have to understand times were extremely different back then. There were no such things as mixed relationships where we lived. His parents weren't racist but they were proud people. They felt like it was the perfect opportunity for their young eighteen-year-old son to get a fresh start on life. Your grandmother, my mother, agreed it was best for our side of the family to keep you and raise you without interference. You have to believe me when I say it was truly the best decision for you and for Charlie."

"So, he unquestionably didn't know I was alive." I felt guilty about all the pitiless remarks I had uttered about him and Mrs. Koperneil.

"No baby, he didn't. He visited the grave site faithfully every week. I didn't see him but I knew he was there because he left fresh flowers every time. My sister used to tell me secrets about how he would woo her with freshly picked yellow daisies on their walk home from school. From then on, yellow was her favorite color. She didn't care that he was a white boy. She cared about his heart. And he had a big heart for your mother. He loved her immeasurably. Times were strikingly different back then. But Charlie was never ashamed of your mother or the color of her skin. He loved her dearly. They were best friends since middle school. He would punch anybody in the face who talked about her beautiful brown skin. He even knocked out the front tooth of one of his closest cousins." She paused for a minute and giggled.

"They were such a cute little mixed couple. He was devasted after the crash. He felt like it was all his fault. Teenage years are tough honey. It is a time where you are transitioning from being a complete child to becoming a complete adult. And sometimes when bad things happen, even if it is not your fault, you think you could have changed the circumstances somehow. Do you remember when you were 16 and what happened? I never bring it up because you never seemed to want to talk about it."

"And I still don't want to talk about it. I try my best to forget about it. I have forgiven him and myself already. I have prayed for both of us and I have let all of that pain go."

"Ok, baby we don't have to talk about it. But Charlie held devoted love for you and your mother. At the gravesite, he left a fresh bouquet of yellow daisies for her and a single yellow rose for you faithfully every week. To this day, even though he is miles away, he has the flowers delivered to the grave. He would have never abandoned you. It took me a lot of years to get over keeping you a secret from him, but my family had made a promise to never tell him the truth. Your grandmother was the main one who agreed this was the best decision for everyone, even for you. Your father and I, well your uncle, made sure you didn't lack for anything. We gave you all the love and affection parents would give their child. I look at you as my own Gretchen. Before you were born my sister used to ask me if I would help her because she didn't know what to do with a baby. She was just a baby herself, like Charlie. They were merely babies. I'm five years older than sissy so of course I promised her I would help her. And I kept my word ever since. I know this is a lot to take in baby, so we can stop if you want to."

"No, let's just finish. I guess it's hard for me to understand why you or somebody couldn't eventually tell me or Mr. Koperneil the truth."

"I thought about it many times. Sometimes it ate me up inside knowing I was living a lie. I truly believe that's part of what made me sick. Anyway, I tried to find Charlie when you were still a baby, but everyone kept telling me he was sent away to college overseas. I even wrote a letter once, but it came back return to sender because it said the address was not found. At that point I figured it was God's will and I left it alone. I never told you because I didn't want you to go out looking for him. I had wasted a lot of years, a lot of painful years, worrying about if I did the right thing. I did a whole lot of praying to stay sane about the whole situation. It hasn't been easy for anyone. I am truly sorry you found out the way you did baby. I hope you can forgive me and everyone else."

I didn't know what to think. I didn't know how to feel. I concentrated on my emotions. I could feel my mother's eyes scrutinize me waiting for a response but I couldn't think of the right words to say. I took a long deep breath and I felt a sense of calmness enter my spirit. It felt like a heavy burden of unresolved issues had been lifted. It was unexplainable what I was feeling at that moment. I literary felt the magnetism of the room pull out all of the negative emotions I was having and I felt a sense of peace. It was so weird. I allowed my feelings to come out across the panel. "I do forgive everyone. And I truly understand. It's still hard, but I get it. I see what Miles is going through with his parents and I wouldn't wish that feeling on anyone. I guess I have been hard on Mr. Koperneil by ignoring him. I know now that none of this was his fault."

"No, it fairly wasn't baby. I'm sure he is going through a million emotions himself if he is the same Charlie I knew back then. But see how fate works, you found each other anyway. My mother always used to say, 'If it's meant to be, it will be.' She was right. And you know what is extra special about everything?"

"What?"

"Everyone, including Charlie's family, wanted what was best for you and for him. Both of you would have had to face so much unnecessary discrimination. It wasn't healthy. I love you like my very own Gretchen. The night of the accident. I lost my sister who was my number one best friend in this whole universe. We kept secrets for each other that I still will not utter to this day. Not even on this freaky panel. (I couldn't help but smile.) But despite that traumatizing lost, I gained her soul through you. You were my saving grace. Your life brought me through all of that pain. Every time I held you as a baby, I felt like I was holding my sister. Your mother. I know that life is hard baby and it is not always fair, but you have to keep pushing and search for the bright light in every single situation. Once you do that, you allow yourself to grow and better yourself above everything."

I sat there pondering about everything. The panel was soothingly empty. My mom stood up and held out her hand. I stood up with her and we walked out together, hand-in-hand.

Chapter 12

Thanksgiving morning was no different from last year except we were at my new home in Mintly, Texas instead of bunched up in the kitchen at mom's house in New Orleans. My mom always reminded me of how my dad used to love her oyster dressing.

"You know your daddy said my oyster dressing is what made him know for sure he wanted to marry me?" she started. I thought to myself, here comes the long drawn out story. "Yes baby, when I would be in that kitchen, he would sneak up behind me while I was mixing up that dressing and he used to flirt in my ear and say, 'let me get a taste of that.' And I would say, what this little simple dressing? And he would say, with his slick self, 'mmm yeah that too.' And I would tell you how the rest of the morning went but you're still too wet behind the ears to know all my business."

I just laughed. "You miss him huh mom."

"Yes, I do baby."

"Me too. I remember like it was yesterday when he was called out to duty for that military mission. He told me no matter what happened he would think about me every day. I believed him too."

"Good, because I know he meant every single word and I believe in my heart he is with us today in spirit. So, who are we fixing all of this food for baby. I know you don't expect me, you and Miles to eat all of this food by ourselves. And you know I'm not down with eating left overs for more than one day."

"I know mom. I invited a few friends over. They need to know what some real cooking tastes like."

"Alright nah baby. Don't skimp on them then. Drop a few more dashes of cayenne in the rice dressing mix." Mom loved to cook her food extra spicy. It was the kind of spice that made your upper lip sweat. I made sure I mixed up a mixture of Hawaiian punch and pineapple juice plus a pitcher of fresh homemade lemonade. I knew the guest would need something sweet to curb the spice from the food.

Carl showed up first and he was accompanied by his new friend.

"Happy Thanksgiving!" I greeted them both as they walked in.

"Happy Thanksgiving!" Carl was flooded with excitement as he gave me a few smooches on each side of my cheeks. "Gretchen this is Greg and Greg this is Gretchen," Carl introduced. Carl held out two bottles of wine. "Look what I brought," he said as if it was some kind of surprise.

"I love it." I pointed to the dining room table. "You can place them on the table."

My mom walked out of the kitchen to the living room area wiping her hands with a dish towel. "Hello," she jumped in as if I had forgotten to introduce her. "I'm Ms. Hall."

Carl gave her a tight hug catching her off guard because she was already in the process of extending her hand for a handshake. "It is so good to meet you Ms. Hall. Gretchen talks about you all the time."

"It's good to meet you too. And who is this handsome guy? Is he one of your college friends?" she pried.

Carl cleared his throat to keep from sounding embarrassed by the question. "Oh no Ms. Hall, this is my friend Greg."

"Well hello Greg. It is a pleasure to meet you." She winked at Carl and tried to whisper to him but everyone could hear her, "Relax baby. I knew he was your friend the whole time. Gretchen mentioned how good you have been to her since she moved here and anyone who takes care of my baby is ok in my book."

Carl looked relieved. Miles came from the room still in his pajamas and rubbing his stomach. "Good morning everybody. What is smelling so good?"

My mom couldn't help but to make a comment, "It's called food son. What do you think it is? It's Thanksgiving for goodness sake. You sure do wake up asking crazy questions for someone who is as smart as you are."

"Momma," I pestered partially laughing because we all knew she was joking with Miles. Luckily Miles recognized her humor too.

"You got me Ms. Hall. Happy Thanksgiving everyone," he sleepily spoke as he yawned.

"Oh, my goodness Miles. Are you still tired?" I asked.

"Yes ma'am. I was up late hoping my parents would call but the phone didn't ring."

Carl and I both looked at each other and didn't say a word because we both knew they weren't calling. They weren't even showing up for Thanksgiving. They had made that clear last week. I still hadn't told Miles. I didn't know how to say it. "Go take a quick shower to wake yourself up so you don't miss out on the whole day."

"Oh no Ms. Gretchen. I might be tired but I'm not missing out on this food." Everyone laughed at Miles. The doorbell rang again. I knew it was Langley and I felt my stomach quiver because I was a tad bit nervous about him meeting my mother. When I opened the door, he was standing there looking just as handsome as could be.

"Welcome," I said. "Come on in."

"I hope you don't mind but I brought Paisley along because she was at the shop all alone."

"Oh, I don't mind at all," I insisted as I pulled Paisley in and gave her a huge hug. "Happy Thanksgiving Paisley. Why in the world were you opened on today?"

"I didn't have anything else planned so I figured I'd open the shop. I didn't have a single customer all morning. I was so glad when Spencer stopped in and asked if I wanted to come here. I hope you don't mind."

"Not at all." I was ashamed I hadn't thought to invite her myself. "Make yourself comfortable and relax. My mom and I are almost finished preparing everything."

Langley was still standing close to the door afraid to move. "Come on in Langley. Let me introduce you to everyone." Langley took a few more steps but still didn't seem too comfortable with interacting with everyone. "This is my mother. Everyone calls her Ms. Hall. And this is Carl and his friend Greg."

My mother stopped working in the kitchen again and went to greet Langley. "Mom, this is Spencer Langley. He prefers to be called Langley."

"Langley," she repeated as if she heard his last name before. "No baby, I don't think we are related to any Langley's. I think this one here is a keeper."

"Don't pay her any mind," I rushed and told Langley as I walked him away from my mother before she said anything else to embarrass me.

Me and my mother finished setting everything up on the table and I overheard the conversation between Langley and Paisley while they were sitting at the breakfast bar. Langley whispered to her and said, "Hey, why were you staring at the that house when we drove by?" "What house?" she asked. "You know. That real colorful house. Do you know who lives there?" Paisley didn't respond. I was almost frozen in my movements of placing the utensils on the table waiting to hear if she would say anything about the lady from the house. She never did answer. Langley continued, "Anyway, it looks like I saw that windchime somewhere before. Like, besides at that house." Paisley gave him a speechless gaze. Langley immediately stopped talking. Carl and Greg were flipping channels and Carl stopped on a channel showing holiday movies. "Not a Christmas love story already," Carl said. Greg added, "I know. We haven't even finished with Thanksgiving and they are already pushing Christmas on us."

"Those Christmas shows are some of my favorite to watch." I added to their conversation. "I watch them every single year."

My phone rang and I heard Miles running full speed towards the sound. "Is it my parents?" he screeched excitedly.

I looked at my phone and surprisingly it was them. They were calling by video. I handed the phone to Miles so he could answer. As soon as he swiped, he put on a big smile and said, "Happy Thanksgiving mom and dad."

Shockingly they responded back, "Happy Thanksgiving baby."

I could tell this melted Miles' heart. "Hey, what time will y'all be here and where is Zach so I can tell him hi."

"Zach is still by Grammy's house in New York. Listen baby, we won't make it back until next week." His dad added, "Miles, we are extremely sorry we couldn't be there today. I know Ms. Gretchen will make sure you have a great meal."

Miles looked a little sad that they said they couldn't make it but he kept his composure. "It's ok. I can't wait to see you all next week. And yes, Ms. Gretchen and her mom has the kitchen smelling extra good." Miles put on another smile while he talked about the food.

"That is so good baby," his mom said. "We have to go now but we love you and we will talk to you soon."

"I love you too," Miles said before they hung up. He called his grandmother and got a chance to speak with his baby brother for a minute.

After dinner the doorbell rang and it was the two oldest kids of the Koperniels with a homemade pie from Mrs. Koperneil. They asked if Miles could go with them to play video games at their house. I was reluctant at first but I agreed because Miles didn't have any kids to play with at my house.

Mom, Miles and I got dressed that following Sunday and went to church. My mom met Mr. and Mrs. Koperneil. When she first saw him, it looked like she was seeing a ghost. He looked at her the same way. It was nothing any of us could prepare for. No one could talk because service had already started. She whispered to me and said all she could see when she looked at Charlie was her sister. Her hands were trembling, and I tried to hold them still on her lap. They felt ice cold. "Mom," I whispered. "We don't have to stay for the whole service. We can leave if you feel like this is not comfortable." She tapped my hand as if to say, no, everything is ok. We stayed the entire service. I looked for Mr. and Mrs. Koperneil when it was over, but I didn't see them anywhere.

When we got back to the house, mom was not her usual self. She was quiet and went straight to the room and changed her clothes. I couldn't think of what to say to make her feel better. I could only imagine what was going through her mind since she was able to see Mr. Koperneil face-to-face. I decided to help take her mind off things. I opened my computer and looked up cruise trip packages to Brazil. I found some interesting information about Brazil. I had no idea it was the second largest black nation in the world.

"Check this out mom."

"What is it baby? Come and show me over here on the couch so I don't have to get up."

I walked over and sat next to her showing her the computer screen. "I found us a week-long cruise to Brazil. Do you want me to make the reservation?"

When I said Brazil, her eyes lit up. "What kind of fool do you think I am to ask me a silly question like that? You already know my answer child. Of course I want you to book the trip. The real question is when do we leave?"

"Well, they have two departure dates to choose from. One is the first week in December and the other one is a few days before Christmas which means we would spend Christmas in Brazil."

"Christmas in Brazil sounds good to me," she said with excitement in her voice. I was happy to see she was getting back to her usual self.

"Instead of leaving to go home tomorrow, do you prefer to stay here until the cruise?" I offered.

"I would baby, but I have a few important doctors' appointments I can't afford to miss."

I booked the reservation and made sure I knew what documents we would need to travel. I was feeling excited about our getaway. I could tell that mom was too. She started telling stories about her great-grandmother. She said she lived to be 97 years old. She laughed because her great-grandmother was convinced that she was already 100. No one argued with her. There could have been some truth to what she believed knowing how inconsistent the birth records were back then.

/ hadn't been jogging alone in a while, so I decided to take advantage of my mother being there to stay with Miles. I woke up, dressed and dashed out of the house. By the time I made it back, Miles and my mother were in the kitchen. She was fixing him breakfast. She kept her eyes on him the whole time. I could tell she still had her doubts about Miles, but it looked like she was starting to warm up to him.

"So, Miles," she opened up with an attempt of a morning conversation. "I keep hearing a lot of great things about you. (Miles looked over at me with question in his eyes wondering what I said about him.) That is an amazing project you came up with. Did you think of that all by yourself?

"Yes ma'am. I thought of most of it by myself."

"What do you mean? Did your parents help you?"

"No, they would never help me. They don't even like my project! I actually had this unexplainable crazy dream. (He started rubbing his wrist while he told his story.) I was riding my bike down the street and I saw a small ball right there in the middle of the street. When I got close to it, it started rolling. It was rolling painfully slow at first and suddenly it started to go super-fast. The wind was blowing by this time and I was starting to lose my balance. I tried to go faster but it felt like my bike wasn't moving anymore. I got scared so I jumped off my bike. The wheels on my bike were still moving exceptionally fast and without interference they just stopped and my bike fell down. I was too afraid to touch it so I ran away. I ran as fast as I could. I could hear my heart beat in my hears. It was so loud. I tried to scream for help but my voice didn't have any sound. My legs started to feel tired so I tried to stop running but the wind was pushing me. I fell down and I when I looked up, I couldn't believe my eyes. It was right there in front of me on the ground. A large shiny key with the words The Cemetery engraved in it. I picked it up and as soon as I was about to figure out what it was for, my mom woke me up. After that dream, I couldn't get the key out of my mind. So, I started doing some research and that's when everything came together."

"Amazing," my mother said as if she didn't wholeheartedly believe his entire story.

I went near the stove and helped with stirring the cheese grits. "I'm sure going to miss you mom. Are you sure you can't stay longer?" I pleaded hoping she would say yes and trying to change the subject. I didn't want my mom to leave thinking she had confirmation that Miles could not be trusted.

"Like I said before baby, I wish I could, but I have a few important doctor's appointments I can't miss. And if I try to reschedule, it might not be until July. I could be dead and gone by then."

"Don't say that mom." I shook my head not understanding why she insisted on being so negative.

"Well it's the truth and the truth is something we can't change no matter how hard we try."

Mom was always dropping some kind of matter of fact point every chance she got. I understood where she was coming from, but I guess some things I naturally didn't like talking about. Dying was at the top of my list with being one of those things. My mother was all packed and ready to go to the airport. We had to drop Miles off at school first, so I made sure he was dressed and ready to go. I also got dressed for work so I could finally make it back to the office. I knew I would have a lot of emails to catch up on even though I knew Lance was taking care of most of the appointments on my schedule.

On our way to the airport, I passed in front of the colorful house one more time at mom's request. She was amazed at the colors all over again as if it was her first time seeing them. Like before, she took out her phone and took another picture of the house. "Mom, didn't you take a picture of that house the other day?" I reminded her.

"I know I did. I'm not crazy," she answered smartly. "I'm thinking about using it to make postcards for the people at the nursing home and I want to make sure I have a clear picture."

"I understand mom. It's nice for you to still think of them."

"Well somebody has to. Hardly any of their children ever bother to visit. I sure hope you don't be one of those children who doesn't visit her poor old mother when I'm in a nursing home."

"And who said you will ever go to a nursing home? We already had this discussion a long time ago mom and I explained that if it ever gets to that point you will just have to come and live with me."

"Ok baby. I won't argue with you about that."

"Good." I said satisfied that she finally let me have my way. I couldn't help but think that she deliberately brought all of that up to see if I had changed my mind since I found out she was not my biological mother. I still couldn't look at her as anyone else except as my mother. She was the only mother I had ever known. When we drove in front of the house, I caught a glimpse of Miles in the rear-view mirror and he was looking down at his bracelet. I still hadn't told Miles about Ms. Hannah. It kind of slipped my mind to tell him with everything that was going on and I didn't want to mention it in front of my mom.

After we dropped off Miles, I headed to the airport and dropped off my mother. I made sure she made it to her gate on time and all of her bags were checked in. I stopped at Han's Café and picked up two cups of coffee. One for me and one for Lance to show my appreciation for all of his help with my clients while I was out. It was still odd knowing the man whom I had met a few short-lived months ago and whom I had grown to admire was indeed my biological father. I know he hadn't told anyone at the office because he wasn't that type of person. I walked over to Lance's office and left the cup of coffee on this desk with a sticky note saying, 'Thank you!' I knew he would be in soon so I wasn't worried about the coffee getting cold.

I stepped in my office and everything on my desk was the same way I had left it a week before. It was funny because I knew where everything was, and I easily picked up where I had left off. While in the middle of checking my fifth email, my phone rang. It was Miles' grandmother. I answered hoping she was calling to tell me when the Sinclairs were returning.

"Hello," I happily answered.

"Hi is this Gretchen?" she asked.

"Yes, this is Gretchen," fractionally listening to what she was saying and reading my emails.

"I hope I didn't catch you at a bad time dear."

I didn't want to tell her to the truth, so I deliberately gave her a false response, "No, it's fine. I wasn't too busy. How is everything going? Did you hear from your son and his wife yet? The last time I spoke with them they said they were returning today."

"Hold on dear. Let me let you talk to my oldest son, Jim." Her voice was shaky and I could hear her whispering to Jim that I was the one who was taking care of Miles.

"Hello Gretchen." His voice was solid when he came on the phone.

"Hi Jim," I answered still hoping for good news.

"My mother can't speak that well right now. I know this is all so unexpected but there has been a huge change in plans."

"What do you mean? Was their flight delayed or something?"

"I wish it was just a delayed flight." Jim's voice was starting to shake too. I painfully stopped reading my emails because up to this point, they only had half of my attention.

"Ok, tell me what happened. Did they decide to stay abroad longer than expected?" I couldn't help my tone but I know I sounded agitated.

"No, Gretchen. The thing is they were on their way back and there was a plane crash."

My heart dropped. "Oh my God." I was in shock.

Jim continued talking straining to get the words out, "They didn't make it Gretchen. They both died in the plane crash. I'm here now with mother to help her figure everything out." His voice had gone from being solid to sounding as if we had a bad connection.

"Oh my God," I repeated. My tone had softened not knowing what to say. "Miles, how in the world will I explain this to Miles? What are we going to do? Miles will be devasted. I can't tell him this. This is absurd. Why did that even happen? How am I going to explain this to Miles?" I could feel myself repeating the same thing over and over again as I started to lose my nerves. Jim could tell by the way that I was talking I was having somewhat of a breakdown.

"Gretchen, listen to me. I know this is hard. It is hard for us too over here. We have Zach who keeps asking for his parents and my mother can't bring herself to tell him they are not coming back. This is a lot for all of us."

"Poor baby Zach." I used my imagination to put myself in a baby's shoes trying to see how he felt not being able to see his parents. "Ok." I tried to convince myself I was calm now. "Ok, what do you need me to do? How can I help?"

"Well." Jim coached. "To be honest Gretchen. That is the reason we are calling you right now. My mother is flying out there first thing in the morning. She has to meet with my brother's attorney. I'm not able to go with her because of a prior commitment I made. Is there any way you can meet mother and Zach at the airport and help her to get around?"

"Sure." I agreed. "What time is her flight coming in?"

"10:20 tomorrow morning."

"Ok, then I'll be there." We were about to hang up and I thought about it. "Wait, Jim. This is going to sound crazy but I don't even know what your mother looks like."

"I'll text you over a picture. I'll make sure she has on a loud orange shirt so you can recognize her. And don't forget, she will have Zach too."

"That's right." I remembered that I could easily figure out who she was because she would have Zach with her.

We hung up the phone and I started pacing the floor back and forth. All I could think about was Miles. I had so much to figure out. I moved my hands vigorously to shake off my emotions. I heard two knocks at the door. I thought to myself, *oh no. Not now Mr. Koperneil.* I turned around to face Mr. Koperneil but it was Lance. I felt a huge relief. Lance walked in holding the cup of coffee I brought him. He was smiling when he first entered but his expression quickly turned into one of concern when he saw my face.

"Gretchen," he began while he softly guided me to sit in a chair in my office. After I sat down, he sat next to me. "What in the world is wrong? I thought you were feeling better since you took some time off. I was stopping by to thank you for the coffee. Is there anything I could help you with?"

I couldn't tell Lance the *whole* story. He didn't know anything about my personal life. I stalled while sitting there silently with my eyes focused on the floor. "Gretchen, I don't usually pry in people's business but I have to go and get Mr. Koperneil and let him know something is wrong."

"No," I rushed and said pulling him on his arm when he stood up to leave my office. He sat back down. "Don't tell Mr. Koperneil. I'm not emotionally prepared to deal with everything right now."

"Ok, Gretchen. I'll hold off saying anything for now. But why don't you go out and take a break and I'll cover for you? When you return, please consider talking with Mr. Koperneil about whatever is going on. It's going to start affecting your client relationships. I know you're one of the best. He just bragged about you last week. He believes in you. Listen, Mr. Koperneil is more than a boss Gretchen. He can also be a compassionate and understanding friend. Trust me. I know. I've been at some pretty low points myself and he was the one to help me during those times. I think he might be able to help you too."

I listened to every word Lance spoke but my thoughts kept creeping back to my visit at the Koperneils when I found out he was my biological father. I still had not spoken with him on a personal level about the whole situation. Lance walked out and I grabbed my phone and purse and took his advice and stepped out for a break. I drove to Han's, ordered a quick coffee and found me a quiet seat in the corner. I guess Paisley could tell something was bothering me so she quickly fixed my order and didn't even bother offering me her special herbal tea. I appreciated that she recognized I wanted to be left alone. I judged my emotions as I looked at my phone contemplating on if I should call Carl and give him the news about the Sinclairs. I had to think. I had a lot to think about and it felt like I was on some kind of timeclock with making my decisions. I had a strong feeling that 10:20 tomorrow morning would be here before I knew it.

I heard the bells to the café chime. I never looked up to see who it was. I was trapped in a space of time still contemplating on calling Carl. I felt a person's body standing behind me and I heard someone clear their throat as if they were trying to get my attention. I looked up and it was Langley. I took a deep breath as if to say, '*oh boy, not now*'. I guess he kind of read my expression. "I apologize. Is this a bad time?" He seemed slightly hurt that I didn't give him an expression of excitement when I noticed it was him. I realized he didn't have anything to do with what was happening so I softened my look and said, "No, no. Have a seat Langley. I'm especially elated to see you."

He leaned his neck back and raised his eyebrows in disbelief, "Really? I couldn't tell the way you looked at me just now."

"I'm sorry. It's a whole lot that has been happening to me in a dreadfully short period of time and I'm trying to figure out how to deal with the whole situation."

Langley took my phone from my hands, placed it on the table then held both of my hands in his. I felt a warm sensation travel through my spine and caught the chills. It shocked me so I giggled a little bit from embarrassment. He jokingly said, "It's ok. I know I have that effect on you."

"Oh boy," I began to accuse Langley. "Here you go again. Thinking you can get a compliment out of me."

"No, my sweet lady. I'm trying to get you to loosen up a little bit so I can help ease your mind. By now you have to know I have feelings for you."

I couldn't respond at all. I felt frozen. He just kept talking. "If you give me a chance, I'm here to help you if I can."

I thought about his offer for a few long seconds and I deliberated in my mind, '*What the hell? Why not? I don't think things can get any crazier than they already have.*' Without even controlling myself, I said, "Ok, I'll tell you. But you have to promise me you will keep an open mind about everything I'm about to say."

"Yes ma'am. I promise."

I didn't even know where to start. First, I told him about Miles staying with me and how that whole thing happened with the Sinclairs popping up at my office. Then I told him how I found out my mother wasn't in all actuality my mother and Mr. Koperniel was indeed my biological father. Mixing in a final touch of perplexity shocking him out of his seat I told him how I found out, about an hour ago, that the Sinclairs died in a plane crash and Miles' grandmother was flying in tomorrow morning with the baby to come and meet with the Sinclair's attorney. It looked like none of this was bothering Langley. He sat there with a serious expressionless face and listened to every word I blurted out.

"There," I said giving off a stressed out laugh. "That's what's going on in my life right now. Do you still think you can help me?"

Langley was leaning forward. It looked like he was at a lost for words. A feeling of guilt was creeping up on me because I trusted him enough to confide in him and tell him everything. He thought about what he wanted to say in response and sat up straight in his chair. "Gretchen," he said not following through with the rest of the words from his sentence.

"I know. It is way more than you thought huh?" I figured I could predict his answer to that question.

"Well." He started speaking carefully choosing his words as if he didn't want to hurt my feelings. "It is way more than I thought. But it is not something I'm afraid of approaching. Obviously, these are unspeakably difficult times for you and the last thing I want to do is watch you go through it all alone." It felt like Langley was simply giving me a politically correct answer instead of being honest. He kept talking and I kept listening wondering if he was for real. "Tell me what you need help with the most and I will see what I can do."

"Ok," I said as I thought about it. "I know the first thing I will need help with is getting over the fear of facing Mr. Koperneil."

"That's tricky," he fessed up. "But if I know Mr. Koperneil as well as I think I do, he won't make the situation more awkward for you than it already is. I'm sure he is trying to think of a way you two could sit down together and discuss everything. How about asking him if he will have a session with you at The Cemetery?"

"I guess I could, but that is still weird. I don't know. I think I will let time take care of everything."

"You can do that too," he agreed. "And like I said before, I know Mr. Koperneil will try to make the transition easier. He is not the type of guy who likes confusion."

"I know. He always checks on me. He has been nothing but kind ever since I met him. And that is before he even found out I was his daughter." I checked the time and it was time for me to return to work. "Oh boy, I'd better get back. Today was my first day back to work in a week." I stood up to leave and Langley stood up with me.

He held me by one of my wrists, "Wait." He was looking at me directly in my eyes. It felt like we had known each other for years. I felt so comfortable around him. "Are you able to meet me for dinner later? I have something I need to tell you."

My mind was wondering because I could not imagine what he needed to tell me. "I'm not sure to be honest. I think I need some time to clear my thoughts."

"Ok, well will you call me and let me know?" He pretty much knew that I wouldn't call but I guess he asked me out of courtesy.

"I will."

Chapter 13

The morning came around faster than I imagined. I felt like I was moving in circles. I couldn't find my keys or my phone when it was time to walk out the door. After the school van picked up Miles, I went straight to work. When I walked into my office, I was shocked to see I had a large bouquet of pink roses waiting for me on my desk. The card read, *"For a Beautiful Lady - Inside and Out - S. Langley."* My heart melted as I smelled the roses and remembered that I had forgotten to call him last night about dinner.

Knock knock. I knew that sound.

"Good morning Gretchen," I heard Mr. Koperneil say before I was able to turn around. "I didn't want to stop by yesterday because I knew it was your first day back." He walked over to my desk admiring the bouquet. "Ah, these are some lovely flowers."

"Thanks. They're from a close friend," I smiled as I thought about Langley and how he made me feel. "Please have a seat Mr. Koperneil. I'm so glad you stopped by." I shut the door to my office for some privacy. Mr. Koperneil took a seat and I sat in the chair right next to him. "Mr. Koperneil, right when I didn't think things could get any more complicated in my life, they have."

"Gretchen," he reached out to hold my hands. "I'm so sorry about everything Gab and I spilled on you. I promise I didn't know. You have to believe me."

"No, Mr. Koperneil," I contended as I slowly pulled my hands back to myself. He sat up straight ready to listen to what I had to say. "I'm not talking about that. I had a long talk with my mother concerning that whole situation and undoubtedly you and I will have to figure it all out at some point. Honestly, I'm sort of over the shock. Right now, I'm about to face a bigger issue."

"What is it?" he asked concerned.

"The Sinclairs."

"What about them?" His tone dropped as if he was as angry as I first was about them leaving Miles while they traveled.

"They were in a plane crash Mr. Koperneil. And, they did not survive."

"Oh my God," he gasped placing one hand over his mouth in shock. "So, now what will happen with Miles?"

"Truthfully, I don't know. I have to pick up his grandmother and baby brother from the airport at 10:20 this morning. I feel like everything is all over the place right now."

"Ok, Listen to me Gretchen. You do not have to go there all by yourself. I will have my driver bring us to pick them up. I will go with you. You shouldn't be dealing with this alone right now."

His gesture was a relief. "I sincerely appreciate it."

"Good," he asserted as he stood up to exit. "We will leave around 9:30," he said checking the time on his watch.

"Ok. I'll be ready."

Carl called and I picked up on the first ring. "Carl!" I was overjoyed that he called because I missed him immensely.

"There's my friend," he enforced. "Where have you been? Did you go on another love date with that sexy ass Langley?"

I was flushed with passion. "No, I have not. But, he did send me a bouquet of roses at my job."

"Ouuweee. That's romantic. What did the card say?"

"Stop it. I'm not telling you."

"Figures. You always leave out the good stuff."

I laughed at Carl because he was sounding like a jealous friend. "Carl, I'm so glad you called because you will not believe what has happened now."

"What baby?" His anticipation spilled through the phone.

"Miles' grandmother called me and told me his parents were in a plane crash and did not survive."

"What the hell?" Carl sounded shock and upset all at the same time.

"I know right. And now Mr. Koperneil and I are going to meet Mrs. Sinclair and Zach at the airport this morning."

"Wait, back up. Did you say you *and* Mr. Koperneil are going to the airport *together?*"

"Yes, I told him what happened and he offered to have his driver bring us to pick them up."

"Well, that was nice. I know you presumably didn't get to talk with Mr. Koperneil about the situation between you two but it seems like things are starting to smooth itself out."

"Yes, it is. I figured I would deal with that as it comes. I'm not going to force it, you know?"

"Yes, I understand what you mean."

9:30 rolled around and I met Mr. Koperneil downstairs. He was already there waiting for me with the driver. When the flight arrived, we didn't have any problems spotting Mrs. Sinclair and Zach. She had on a bright orange sweater like her son had said she would. She was of tall stature and walked with a firm steady pace for someone her age. I walked up to her and said, "Mrs. Sinclair, right?"

"Yes, and you must be Gretchen," she guessed.

"I am and this is my (I cleared my throat because I almost said something else.). This is my boss Mr. Koperneil."

"It's very nice to meet you both. Just call me Ms. Nancy," she insisted. "The flight was hectic. These tired old legs were already aching from chasing this little fellow around." She passed Zach's hand over for me to hold. I knew Zach from seeing him with the Sinclairs but I had never been this close to him. I didn't know how he would feel holding my hand. In all his innocence, he gave me a sweet smile letting me know he approved. I smiled back at him.

We loaded up her bags of luggage which felt extremely light and drove her to the Sinclairs. When we passed in front of the lake she recalled, "The last time I came to Mintly, Texas was when Zach was born. I remember coming to this lake with my son like it was yesterday." She took out a white handkerchief from her purse, blew her nose and wiped the tears falling from her eyes. "It's too bad I had to return here in these circumstances." She released a hard cry and apologized for not controlling her emotions.

"It's ok," Mr. Koperneil consoled Ms. Nancy. "It is much better to cry and let it all out. This must be an extremely difficult time for you right now Ms. Nancy. Believe me when I say I feel your pain."

I turned around and observed how affectionate Mr. Koperneil looked while comforting Ms. Nancy. This is a lady he legitimately just met and he treated her as if he had known her a vastly long time. I thought about what Langley said about Mr. Koperneil having a big heart and I was witnessing exactly what he meant by that comment. Zach was sitting between them in the middle playing with his miniature toy truck. He didn't have the slightest clue he would never see his parents again. In that instance, I also thought about Miles. He still did not know what had happened.

We dropped Ms. Nancy and Zach off at the Sinclairs and Mr. Koperneil made arrangements for another driver to take her wherever she needed to go. It was a quiet ride back to work. When we reached the office, I thanked Mr. Koperneil for helping me this morning. I walked into my office and started to read one of my contracts for a client who was scheduled to meet with me that afternoon. I cleared my mind and focused on work. My cell phone buzzed alerting me I had a text message. I didn't want to check it right away because I was almost finished reading the contract. It buzzed two more times back to back. I picked up the phone quickly to put it on silence because it was starting to annoy me. I felt like I couldn't breathe. I couldn't help but notice it was Langley's name blasted across the screen for the message. Instead of feeling agitated, my mood immediately changed. I opened the messages and read each one. Langley seemed desperate to meet with me for lunch. I had only been back at the office for an hour. I sent him a reply text message and asked if he wanted to meet for a late lunch around 2:30. He agreed. I finished making all the necessary revisions I needed to make to the contract.

I met Langley at Han's and we split a club house sandwich. He seemed especially nervous and I couldn't figure out why.

"Langley." I felt a twinkle of curiosity. "Is everything all right? I mean, don't get me wrong. I was flattered by the multiple text messages but it was a bit out of character for you."

Langley looked like he was a kid afraid to tell me he broke my favorite vase then he set free a full-fledged babble. "Gretchen, ever since our lunch date I've thought about you every single second. I simply can't get you out of my mind. And as crazy and bizarre as this will sound, I don't want to ever stop thinking about you. I want to see you more often. I'm not any good at this at all."

"Slow down Langley. You are talking so fast. You are scaring me." It felt like Langley was damn near prepping me for a proposal to be his wife.

"I'm sorry," he pleaded. "It's simply that I enjoy your company."

"I enjoy your company too Langley."

"Do you?" His eyes yearned to hear it again.

I giggled, "Yes, I do."

He stood up unexpectedly, reached in his jacket and placed a small box on the table. He partially sat back down, pulled his chair closer to mine and half knelt on one knee, "Will you please say yes and spend the rest of your life with me?"

I could not believe my ears. I had developed strong feelings for Langley but I never imagined everything would start happening this fast. The memories of my last three-year engagement to that low-down dirty Ralph rushed into my mind clouding my decision. I glanced over at Paisley and she was pretending to wipe down the counter but I could tell she was listening to every single word. I looked back at Langley and he had desperation in his eyes making it intensely difficult to disappoint him. I slid the unopened ring box back closer to his seat and softly answered, "Langley, as much as I would like to say yes. I just can't. I mean, we only had like one or two real conversations. We don't even know each other."

"I know Gretchen, but tomorrow is not promised and I would hate for anything to happen to either one of us. I would hate for circumstances to change and I miss the opportunity to prove just how special you are to me." I sat there stunned not knowing how to feel. I never believed in love at first sight but I had to be honest, this felt more real than any long-term relationship I had ever been in. Langley kept talking and I listened not able to finish my sandwich. He was pouring his heart out to me and I did not know how to respond.

"Langley, I'm truly sorry. But maybe we can take our time with this and start off by doing normal things people do in a relationship."

"That's the thing Gretchen. I'm not sure I have that kind of time."

"What do you mean?"

"I wanted to tell you all this yesterday over dinner but you never called me back. Now, it's just not fair to keep this information from you any longer. You deserve to know the whole truth." I was all ears as Langley premised his story. "Like most people, I have secrets Gretchen. Before I moved to Mintly, I discovered I was different from everyone else. I mean extremely different. It started when I was in high school and progressively got worst when I was in college. After the doctors could not figure out what was wrong with me or what was causing it, I decided to keep a journal and try to figure things out for myself."

"I'm not following you Langley. What are you talking about?"

"I'll be straight with you Gretchen because you have been open and honest with me. I have an isolated disease which attacks my nervous system. If you notice, and I think you have because you sort of made some remarks about it, I don't usually talk much. During my journal writing and observations, I discovered the less I thought about ideas or expressed my emotions, the more I was able to control the affects of my nervous system. Before then, I was a social butterfly. The problem with that was I had way too many ideas I would get excited about. I used to think of new inventions all the time. I had to force myself to stop thinking of new things. My emotions and ideas were causing me to get sick. It would start off with my sight. I used to have perfect vision. Out of nowhere, my vision started to go in and out. The blackouts wouldn't last for more than a few seconds at a time but it happened often enough for me to be scared out of my mind. I did some research but couldn't find anything on my own. Luckily, I learned about a special blended tea. It is a true secret blend and the government doesn't even know about it. You have to promise never to tell anyone about it because the wrong people don't need to find out. You know how it is sometimes. People just want to exploit things for their own financial gain."

I listened in amazement. "It sounds like you have ultimately found a cure."

"Sort of. The tea is enough to keep my nervous system in tack. The doctors said if my nervous system continued to deteriorate it is highly likely I would not survive beyond three more years. This was over ten years ago."

"Who else besides me knows about this special tea?"

He looked over at Paisley. When I turned around to see her response she simply winked and continued to wipe down the counters. "So, let me get this straight." My mind felt twisted in knots after listening to everything Langley had just told me. "Do you mean to tell me if you think too hard or get too excited you will get sick?"

"Precisely," he firmly responded.

"So sick, that it might cause your life to end?"

He thought about what I asked for a second and admitted, "Yes, pretty much. If I overwork my brain, it pushes my nervous system and causes damage to my heart. The only solution the doctors gave me was to train myself on how to numb my thoughts and my feelings."

"So that explains why you are usually so stiff and emotionless."

"Right," he answered happy to see I was finally understanding. "After I learned how to control my thoughts and feelings I had to move away from my family and friends. I had to isolate myself in a place where I didn't know anyone in order to save my life. That is when I moved to Mintly. I didn't tell my mother why I moved so far away because I didn't want her trying to figure out what she could do to fix my problem. She had enough to deal with raising my two younger sisters. It got to a point where I only spoke with her once a year. I know it broke her heart but it was the only thing I could do to keep myself from getting sick. I hated not speaking to her or seeing her. She deserved much better. My mom had me at a drastically young age and it was just us two for the longest time. After she married my step-dad, they had two girls. I learned later that she was pregnant with my baby brother when she died while giving birth. I felt so guilty for not talking to her all that time I didn't even go to her funeral. It has been ten years now since she passed away but I feel the same stinging pain today I felt back then."

"Wow Langley, that's crazy." I thought about my comment, "I'm sorry. I mean, it's not crazy. It's just ..."

"You're right, it's crazy. There is no other word for it." Before he placed the box back in his jacket pocket, he looked at me again, "Are you sure you don't want to marry me?"

I could not speak. I did not want to say the wrong thing. My heart pushed me to go ahead and tell him yes. Who said you have to date for years first? My meddling mind jumped in with the voice of my mother and said you'd better not go and do something like that. You don't even know this man.

"It's ok," he rationalized while I sat there unable to speak. He placed the box back in his jacket. "This was a bad idea in the first place. I should not have put you in a position like that. It's just that I have never felt like this about any woman and I didn't want to lose you."

"We can spend time with each other for now." I tried to sound convincing.

"Sure." His feelings seemed crushed but he held his composure. "Let's just finish our lunch."

"I hope you're not upset with me Langley."

"Oh no Gretchen. You are way too beautiful for me to be upset with you. You are beautiful inside and out, just like the card said. But I also know you have to eat because while we've been talking your stomach has been chiming in with some strange sounds."

I laughed. "I didn't know you could hear my stomach growling."

"Oh yes, all the customers in here heard the strangling howl from your stomach."

"Whatever." I felt content that Langley's feelings were not miserably damaged by my rejection to his proposal.

We finished our lunch and Langley walked me to my car. He was like the perfect gentleman. We both walked slowly and there was a warm breeze blowing. Langley reached out to hold my hand while we walked down the street. "You don't meet anyone by chance," he said. "Everything around us happens for a reason. Good and bad. The key is to pay attention to the signs and figure out its meaning. Once you unlock the true meaning of why things happen, when they happen and with whom they happen, then and only then will you be able to live life to its fullest. And I don't mean live like some crazy rich person. (laughs) I used to think being rich meant only having a whole lot of money. That's why I worked hard to become one of the top brokers."

"Oh my God Langley. Are you bragging on yourself?" I found his arrogance charming.

"No, not at all," he said. "I'm only saying that I learned later on in life that there are other ways to be rich. Everyone has to figure that part out on your own. Hopefully, everyone does get a chance to figure it out. I learned what it truly means to be rich when I met you."

"Aww Langley, that is the sweetest thing anyone has ever told me." He gave me a peck on the cheek, opened the door to my car and made sure I was in ok.

"I'll talk to you later, right?" he enchanted a positive response from me before I drove off.

"Yes, you will."

"You told me the same thing the other day. Don't have me waiting all night," he said jokingly.

"I won't," I laughed.

Later in the afternoon Ms. Nancy came by to pick up Miles. I was relieved because I still had not told Miles about his parents and I didn't want to be the bearer of bad news. Miles was so excited to see his baby brother. He gave Zach a big hug and kiss. Zach held him tightly by the neck while Miles tried to lift him up. His grandmother said in a kind tone and admiring their cuteness, "Put him down Miles. He is almost as big as you."

Miles tried to prove her wrong by using all of his strength.

"No, he's not Grandma." He lifted Zach two inches from the ground.

"You're right baby." She amused Miles concerning his strength. "You are so strong Miles."

"I know." He posed with his arms to show off his muscles. "I can't wait to show mom and dad how strong I am. Are they at home?"

Ms. Nancy and I both looked at each other at a loss of words. She composed herself and answered Miles, "Come on dear. Let's get out of Ms. Gretchen's way so she can have her house back." I could tell she was trying to change the subject and didn't mean it in an offensive way. I gave Miles a big hug and walked them out to the car with his things.

"I'll see you at the center tomorrow." I gave Miles a quick hug.

"Yes ma'am," he cheered. They all got into the car and drove off.

I went inside, shut the door, took a deep breath and stood by the door resting the back of my head against it for support with my eyes closed. This was the first time in what felt like forever that I had some alone time. I called Langley as promised and explained how I was mentally drained and I just needed to stay in and rest. He gently understood.

Chapter 14

The doorbell rang at 6:00 in the morning. I was in the process of putting on my tennis shoes getting ready for my morning jog. I walked over to the door wondering who it could be. When I opened the door, Miles and Zach were standing there with Ms. Nancy. I didn't even have a chance to invite them in before she guided them into the house explaining why they were all there. "I'm so sorry to barge in on you like this Gretchen and I know it is early. Miles told me that you would be up already so I figured it was ok. Look, I have to leave them with you for now because I realized I don't have anyone to watch Zach when I go to meet the attorney this morning. I have to be there for 8:00. I hope you don't mind dear. I don't know what to do right now. I'm not used of all of this."

At first, I shook my head in disbelief. I thought about the kids and I saw how distraught Ms. Nancy was looking. My guess is that losing her son in the plane crash miserably hit her even harder last night while they were at their house all alone. Miles was extra quiet and withdrawn. He held his brother's hand and they went to the sofa. "Does Miles know yet?" I whispered to Ms. Nancy.

"No," she said. "I can't bring myself to tell him." She was starting to cry again. I felt horrible. She was all alone and was having to deal with everything by herself. "Can you please tell him Gretchen? I don't know how to say it." She walked out without even waiting for my response to her question. I watched as the driver took her away.

I went to the garage and pulled out a foldup wagon I had stored. "Come on kids. You will both come with me for a walk this morning." Miles picked up his brother and helped him get into the wagon.

"I'll pull him Ms. Gretchen," he vowed.

"Ok baby." I rubbed Miles' curly hair. "I will walk and you can follow close behind me. Ok?"

"Ok," he approved.

We walked a few blocks quietly then I felt Miles tug on the back of my shirt. I stopped and looked at Miles. He burst out in tears and grabbed me. I held him back extra tight. "I know what happened," he said with his voice partially drowned out since his face was still pressed against my body.

I squatted down so I could look up in his face. "What do you mean Miles?" I listened but I was afraid to hear his answer.

"I know what happened to my parents." Miles was wiping the tears from his face. "I heard Grammy on the phone with my uncle this morning and she was saying she didn't know how to tell me that mom and dad were not coming back."

"What else did you hear?" I investigated.

"That's it. I ran to my room after that. Why did they leave me and my brother Ms. Gretchen? We are not bad kids. I mean I know I don't clean my room everyday but it's not super messy. Why didn't they send for us to go and meet them? We are good kids."

I realized at that moment Miles did not know about the plane crash. He only thought his parents did not want to ever come back home. I held him close trying to think of how I would give him the news. I thought back to how I felt when my grandmother died. I knew I had to be honest with Miles so I didn't hold back.

"Miles." I rubbed the curls from his forehead. "Your parents didn't leave you. They were trying to get back home to you and your brother. There was a plane crash Miles." His eyes were starting to water all over again. "Listen Miles. I know your parents did not intend for this to happen. I'm here ok. I'm here." A warm breeze started to blow while I comforted Miles. We heard the wind chimes. It was coming from the colorful house. Miles stood up straight and engaged with the chime. I noticed the stone on his bracelet was getting brighter.

"Zach...no...!" Miles screamed breaking me out of my trance looking at his bracelet. Zach had jumped out of the wagon and was headed straight for the house but Miles stopped him.

"Where were you going Zach?"

"To the house. The lady waved." Zach's voice was still like a baby's but he spoke clearly.

"What lady?"

"In the window," Zach pointed. Miles looked at all of the windows but he didn't see anyone.

"Come on Zach. Get back in your wagon," I encouraged while picking him up to put him back in the wagon. I realized I still hadn't told Miles I met the lady who lived in the house. The windchime was still moving and the stone in the center was glistening. Miles was so busy looking for the lady to show up in a window to the point he didn't notice the glow from his bracelet.

"Let's go Miles." I tried to grab his focus away from the house. Miles turned around and started to follow me while I pulled Zach. I could tell he kept looking back at the house. The glow from his bracelet was starting to fade. Miles did not notice it all because he was zoned in on the house.

The alarm on my watch went off. I had set it for 20 minutes. I knew I had to cut my morning routine short since I had Miles and Zach to take care of this morning. We kept walking and suddenly Miles screamed, "Ms. Gretchen!"

He startled me, "What is it Miles?"

The glow from the bracelet had stopped. Miles was too afraid to say what happened because he didn't want to seem crazy so he responded, "I thought I saw something."

"Something like what?" I wasn't prepared to hear the truth but my question slipped out anyway.

"Nothing. Never mind. It's nothing." Miles seemed disappointed that I hadn't noticed the same thing he had seen. Miles looked at the house one last time before it disappeared from our sight. He could not figure out if what he saw was real or his imagination.

Before we made it home, I called Carl to see if he could meet us at the house to help me watch Zach while I dressed for work. He drove up at the same time we were getting back.

"Good morning darling." He kissed me on my cheek.

"Good morning Carl." I was relieved he showed up. "Thanks for coming at such short notice."

"Anytime darling. Don't worry about it." Carl picked up Zach and brought him inside. Zach held onto him as if he knew him already.

Miles commented, "He goes by everybody."

I whispered to Carl letting him know I told Miles about his parents. Miles did not seem to hear us talking. It looked like he was taking everything pretty well. I asked Carl to fix a quick breakfast for the kids while I showered and dressed. Ms. Nancy called right before I got in the shower to tell me which drop-in daycare to bring Zach and she would pick him up after she was finished running errands. After we left the house, I dropped off the kids to school and daycare and Carl met me at Han's for a quick coffee before work.

"Carl, it has been a crazy couple of days."

"More like a crazy couple of weeks honey," he added.

"You're right about that. Guess what else happened to me yesterday right over there at that table." I pointed to the table where Langley and I sat for lunch.

"What?" he waited to hear more shocking news.

"Someone proposed to me."

"What?" Carl was utterly surprised. "Are you telling me Mr. Look Good Himself asked you to be his wife?"

"Yep." I was proud to announce the news about the proposal to Carl.

Carl lifted up my left hand. "Well then, where is the ring girlfriend?"

I pulled my hand back laughing, "Now you know I didn't say yes. I mean, we don't even know each other that well."

"So."

"So?"

"Yes, you heard me. Listen, I have way too many clients who come to me wishing they hadn't waited so long to marry the person they loved. My suggestion to you is to give it a try. I see how you light up when you talk about him."

"That's crazy Carl. I can't marry that man."

"All I'm saying is to think about it."

"Yeah, ok." I was being sarcastic knowing good and well I was not going to marry Langley. At least not until we had a chance to get to know one other.

"Will I see you for lunch today? I know you have been super busy but I miss my friend."

I guess I had been extra busy lately and knew we hadn't been spending as much time together. This made it easier for me to accept Carl's lunch offer. "Jazzes?" I suggested.

"Yes, by all means Jazzes. I could use some of that good soul food today," Carl publicized.

"Me too. Let's meet at 1:00."

"Ok, sounds good," Carl answered. We walked out the café and I looked across the street at the cemetery. I noticed Carl was looking at the building too. "Gretch, it feels like that place is calling my name."

I kept penetrating my eyes on the building, "As crazy as it sounds Carl. I feel the same way."

"Girl, it's clearly in our heads," Carl laughed. "I'll see you at lunch."

"Ok." I couldn't resist that Carl was right. "See you at lunch." I got in my car and arrived at the office with a clear mind because I knew I had to meet a client for 11:00. After the meeting I called and checked on Langley. The phone rang a few times and went to his voicemail. Leaving a voice message was not in my plan because I hadn't prepared anything in my head. My expectation was that he would answer my call as usual. After about twenty minutes I tried calling him again. This time the call went straight to his voicemail. That was strange. I couldn't help but wonder if he was ignoring my calls or simply blocked my phone number. My mind was developing paranoia conclusions. I decided I wouldn't worry about it right now because I had other things to deal with. My phone rang and it was him.

"Hello." I suppressed any hint of expression he might hear in my voice. I was suspicious as to why he didn't answer my calls earlier but I didn't want to question him. Plus, I didn't want him to think that it bothered me.

"I noticed you called earlier but I was in a meeting and couldn't answer. This is my second time calling you. The first time it went straight to your voicemail but I didn't leave a message. I called right back." I started to smile because I realized we must have been calling each other at the same time. I guess our calls crossed when my call went straight to his voicemail.

"Oh." I pretended to be nonchalant. "I was just calling to check on you. I know we never openly had a chance to talk since yesterday."

"I'm ok Gretchen," he assured me. "I knew before it even happened that you would feel more rational by answering no. But I'm a man of patience. How are you today young lady?"

"I guess I'm ok."

"Just ok?"

"Yes, Ms. Nancy showed up at my house early this morning and dropped off both Miles and Zach."

"Miles *and* Zach?" he asked in surprise.

"Yes, she said she couldn't deal with them right now."

"I see," he sounded as if he didn't want to make the wrong comment about the whole situation.

"Yes, but it's fine. I dropped them both off this morning. As much as I hated to do it, I had to end up telling Miles about his parent's death."

"Oh, my Goodness Gretchen. How did that go?"

"I'm not sure he understood the whole concept. His baby brother started running towards that house so it kind of distracted his attention."

"What house?"

"I'm sorry. I'm talking to you like you were right there with us. There is a real colorful house a few blocks away from where I live."

"Oh, do you mean that extra colorful house with the angel winged shutters?"

"Yes." I was surprised he knew exactly which house I was talking about. "Do you know who lives there?"

"No." He explained, "Whenever I drive by, which is not often, I never see anyone coming out or going in. I do like all the colors though. It reminds me of a flower garden from my childhood I planted. I had to do it for a school project and I used a whole bunch of seeds from all kinds of flower packs I found in my mom's kitchen drawer. When the flowers bloomed, I had the most colorful flowerbed out of the whole class. All the other kids loved it too. I was so proud of my flowerbed."

"That's amazing." I was astonished. "Well, one day while I was jogging past that house, I got caught up in looking at the windchime and ended up in the yard right near the porch."

"You went in those people's yard?" Langley sounded as if he was there and ashamed for me.

"I know." I still felt the embarrassment just by bringing it up. "I didn't realize it until it was too late."

"What do you mean too late?"

"The lady came outside."

"What lady?"

"The lady who lives there," I defended.

"So, you physically saw the person who lives there?" Langley questioned surprisingly.

"I did. I was so nervous and mortified all at the same time."

"So, what happened? Did she tell you anything about trespassing in her yard?"

"No," I thought back to that day. "She was amazingly beautiful and sweet. She told me her grandmother made the windchime was on her porch."

"The windchime?" Langley was acting like he hadn't seen it for himself.

"Yes, there is a wooden windchime hanging on the porch and it has some kind of stone in the middle. Anyway, the stone caught my eye and to my surprise Ms. Hannah came out and caught me standing in her yard."

"Ms. Hannah?" he copied.

"Yes, she said her name is Hannah." Langley was extra quiet on the other end of the phone. "Are you still there Langley?" I was unsure if he would answer.

"Yes, I'm still here." There was a window of hesitation. "Gretchen, my mother's name was Hannah."

"I'm sorry Langley. I didn't know."

"No, it's alright." I could tell that the memory of hearing her name was bothering him but he didn't shut me out. "I think the lady you met is my mother."

"Wait." I was confused. "I thought you said your mother died during childbirth?"

"Yes, but what if ..."

"What if what?" I waited for Langley to finish his thought.

"Gretchen, please hear me out and don't think I'm losing my wits or anything but I'm wondering if the lady you met is indeed my mother. Maybe she didn't die. Maybe, somehow, she is here. Living all this time in that house."

"Langley, I'm not following your train of thought. What you are saying does not make any sense."

"It does." He tried to reason as if he was figuring out some kind of mystery. "When my mother died, or at least when I was informed that she was dead, I never felt in my heart like she was gone. I've had close relatives die in my family and it brings about a certain feeling of emptiness within my soul. I didn't have that feeling with the news about my mother dying. Then when you told me about the windchime just now I remembered she used to have a wood windchime when I was kid. It is all making sense now. The colorful wood front is like the flower garden I made when I was a kid."

"Langley," I spoke gently not to discourage him. "Don't you think everything you are saying is a little far-fetched?"

"Check your messages," he dictated.

"What?"

"I just sent you a text message with a picture of my mother. Look at it and tell me if she is the lady you saw."

I opened my text messages and loaded the picture onto my phone. The picture was faded but I could still make out the lady's face. "I'm not sure Langley. It looks like it could be her, but I don't want to say for sure because this is serious and the picture is a tad bit faded."

"I think it's her Gretchen." Langley got quiet again on the phone. I didn't know what to say or think. Langley's rambling took over, "And if that's true, maybe the baby is alive too. That means he would be around ten years old." He was trying to connect all the dots in his mind out loud. The more he talked the faster the words gushed out. "Both of them are alive. No one died. This is a miracle. Oh my God Gretchen. Miles."

"What about Miles?"

"Miles is my brother."

"No way!"

"Yes, Gretchen. Think about it. Miles does not look anything like his parents. Zach on the other hand has all of their features. And the more I think about Miles, the more I realize he looks strikingly similar to my youngest sister. Check your phone again."

I looked at my phone and a picture came across of a pretty little girl with big eyes and large ashy brown curls. "Oh my God Langley. He does resemble her a whole lot. Now you have me thinking that there is some truth to what you are saying." I kept looking at the picture. The more I looked at it the more I could see Miles' smile and all the rest of his facial features. "I do remember Miles confiding in me saying he looked different. And Langley please don't tell a soul about this."

"I would never do that Gretchen. I know how much he means to you."

"Yes, he is a special kid. But he knows he is different. He said he asked his parents if he was adopted or something and they insisted he wasn't. He also said he overheard her arguing with someone at the hospital demanding to know everything that happened when she delivered him."

"Gretchen!" Langley's excitement burst through his voice over the phone. I got worried because I remembered what he told me about his condition. I did not want his excitement to trigger anything that could jeopardize his health.

"Wait Langley," I interrupted him in mid-sentence. "Don't get so excited. I don't want anything to happen with you. You know. Remember what you said about your nervous system."

He calmed down and I could hear him taking a few long deep breaths. "You're right Gretchen. But listen, I know Miles is my brother. He looks like my younger sister when she was his age. I don't know why I didn't figure this out sooner. Plus, he has the gene."

"What gene?"

"The genius gene. He thinks of things kids his age wouldn't normally think about. I sure hope it does not affect his nervous condition the way it affects mine. If it does, he might not even realize it until it's too late."

"What do you mean too late?"

"Too late as in there is no turning back."

"Are you saying if Miles is your brother there is a possibility that he has the same condition you have and he might die at any moment?" I was feeling hysterical and overwhelmed with the need to find out if everything he was saying was true.

"That's exactly what I'm saying Gretchen."

"What are we going to do?" It felt like we had already mutually agreed we would save Miles. We had no clue if these thoughts were even true but I was willing to take a chance and find out in case it was because I cared deeply for Miles. I couldn't imagine how I would emotionally be able to handle if anything ever happened to him.

"What about The Cemetery?" Langley suggested.

"What about it? The Sinclairs are dead. We can't talk to the dead remember."

"I'm not talking about the Sinclairs. I'm talking about my mother. Hannah."

"Yes! That's true. Ms. Hannah. If my mother heard about The Cemetery all the way in New Orleans, hopefully Ms. Hannah also saw it on the news and registered too. This is brilliant Langley. I can go to meet you at The Cemetery when I get off of work if you like."

"Ok," Langley agreed. "Don't tell anyone about this right now. We undoubtedly need to make sure first."

"Ok, I promise I won't tell anyone."

"Good. I will see you at The Cemetery later."

"Ok, see you then."

My nerves had my hands shaking. I kept looking at the pictures on my phone that Langley sent me of his mother and sister. I noticed the time and I only had a few minutes to meet Carl for lunch. I rushed out and found a place to park. Jazzes was crowded as usual. I looked for Carl and he already had a table for us and had ordered my favorite meal.

"You're the best Carl." I gave him kudos for taking care of my meal order before I arrived.

"Are you ok baby?" He looked troubled by my appearance. "It looks like you ran into a ghost."

I gave Carl a fake laugh saying, "You're so silly Carl." I knew he could read straight through me, but he respected me enough not to keep pushing the issue. "So, all we've been talking about lately is me and all the drama that has been going on in my life. Let's switch up this time and talk about you. What's going on with you?" I squeezed a few lemon slices into my glass of sweet tea. I loved the fact I never had to ask for extra lemons because they were readily available right there on the table in a small jar.

"Well," Carl started. "You remember my new friend, right?"

"Greg?"

"Yes, my darling Greg." Carl put on a dreamy look. "He is the best thing that has happened to me in a long time. He is talking about moving here and I don't know how I feel about that."

"What's wrong with that? Won't you have more time to spend with each other?"

"Yes, but I don't know for sure if I'm ready. That last relationship I had nearly drained the spirit out of me." Carl's whole demeanor started to change thinking about it.

"We don't have to talk about it if you don't want to."

"No, it's fine. I'm dealing with it all in my own way." The waiter came to the table and brought us some fresh bread. "Gretchen, I never mentioned this before but the guy I used to date was abusive."

"Abusive how baby?" I needed to know what happened. "Did he tell you some insulting things? Because if he said negative things about you, I know for sure none of it is true at all. You have to believe that."

"You're such a sweetie Gretchen. If I were a straight man, I would confidently give Langley a run for his money." I laughed. "But seriously Gretch, that man ripped out my soul. I don't know if I want to let anyone else in like that. I can't go through physical abuse like that ever again."

I almost choked on my tea. "Carl?" I immediately tried to console him. "I didn't know you were in a physically abusive relationship. That is serious honey. How long did that go on?"

"Too long. But thank God I was able to let him go."

"What do you mean?"

"It's crazy Gretchen. I knew I didn't deserve any of that abuse but I felt like it was my fault sometimes so I would beg him to stay."

"I can't believe this. Carl, no one deserves to be treated that way. I mean no one."

"I know. I knew better. I was in the typical false sense of love relationship. That is why I'm so afraid to get too close to Greg. I don't want to end up back where I was before."

"You don't have to Carl. Listen to me, every relationship will not be the same. You have to at least give you and Greg a try. If you see things are starting to make a turn for the worst just end it before it gets too complicated."

"I hear what you're saying Gretchen but I don't know. I will think about it though."

I smiled at Carl. "You'll be fine. You know you can always go to The Cemetery, like you told me."

"I know. I've miraculously been giving it some thought. I don't want to go alone. Will you come with me?"

"I sure will. Just let me know when."

The waiter brought our food to the table and everything looked and smelled delicious. We both left there stuffed as usual. After we left there, I went back to work and finished everything I planned. I rushed out so I wouldn't be late to meet Langley at The Cemetery.

When I got there, he was walking out of the building towards me. "It won't work Gretchen. She's not registered." He seemed discouraged.

I held him by his arm, "Come on, let's go walk across the street to Han's and get a hot cup of tea."

We entered the café and Paisley was at the counter talking with Lance. I said hello to Lance and waited to see where Langley wanted to sit. When I turned around, I noticed Langley had tapped two times on the counter. Paisley responded as she always did and reached for the unmarked jar. As I watched Langley and his process of pressing the bags together with the spoon, I realized this must be the special cure he told me about. I looked up at Paisley and she was watching my expression. She winked at me and went back to finishing her conversation with Lance. I watched Langley as he stood there and prepared his tea. It was mesmerizing. I could hear Miles' voice tell me that Paisley gave him a cup of the special herb tea she usually offers to me and Carl. I looked up at Paisley again but she wasn't looking my way. "Langley," I whispered. "Is that...?" He stopped me before I could finish asking the question by raising one finger in the air. I kept whispering, "If that's what I think it is, I think Miles already had a cup while he was here."

Langley never looked up at me until he finished the full cup of tea. I felt awkward standing there so I excused myself to the ladies' room. When I came back out Paisley said Langley left a message for me. She handed me a note which read, "*I'm sorry I had to rush out. I will call you later to let you know what I figured out. Love, Langley.*"

I rushed out of the café holding the note in my hand and looked everywhere for Langley but he was no where in sight. *Love, Langley* I thought. Does he love me?

I checked my phone and the only message I had was from Carl asking me to meet him at The Cemetery for 8:00 in the morning. I agreed and looked over at The Cemetery. I thought I saw the back of Ms. Hannah enter the building so I ran across the street. I looked both ways in the hall and I didn't see anyone. I asked the receptionist if a fair skinned lady wearing a hat just entered the building. She told me based on privacy reasons she could not release any information. I didn't push the issue because I knew the building was scheduled to close in a little over an hour. I camped out in my car on a mission to catch Ms. Hannah when she came out. The time crept by like a snail crossing the street. I heard a tap on my car window that startled me. Paisley was standing there waiting for me to put my window down.

"Are you ok?" she asked.

"Yes, I'm waiting for someone."

"Ok, It looks like you were sleeping. I stopped by to check on you. Good night."

"Good night, Paisley." I looked at my watch and it was ten minutes after seven. "*No way,*" I said out loud to myself. I picked up my phone to make sure it had the same time as my watch. It did. I couldn't believe that I fell asleep.

Chapter 15

I got to The Cemetery early the next morning waiting for Carl to show up. It was before 8:00 but I didn't want to miss him. I saw his car pull up in my rearview mirror. I stepped out and greeted him.

"Good morning." I gave him the usual smooches.

"Good morning Gretch. Thank you so much for coming here with me. I am still having second thoughts."

"I figured you were. Let's go in and give it a try. If you start to feel uncomfortable tap your foot two times so I can know you want to stop."

"Ok," he agreed.

We walked into The Cemetery and the walls felt especially cold this morning. As soon as we sat in the designated room, the panel started showing Carl's thoughts.

"Everything will work out fine. You have been through a lot and have overcome every obstacle. You are a successful psychiatrist. Wait a minute. These are all affirmations I tell myself every morning. Why are these the only thoughts?"

"Take your time Carl. You are doing fine. Just let your mind flow freely."

Carl closed his eyes to concentrate. "I'm remembering my mother. I remember the day I lost my mother. I was playing at home and singing those high notes of one of her favorite female singers. My mom was encouraging me to sing on because it was her favorite song. She believed in keeping a record player in the house and kept playing the song from the vinyl single so I could keep singing. At that time, my mom was dating an abusive guy. When he heard me singing, he went into the living room, took the record from the turntable and started scratching it with a knife. My mom tried to stop him, but he kept scratching the record over and over again with that knife. Him and my mom got into an argument later that night. I stayed in my room and tried covering my head with a pillow to drown out the noise. I heard a gunshot go off but I still didn't move. In my heart, I was hoping he was dead. I was seven years old. Everything was extra quiet. I hid deep under the covers when I heard footsteps coming to my room. I remember the door opened and closed then the footsteps went away. After a while I heard the guy saying he was sorry. He kept saying it until I heard police sirens. It was the same words he always said after a fight with my mom. But this time, I didn't hear my mother's voice. I peaked out of my room and saw the police putting handcuffs on the guy. That low-down dirty animal turned around towards my room and said "I'm sorry" as he looked at me. The crazy part is I essentially believed him. I believed he was truly sorry. I guess that's why I was willing to stay in the abusive relationship I stayed in for all that time."

Carl paused staring at the panel in disbelief. It looked like he was reliving that day all over again. "We can stop if you want to Carl."

He ignored my thoughts and kept going, "After the police took the guy away, my grandmother showed up and covered my head with a towel while she walked me to the car. I did not ask any questions. I remained quiet and held my grandmother's hand. The next time I saw my mother was at her funeral. She was sleeping peacefully. At least that's what my grandmother told me. My grandmother told me she will wake up in Heaven."

Carl started crying, "I felt guilty for years. I felt like I could have stopped him from killing her. I don't know why I didn't help her. She needed me and I didn't move. I hid like a coward. When I was in that abusive relationship, I thought about my mother every time he would hit me. A part of me felt like I deserved each blow because I needed to know what my mother went through while I laid there in my room with my pillow smashed against my head. I felt like

I deserved to die. I believe I wanted to die. I wanted to die and go to Heaven so I could tell my mother how sorry I am for not being there for her. She died protecting me. She was my shield. I'm so sorry momma. If you can hear me at all, I'm so sorry momma."

We sat there quietly while Carl recomposed himself. When I felt like he was feeling better I allowed my thoughts to come across the panel. "I'm greatly sorry you went through that Carl. You have to believe me when I tell you none of this is your fault. I'm sure your mother knew you loved her dearly. Didn't you make her proud when you sang her favorite song?"

"I did. She wouldn't even join in. She would pull up a chair and watch me perform over and over again. She never got tired of loving me."

"And that's what you need to remember. It's what you need to focus on. It is what will help you get through and have a healthy relationship. I can tell that your mother loved you with all of her heart and she would do anything in the world for you."

Carl smiled, "You sound just like her right now."

The panel cleared and the door opened. We left the session and I could tell that Carl felt relieved he let all of that out. His phone rang as soon as we walked out of the building. It was Greg. Carl's face lit up.

"Go on and answer the phone Carl. I'm about to run and grab us a coffee. I will meet you by your car."

"Ok doll," he replied before answering the call.

I walked across the street and ordered two cups of coffee to go. I noticed Langley had been there already because his double spoon and drained tea bag with the distinguished purple string was left on a napkin still sitting on the counter. I looked around the café to see if he was still there. I didn't see him at all. Paisley was busy helping the morning crowd so I didn't bother asking her about Langley. I walked over to Carl and gave him his cup of coffee through his car window. He was still on the phone with

Greg so he blew me an air kiss. I caught it and put in my pocket and he smiled as he drove off. Before I got in my car, I heard a small voice yelling my name. I looked up to see where it was coming from and it was Miles running towards me with his backpack. I put my coffee cup on top of my car and hurried over to meet Miles.

"What are you doing here?" He jumped off the steps and ran into my arms.

"I told my Grammy to drop me at the center because we had a field trip today?" he sounded scared.

"A field trip?" I looked around for other kids.

"Yes, I made up the whole story so I could see you," he confessed.

"But Miles, you have to go to school baby."

"I needed to talk to you Ms. Gretchen. Grammy was on the phone talking with my uncle again and I heard her say she couldn't take care of both me and Zach. She said I would have to go live with my uncle. I don't even know him Ms. Gretchen. Can't you do something? Can you just ask her if we can both stay with you? Pleassee?" Miles pleaded.

"Miles, I would love to do that baby but it's not as easy as it sounds. Plus, I don't know anything about taking care of a three-year-old. It was ok when it was only you because you are older and don't need as much attention. I don't know if I could manage taking care of both of you together." I tried to make Miles understand my point of view.

"Ms. Gretchen, I will help you with everything. I know how to take care of my baby brother. He needs me. You should have seen how excited he was when he saw me. Plus, I need him." Miles' expression was gloomy and it was something I wasn't used to seeing. "I need Zach, Ms. Gretchen, because he is all I have left."

I wanted to tell Miles badly he had more family than he thought but I had made a promise to Langley. "Come on Miles." I led the way to my car. "I will bring you to work with me until we figure everything out." Miles jumped in the passenger seat and didn't say a word. He looked satisfied that I hadn't decided to bring him to school. This was now bigger than me. I texted Langley and asked him to meet me at my office. Miles and I met up with Mr. Koperneil on the elevator.

"Good morning," Mr. Koperneil greeted us both while smiling but still giving me a questionable look as if to ask what is going on. He read my lips saying, '*I'll tell you later*'. We reached the office floor and I held Miles' hand as we walked briskly straight to my office. He told everyone good morning as we passed by. I shut the door behind us and made space for Miles at the extra desk in my office. I checked my phone to see if Langley replied but no messages were there. I checked the messages on my office line to see if he had left a message skipping through as soon as I recognized it wasn't his voice. None of the messages were from him. *Think, think, think* I said to myself. I opened my desk drawer fumbling around papers not even knowing what I was looking for. My nerves were bad. I came across the envelope from the Sinclairs. I opened it and started reading the document they gave to me the day they were in my office. I couldn't understand how my life had gotten to this point. I merely moved to Mintly to live out my dream job and be a successful sports agent. I kept reading and when I got to the end, I noticed Zach's name was also written on the document. I hadn't paid attention to it before so I backed up and read it slowly. It stated this document is to serve as a last will and testament regarding Miles Sinclair and Zach Sinclair if anything should happen to their parents. The Sinclairs had not only given me full custody over Miles during their absence, they had given me full and sole custody over their children if they died. I read it again to make sure my eyes were not deceiving me.

"Gretchen," the secretary buzzed in.

"Yes," I answered.

"You have a Mr. Langley here to visit you." Stephanie sounded unsure if she should let him in.

"Thanks Stephanie. Please send him in," I reassured her.

Langley walked in and was surprised to see Miles sitting in my office. "I didn't realize you had company," he announced. Langley walked over to Miles unsure of why he was there. I'm sure he thought it was some kind of set up on my part to reveal their relationship. His suspicious tone seemed to take over his personality. Langley reached out to give Miles a handshake. Miles shook his hand and Langley looked down at his wrist. "That is an odd bracelet you have there Miles," Langley commented.

"I know." Miles focused on the picture he was drawing on a sheet of paper. "I've been having it since I was baby."

Langley took a step back and couldn't get his eyes off of the bracelet. He came over to my desk and opened his phone. He scrolled to the picture of his sister and zoomed in for a closer look. He slid the picture over to me pointing at his sister's wrist. She had on that same bracelet. My eyes stretched wide with amazement. He whispered, "Do you believe me now?" I nodded my head yes. I could tell Langley was filled with excitement. I felt like it was the perfect time to show him the extra wording I found on the document from the Sinclairs. He sat there and followed my finger as I moved it across each line I wanted him to read. A broad smile snuck across his face. He reached into his jacket pocket and half-way showed me the small box. "Now?" he hinted partially joking and partially serious.

"Stop playing," I whispered.

"Oh, I'm not playing," he whispered back. Langley stood up and went back over to where Miles was sitting. He pulled a chair and sat on the other side of the desk. "What are you drawing?" he admired Miles' artwork.

"Just a picture for Ms. Gretchen." Miles remained focus and concentrated on his drawing.

Langley studied the picture. Miles had a large heart covering the whole page with a lady in the middle and two boys on each side. One boy was standing next to his bike and the other boy was smaller holding a stuffed animal. He colored only the red heart and he placed a batch of yellow daisies on each side of the heart. After he finished, he took his time to fold it in half and brought it to me. I opened it and the first thing I noticed were the bright yellow daisies. Tears immediately swelled my eyelids.

"Stay right here Miles." I instructed Miles not to leave my office. "Mr. Langley and I will be right back." I signaled for Langley to follow me and I brought him into a private small conference room. "So, what happened last night?" I hounded. "I waited for you to call me."

"I know. I'm sorry about that. I got discouraged because I looked on public internet resources and I checked with the local hospitals to see if I could find any information about Miles. The hospitals kept telling me I had to fill out a written request and it had to be authorized by the participating parties. I didn't have any luck with anything. But now, do you see what I mean?" he pointed at the bracelet again on his sister's wrist in the picture on his phone.

"Yes, that is so bizarre. I mean, what are the chances of someone else even having a bracelet like that?" I was puzzled because I still couldn't believe that everything Langley thought about was true. The part about the health condition dawned on me. "Langley, we have to figure out a way to tell him. But we have to be careful because we don't know what that kind of information will trigger. You did say you felt like he has the same genetic trait you have with the nervous system condition, right?"

"Yes, that's exactly right." Langley sat there thinking of what we could do. "I have an idea Gretchen, but we have to make sure we take our time so it can work out in Miles' favor.

"Ok, I'm all ears." I erased all distractions and waited for the instructions on our plot.

Someone knocked on the door before Langley could tell me his plan. It was Ms. Bernette. "Excuse me Gretchen. I hate to barge in like this but I think Miles' grandmother just walked in." I didn't even know Ms. Bernette had seen Langley and I go into that conference room. I jumped up and rushed to my office. Ms. Nancy was already there talking with Miles.

I could tell by her tone that she was upset but she controlled her pitch and made sure she didn't raise her voice. "Why did you tell me you had a field trip Miles? The school called looking for you and I sounded like a fool telling them I had dropped you off at the center. But I can't blame you. You're just a child. I'm sorry Gretchen. I'll get Miles out of your way."

"He can stay Ms. Nancy," I responded. "As a matter of fact, I'm glad you are here because I have something I need to share with you." I went to my desk and showed Ms. Nancy the document her son and his wife gave me before they had left town. She started reading it standing up and the closer she got to the end, she started to sit down.

"I can't believe this." She was disoriented. "Why would Chris and my daughter-in-law put this burden on you? None of this makes sense to me. I had no idea Gretchen. I asked about Miles when they stopped by to drop off Zach. They claimed he couldn't afford to miss any days of school."

I noticed that Miles was tuned in fervently to our conversation. "Ms. Nancy, perhaps we can talk about this some other time. You can leave Miles here if you like. He is not in my way at all. He is a joy to have around."

"Well," she started unsure if she was making the right decision. "I'll leave him here for now because I do still have some things to resolve with the funeral arrangements." She walked over to Miles and gave him a big hug. "You scared Grammy. Next time just tell me what's going on ok baby?"

"Yes Grammy."

Chapter 16

Mile's grandmother picked him up from my job after she finished running her errands. I called my mother later that night and my cousin answered her phone. "Gretchen, I'm so glad you called. Your mom is in the hospital. It's nothing serious. The doctors are merely taking precautions because they saw something in her lab work."

"Oh boy. Please tell me you are there with her so I can speak with her."

"Yes, she's right here."

"Hey baby." My mother's voice sounded weak but sweet.

"Hey momma. What happened?"

"Well, I was sitting there watching one of those emotional movies and my heart started feeling like it was going to pop right out of my chest. It wasn't tight or anything. It just felt like it would pop out."

"Momma. Why didn't you call me or at least tell Tasha to call me?"

"I'm the momma, right?" she reminded me.

"Yes, you're the momma." I was annoyed that she refused to call me when it happened. "But what if something would have happened to you? Don't you think I need to know when something is going on with you?"

"And exactly what were you going to do about it hundreds of miles away. Child, you stay put. That's what's wrong with y'all young people now. Y'all think that y'all can fix the world when you can't even fix yourselves. Now look baby, don't make momma talk all ugly to you right now. Your cousin has been begging me for hours to give her the password to my phone so she could get your number."

"Momma." I became more agitated. "Why didn't you just give her the password?"

"Now you know I'm private. I don't trust Tasha like that."

"Where is she right now?"

"Right here. She can hear our whole conversation because I have you on speaker. I can't hold this phone to my ear with all these needles hooked to my hands."

"But I thought you just said you are private?"

"Look child, don't get smart with me." Momma started coughing. It sounded like she was getting short of breath.

"Tasha, write down my number so we can talk later." I gave Tasha my number.

"Ok Gretch, I have it. I promise you I will stay here all night and keep you posted," Tasha shouted from the background easing my mind.

"Gretchen," momma called out before I hung up the phone. "I will text you those pictures I took of that house. Look at the details of the colors of the house and let me know what you think."

"Ok." I wasn't sure what she wanted me to see in the pictures. "I love you momma."

"I love you too baby and don't worry about me. I'll be fine."

We hung up and I waited for the pictures of the house to come through my phone messages.

I had invited Langley over for dinner. I cooked up a quick pasta and chicken dish. Langley showed up right when I was finished. I opened the door and he greeted me with a single pink rose.

I smelled the rose and invited him in. Langley looked around and complemented my place. "This is nice Gretchen."

"Thank you." I placed the rose in a thin vase and placed it in the center of the dining table.

"Dinner smells delicious baby."

He kind of caught me off guard with all the sweet talk because our relationship was still pretty new. I liked it. He walked over to the edge of the kitchen and asked if I needed any help. I directed him to open the wine and pour us each a glass. I served our plates of food and we sat at the table. Langley bowed his head and I followed through while he blessed the food out loud. After we ate dinner, I turned on the television and we both slouched onto the sofa. We were stuffed. I couldn't help but turn the television to the channel showing the Christmas movies.

"You too?" he quacked.

"Me too what?"

"I love these movies too. I wish they would play all year round."

"Ahhh..., I see you're all into the romantic stuff.

"Well, I am a romantic guy," he snared with sexy confidence.

"So far, it does seem that you are."

"You're just determined not to give me any compliments, aren't you?" he accused me point blank.

I laughed at how cute he looked waiting for me to honestly answer that question. "Why don't you just relax and take off your shoes? You don't have to be all professional and everything around me." I reached down to help him slide off his shoes and I remembered I needed to check the message from my mother. I picked up the phone on the coffee table and explained I was only looking for a message from my mother. I opened the two pictures and kept swiping left and right between the two so I could see what she meant. I showed the pictures to Langley and he snatched my phone, "That's the house?"

"Yes, that's it. My mother was amazed by the colors when she was here so she took a few pictures. Now she claims there is something peculiar about the pictures. I don't see anything. Do you?"

Langley swiped left and right slowly studying each picture. He was about to put the phone down before he said, "Wait a minute." He started swiping back and forth again. "No way," he argued.

"What is it?" I was hoping it wasn't anything bad.

"The colors on this house change from one picture to the next."

"Let me see." I leaned over his lap while he showed me the difference between the two pictures.

"Do you think it has something to do with the time?" Langley was determined to figure out why the colors changed on the house.

"I'm not sure." I grabbed my phone and placed it on the coffee table. "But one thing I am sure about is we are not going to sit here and waste this good movie watching time worrying about some colors on a house."

Langley laughed, "You're right baby. Let's enjoy this peaceful time we are sharing together right now. It feels so good to be here with you right now."

Without even thinking about it I responded, "Thanks baby." Langley pulled me closer to him so I could lie on his chest while we watched the movie. I could feel the warmth of his body and I didn't want to move. It was exactly as he said. The moment felt so good.

After the movie ended, Langley reminded me about his plan. "Hey. I never did get to tell you about the plan I have."

"That's right," I acknowledged. "Tell me now." I sat up and pushed away from him so we could see each other's faces clearly.

"Ok. The first thing we need to do is see if we can get Miles and my mother to see each other. We have to get them in the same place at the same time. If she sees his face, I know she won't be able to resist saying who she is and what happened in reality. She didn't come all the way here for nothing. She vibrantly figured out where I lived and flew here to find me and ended up going into labor. Who knows? But, the second thing we need to do is find out if it is her, why didn't she come out and say who she was in the first place."

"Well." I tried to be as non-discouraging as possible. "Both of those things are going to be a challenge but first we have to figure out when she will come out of that house." I started thinking about the custody papers the Sinclairs left for me. I thought about how Miles pleaded for me not to separate him and his brother. *If Ms. Hannah was indeed his mother, there might be a chance she would want to take him back. What will happen to Zach? He can't go live with Ms. Hannah. She doesn't even know him. She doesn't even know Miles as far as that's concerned. Now, I'm not so sure it's a good idea for her to see Miles.* I looked at Langley and I could tell he was trying to play out the whole scenario in his mind. *Should I tell him how I feel about this whole getting them to meet situation? He might not understand my point.* "Langley, I'm thinking about this whole thing and I'm not so sure it is all a good idea."

"What do you mean?"

"I mean, what if we go through everything in your plan and she wants him to go live with her or something. What about Zach? Miles just begged me yesterday not to let them separate him and his brother. Ms. Hannah won't know Zach. I don't know Langley. I know you want to find out the truth about everything but think about what it will end up doing to Miles and his brother. Think about how you felt when you had to isolate yourself from your family."

Langley started drifting off while I talked. "Dammit, you're right. We can't go through with that plan. I have to think about Miles and his brother. They are kids. They just lost their parents in a plane crash or at least the only people Miles knew as his parents. That *would* be devasting to spring up all this new information on him now." He was silent for a moment. "So, Gretchen, are you seriously thinking about keeping Miles and Zach and raising them?"

"I think so. I hardly haven't given it a full scope thought. I kept Miles for a little over a week and it wasn't so bad."

"But this would be full-time Gretchen. Plus, it includes a little one. That is a big responsibility. Are you ready to be a single parent?"

"I am if that's what I have to do."

"Well." Langley reached for his jacket. "You don't have to do this alone."

"You better not pull out that box again," I laughed.

He pulled it out anyway, got on one knee and opened the box. "Why not? I know this is all moving so fast but I know what I'm feeling." My mind applauded the huge diamond ring which was staring me right back in the face. He had never opened the box before. Seeing the ring made everything magical. "Gretchen, will you please marry me?"

"Langley, you don't even know if I love you."

"Oh yes I do. I knew you loved me when we went on our first lunch date."

"First lunch date? What? Out of two? Seriously Langley. I like you a lot. A whole lot. But we don't even know each other."

"But think about this for a second and just hear me out ok."

"Ok."

"I know for sure I love you. I also know that even if you don't love me now you will grow to love me. I've read a lot of statistics Gretchen and they say more spouses grow *in love* than *out of love*. Plus, let's not forget the fact I am Miles' older brother. I would make the perfect "Big-brother/Father" for him more than anyone else."

"You do have a point there. But what about Zach?"

"I can be the perfect father for him too. He is still young and don't forget I'm incredibly patient. You can use the help Gretchen if you are seriously planning on keeping Miles and Zach. And, I know I can be the perfect husband to you."

I had to admit that Langley was laying it on thick. "I guess I'm obviously old-fashioned when it comes to marrying someone. I feel we should date first and get to know each other."

"That's not old-fashioned. A long time ago, people used to get married for reasons that didn't have anything to do with love or getting to know the person. How long did it take you to become close friends with Carl?"

"We became close friends right away."

"And do you plan on ever ending that friendship or do you think you could see yourself as being friends forever?"

"Carl and I will most likely be friends forever. But that's different."

"How is it so different? You just said you wanted to get to know a person first before you would marry them but you didn't worry about getting to know Carl first before you knew he would be a close friend."

"You're just trying to confuse me. Let me think about it and I'll give you an answer."

"Ok, fair enough. But I will leave this opened box right here and please know there is large invisible writing hovering over it asking will you me marry."

I laughed at the thought of even picturing the invisible writing. "Ok," I said still laughing. "I will happily keep that in mind."

Langley stayed over and watched movies with me until I fell asleep. When I woke up, I had a blanket draped across me. I smiled at the thought of him taking the time to cover me up. I looked at the coffee table and the opened box was still where he left it with the diamond ring sitting there waiting for a response. I could still see the invisible writing. I picked up my phone and without even thinking I sent Langley a text. *Yes.* Before I could change my mind, I realized I had already pressed send. The message was delivered. I sat up and looked intently at the ring in the box and quickly talked myself out of the response. I tried to text Langley again to let him know I sent that by mistake but the doorbell rang startling me. I dropped my phone and went to the door and looked through the peephole. It was Langley. I didn't know what to do. My instincts made me open the door and as soon as I did, he lifted me up just like they do in the movies. "You've just made me the happiest man in the world."

"Where did you come from?" I wondered. "I just sent you that text like a few seconds ago."

"I know and I had been sitting in my car right out-front hoping you would wake up and respond. And you did baby. You did respond."

"I know." I thought to myself that this was all so weird. "But listen Langley. I think maybe I shouldn't have..."

"Shhhh," he said lightly pressing his finger on my lips before running to the coffee table. He quickly took the ring out of the box, got on one knee again and placed the ring on my finger before I could utter another word. "There." He dusted off his hands as if that sealed the deal. "We are officially engaged."

I kept looking at my hand and how beautiful the ring looked on my finger. "Soooo," he asked with excited anticipation. "How does it feel?"

I couldn't resist. The moment was perfect for me and he was a spectacular guy. "This feels amazing," I said heightening my answer to a slight scream.

He picked me up again, "Thank you so much baby. I promise you, you won't regret this." He was circling back and forth like he didn't know what to do with himself. "I'm so excited right now I don't know what to do."

"I can see that," I said. "I'm excited too."

"Are you sure?" he came closer to me and held me by my shoulders.

"Yes, I am." Langley pressed his lips passionately against mine and it felt righteously satisfying.

"Ok baby. It's late." He kissed me on the forehead. "I'll see you tomorrow, right?"

"You sure will."

I closed the door after watching him blow me a kiss before he got in his car. I stared at my hand the whole time I walked to my room.

/ met up with Carl at Hans Café the next morning and the first thing he noticed was the ring on my finger. "What is this?" he excitingly grabbed my hand admiring the ring.

"I said yes Carl."

"And I see why my darling. That's what I call a rang." Carl gave me a big hug. "I'm so happy for you Gretchen. You deserve it."

"I guess you're right. We have so much to talk about Carl. I hate that I have to rush off but I have to meet with Ms. Nancy this morning."

"Ms. Nancy?"

"Yes, Miles' grandmother."

"Ok doll. I'll catch up with you later."

I rushed off so I could be all settled in my office by the time Ms. Nancy showed up. As soon as I stepped off of the elevator Ms. Bernette called out to me from her desk. I walked over to her to see why she was calling me. She smiled at me the whole time. When I got to her desk, she pointed at my finger and cleared her throat, "Is that what I think it is?"

I tried to smother my excitement, "Yes, Ms. Bernette. But don't make a big deal out of it ok?"

"Ok honey. I won't. Congratulations!" she spoke slightly above a whisper as if she were keeping a secret for me.

"Thanks Ms. Bernette." I walked to my office wondering how in the world she noticed the ring and I had gotten off the elevator precisely two seconds ago. She doesn't miss anything. After I settled in, I picked up the custody document from the Sinclairs and read the ending part again. I closed my eyes and said a prayer asking God to please guide me and help me to make the right decision. About thirty minutes into my day, Ms. Nancy showed up. She looked much better than the other times I had seen her.

"Good morning Ms. Nancy," I greeted her with a hug.

"Good morning dear."

"How is everything going? Were you able to get all the arrangements completed?"

"Yes, I did. And I'm feeling much better now. It is one thing to lose a friend or even a spouse, but it is an indescribable feeling when you lose a child. I'm dealing with it better each day. Listen

Gretchen, I know you didn't ask for any of this burden to come into your life and I will understand if you are not able to keep the kids."

I stopped her before she continued talking because I knew I had already made up my mind. "Ms. Nancy, I've given it a lot of serious thought. And although I haven't known Miles that long, I feel I've known him long enough and he does hold an exceptional place in my heart. What I am saying is I'll keep the kids."

Ms. Nancy was overjoyed by this news. "Thank you, God," she exclaimed. "I have been praying about this and I just didn't have any answers. I know this is the best thing for everyone. And listen to me Gretchen, you are not in this alone. I am still their grandmother. I am here for anything you need. If you need a break, call and I can fly here and help out. If you want to send them by me for the summer, I'm all for it."

"Yes ma'am," I answered. I hadn't even thought as far as the summer with school being out and all.

She opened her purse and pulled out a folded paper. "This is the paper the attorney gave me for you to sign stating you accept the guardianship over the kids. If you want to take your time, I understand."

I opened the paper and read it. The language was simple for me to understand since I was used to dealing with contracts. I took out my pen and signed it without a second thought. "Let me make a copy right quick and I will give you the original to take back to the attorney." I placed the original on the personal copy machine I had in my office. I handed the original back to Ms. Nancy for her to bring to the attorney and I kept the copy. "Can you please ask the attorney to have the original recorded in the court records?"

"I sure will Gretchen. The families are coming here for a small private funeral next week. Miraculously, the authorities were able to find their bodies but we chose to have the ashes shipped here for the burial. It didn't make sense for anyone to see them in such a way."

Ms. Nancy was starting the get teary eyed. It was unimaginable how well she held her composure, especially, dealing with preparing for the burial of her son. "I'll get their room ready for when they move in. I'll try to make the transition as easy as possible. If you like, I can pick up Miles from the center this afternoon and maybe he can ride with me to the store. We can pick out some things to put in the room for him and Zach."

"Miles would surely love the outing. You can drop him back at the house afterwards so you can finish putting things in place for their arrival."

"Ok," I agreed. "Sounds like a great plan."

/ went to the center after work and Miles was sitting at a table by himself writing in a journal. He closed it quickly and put it in his backpack when he noticed I was there.

"Are you ready to go?" I asked.

"Yes ma'am."

We walked out to the parking lot and right before we reached my car Miles jerked at my hand excitedly, "Ms. Gretchen, look. That's her. It's the lady from my dream. She is going into The Cemetery." He pulled me by the hand running towards The Cemetery. "Come on. Hurry up. We have to follow her. I just want to see her face."

Miles still didn't know I had already met Ms. Hannah. He looked all over in The Cemetery and could not find her. When we were leaving out, he kept looking back to see if he could get a glimpse of her. While he was looking back, I spotted her going into Han's Café across the street. I felt guilty about my actions but I didn't tell Miles.

Chapter 17

I stopped at Han's Café the next morning for my usual coffee on the way to work. I bumped into Lance at the counter.

"You like the coffee here too?" I asked Lance.

"I'm more of a tea person," he objected. "I've been coming here ever since Paisley opened up the shop."

"Wow. So, you know each other pretty well then?" I queried.

"Yes." He glanced over at Paisley. "She introduced me to this special blend of tea and I've been hooked ever since."

"Really?" I asked.

"Yes, have you ever tried her tea before?"

"Is he talking about the one you always offer to me and Carl?" I questioned Paisley.

"Yes, that's the one," she boasted proudly. "I keep telling you to give it a try."

"She's right Gretchen. It gives you a boost of energy that is way healthier than coffee. You should listen to her and try it out." Lance walked out after leaving Paisley a tip in her tip jar.

I thought about it for a second, "Nah, I'll just stick to what I know for now. Maybe another time."

"I'll hold you to that." Paisley handed me the cup of coffee in exchange for my payment. "Beautiful ring by the way. Who's the lucky guy?"

I didn't even see her look at my hand. I cupped my hands over my mouth so no one in the café could read my lips, "Spencer Langley."

"What?" she shouted in delight. She came from behind the counter and gave me a dancing hug. "Welcome to the family. I knew it the whole time I asked you. I saw him get on one knee the other day. I told him not to give up on you. I guess he listened."

"Hold on." I was puzzled. "Back up. What do you mean welcome to the family?"

"I mean like you are about to be my sister-in-law. What do you think I mean? Spencer is my brother. But listen, he doesn't know he is my real brother. He thinks he is purely my pretend brother. Momma doesn't want him to know because he has this condition."

I put my coffee down and sat at the bar holding my head trying to grasp everything she was saying. "Paisley, you have to forgive me because what you are saying sounds crazy as shit." A few customers sitting near me gave me a nasty look for cursing. I propped my elbows on the counter and pressed my fingertips up and down my forehead to try and rub the stress out of my mind. "Wait a minute, wait a minute," I kept repeating. "I am so confused."

"I know," she said. "Just imagine how Spencer would react if he found out the truth."

"But how does he not even know about you?"

"Well, it's easy. When he disappeared, mom was only a few months pregnant with me. No one even knew she was pregnant. I was born when she was barely four months, so you can imagine how small I was. The doctors didn't think I would make it. Mom, on the other hand, made sure I made it." Paisley tapped on the unmarked jar.

"Oh my God Paisley. So, your mom is Ms. Hannah?"

"Yep. That's her."

"No wonder I saw her coming in here yesterday." Everything started running in circles in my mind. "And Miles?"

"Yep, Miles is my baby brother?"

"Oh. My. God." I sat there in disbelief. The door to the café chimed and when I looked up there was a blinding glare. This was my first time noticing the chime in the door had the same stone as the windchime. It had the same stone as Miles' bracelet. I looked at Paisley's wrist for a bracelet but she didn't have one on.

"Paisley, if you knew Miles **and** Langley were your brother's all this time, why haven't you ever said anything."

Paisley brought me to the back of the café in the small prep kitchen. "Gretchen, you can't say anything ok. Mom will never forgive me if something happens to Spencer or Miles. They both have the condition. If they find out all this information, it can trigger a reaction that can kill them. Do you understand what I am saying?"

I didn't but I responded, "Yes."

"Good, we have to keep this a secret. I'm sure when the time is right, mom will straighten this all out."

"Ok, I won't say anything. But let me ask you this."

"What?"

"How are you surviving with the condition?"

"Oh, I don't have the genius trait. I'm just a regular person who was born too early. Miles and Spencer are the only two geniuses in the family. I was the one who found Spencer. Mom insisted on finding him while she was pregnant with Miles because she wanted to make sure he knew about Miles. Things changed after we got here so we've just kept it a secret this whole time."

We walked back out to the front because I had to get to work. I looked across the street at The Cemetery. "Paisley," I suggested. "Why don't you try meeting with Langley at The Cemetery and you can tell him during a session?"

"That place seems eerie to me," she answered laughing at herself.

I laughed with her, "Ok, I'll talk to you later. I have to get to work."

"Don't forget your coffee." She handed me the cup I had left on the counter.

When I got to work, I saw Mr. Koperneil go into his office. I decided it was time for us to have a conversation. I went over to Ms. Bernette's desk, "Can you see if Mr. Koperneil is free to speak with me right now?"

She buzzed his office, "Mr. Koperneil?" I could see she waited for him to respond.

"Ms. Gretchen would like a moment of your time if you are not too busy right now." She paused for a second to listen to his answer. "He said for you to just go right on in dear," Ms. Bernette said with a smile.

I walked into his office not knowing where I would begin our conversation. "Mr. Koperneil, a lot has been going on in my life lately. And, ironically, it's made me realize every circumstance will not always be perfect." He listened attentively with caring eyes. "I've learned that love for people can develop into unexpected relationships. After I found out you are my real "father" I initially felt betrayed. I felt betrayed by everyone from robbing me of the chance of getting to know you from when I was a child. And now that I am in this situation where I am straight overnight about to become a "parent" myself, I realize you were also robbed."

He walked over to me and gave me a big hug rocking me side to side. "But you know the beautiful thing about all of this Gretchen? The beautiful thing is that it is not too late. We still have time to spend the rest of our lives as father and daughter. Oh, that felt so good to say just now. My daughter. Gretchen, even though I didn't know you were alive and I didn't have a chance to watch you grow up, my love for you began when you were in your mother's womb. And it has *never* faded."

We stood there like two old friends holding each other for what seemed like eternity. "I love you dad," I whispered.

"I love you too baby," he whispered back. He grabbed us each a napkin to wipe our face and regroup. He walked over to his bar and poured us each a splash of wine. We lifted our glasses and he made a toast, "To our family journey of love and growth."

"Cheers," I said as we clanged glasses and drank the wine. "Now, let's get down to business 'Dad'." I laughed and he did too because it sounded distinctly strange since I was so used of calling him Mr. Koperneil. "While at work, I will still call you Mr. Koperneil."

"Ok, it's fine with me." He admired my demands.

"Also, you are about to gain two new grandkids because I've signed the custody agreement papers."

"Oh, my Gretchen. This is wonderful news." He slapped his knee with joy. "I know I will make the best grandfather and Gab will be beyond delighted to have the kids over."

"Good, because I will need all the help I can get. And the last thing is, I am getting married. I would love for you to walk me down the isle with you on one side and my mother, well my aunt but you know what I mean, on the other."

"Yes of course Gretchen. This is so wonderful. You have made my day. Don't hesitate to let me know what you need for me to do."

"Ok, I will. We haven't officially set a date yet but we are taking the brave route and planning for it to be soon because he doesn't want circumstances to interfere."

"Is the lucky fellow Mr. Spencer Langley?"

"Yes." I was surprised that he already knew. "How did you know?"

"I guess you can call it Dad's intuition," he said slyly.

I left out of his office with a big smile and a happy feeling in my heart. I called Carl as soon as I got in my office and asked him if he wanted to meet for lunch. He apologized because he had already made lunch plans with Greg.

"Well, it sounds like you are considering giving Greg a chance?"

"Yes Gretch. I had time to think about everything. I made my decision when I saw how happy you looked after getting engaged to the love of your life. It made me want to have the same kind of happiness for myself."

"That's right Carl. You should want the same happiness for yourself. But who said Langley is the love of my life?"

"Well, honey. From the looks of that rock on your finger, it looks like you said it."

I laughed at Carl and played with the ring on my finger thinking about how Langley made me feel. I still had a bouquet of fresh roses sitting on my desk. He was in total agreement with me keeping the kids and helping me to raise them. When I thought about it, he was pretty much my dream guy. Plus, I couldn't deny the fact he was appealing to my eyes.

"But seriously Gretchen, let me ask you a personal question."

"Go ahead Carl. You know you can ask me anything."

"How is that sexy thang in bed?"

"Shut up Carl. We didn't sleep together."

"What?" Carl screamed on the other end of the phone.

"No, we didn't. We cuddled like two love birds."

"Ok, clothes on or clothes off?"

"Clothes on Carl. Bye. You are too much." I laughed at Carl's silliness and hung up before he could ask me any more questions.

Chapter 18

After the funeral, Mr. & Mrs. Koperniel opened up their home to the grieving family for a repass. Mrs. Koperneil prepared the entire meal and it was well appreciated by everyone present. All of the children played well together and Ms. Nancy shared some stories with us about Chris and Susan. Susan's only brother was there as well but he didn't talk much. Ms. Nancy did most of the talking. Jim, Ms. Nancy's other son, left early because he had to travel for work. The one story which stuck with me the most was how proud Chris and Susan were when Miles was born. She claimed they bragged about Miles every time they called. Miles was reading books at age two. He was solving calculus math problems at age three. Everyone knew Miles was exceptional. I now knew Miles was beyond exceptional, but I had to keep that information to myself. Langley sat next to me the entire time, but he kept his conversations to a minimum. I knew he wasn't a talkative person with others, so it didn't bother me. Langley excused himself because he said he had some important business matters to tend to.

After everyone left, I helped Mrs. Koperneil clean the kitchen.

"Charlie told me you two had a nice talk in his office last week."

"We did," I smiled.

"I'm so happy for both of you. And Gretchen, I never got a chance to apologize to you for the way we pushed all that information on you."

"It's alright Mrs. Koperniel. Everything is working out. I look at it this way. I have gained a whole new family."

"That's right dear. You sure have. And I know I am not your mother, but I will love you as if you are my own daughter. And with that being said, you can stop calling me Mrs. Koperniel."

"What should I call you?"

"Let's see." She thought for a minute. "How about Gabi? Those babies can call me Gabi too."

"I like that. Gabi." I gave her a hug and we finished cleaning the last bit of the dishes.

Miles ran up to me in the kitchen looking frightened, "Ms. Gretchen, look!" he screamed showing me the bracelet on his arm. The stone was glowing the same way it did the day we were in front of the house. I tried to hide it from Gabi by covering it with my hand.

"What is that?" she asked.

"Oh nothing." I kept covering the bracelet with my hand and pulled Miles to come with me. "We'll be back in a little bit," I explained to Ms. Nancy as we dashed out of the house. When we got outside, there was a warm breeze blowing. I knew the windchime was simultaneously going off at Ms. Hannah's house. We were too far from it to hear it. I was trying to figure out what to do and I thought about Paisley. I called the café and was glad she picked up the phone. "Paisley." I knew I sounded panicky.

"Yes, who's calling?" she asked not sure who it was.

"It's me, Gretchen."

"Oh, hi Gretchen. Is everything ok?"

"No. Do you have any idea why the bracelet Miles is wearing is glowing?" She could hear I needed straight answers so she didn't delay.

"It can only mean one of two things. Either Miles is on the verge of a nervous breakdown or something has happened to Spencer."

"What?" My nerves were rattled. "What does that mean?"

"It means exactly what it sounds like it means. How does Miles look?"

"Uh," I said while I sped towards the café and looked quickly at Miles and watching the road at the same time. "I guess he looks ok. How do you feel Miles?"

"I feel fine." I could tell he didn't know why I was asking.

"Where is Spencer?" Paisley was jumpy and not her normal self.

"I'm not sure. He left the repass a little while ago and said he had some kind of business to take care of."

"How long ago was that?"

"Uhmmm, I guess about thirty minutes."

"Ok, thirty minutes. That's good. We still have plenty of time."

"Plenty of time for what?" At this point I'm screaming hysterically and it's scaring Miles.

"If Spencer is in trouble, we have three hours to help him by getting him to drink the tea."

"Ok, I'm about to call him and see where he is."

I hung up with Paisley and dialed Langley's number. It went straight to voicemail. *Dangit.* I called it right back and the phone was ringing. A lady answered.

"Hello." Her voice was pleasant.

"Hello. Who is this? I'm trying to reach Langley."

"Spencer Langley?"

"Yes."

"Who is calling?"

"This is his fiancée. Now where is Langley?" I was feeling agitated because another woman had picked up his phone.

"I'm sorry ma'am. This is the nurse's station at Memorial Hospital. Langley was found collapsed on the sidewalk. We admitted him a few minutes ago. He is in critical condition and the doctors are trying to figure out what has happened."

"I'll be right over," I said.

I called Paisley back and told her everything that happened. She asked me to pick her up because it was on the way to the hospital. She was standing outside the café when I drove up and she hopped in the backseat as soon as I pulled up. She was holding a large covered cup. I could tell it was the tea Langley usually orders because the purple string was hanging out.

"I can't lose him Paisley. I love him." This was the first time I had emotionally expressed those words out loud. I realized I did indeed love Langley and I wanted to make sure we didn't miss out on spending the rest of our lives together. We pulled up at the emergency exit and rushed to find his room. The receptionist said he was just placed in a private room because he was no longer in critical condition. She said they had to keep him because his vital signs were not stable. When entered his room, Langley was not in the bed. I knocked on the bathroom door and no one answered. I opened the door slowly afraid to find him dead on the floor. "He's not here," I said in a panic. We went back to the receptionist desk to ask her what happened. She claimed she gave us the wrong room number by accident. They had switched his room at the same time we came in but it hadn't updated in her system yet. She gave us the updated room number. It felt like I was in a horror movie. We ran to that room and he wasn't in there either.

"This is ridiculous." Paisley was losing her patience.

"I agree." I stumped off in a tantrum.

The authorities met us at the room door when we were trying to leave.

"Stay right where you are," they yelled.

"What is going on?" I couldn't understand why they were yelling at us. "We came here looking for my fiancé and now he is nowhere to be found. Can someone please tell me what is going on here?"

One of them questioned us as if we had committed some kind of crime, "So you weren't the ones who helped him to leave the hospital without authority?"

"No," Paisley and I both answered in unison.

I tried to explain our situation, "We just got here but we need to find him quickly."

"Well, we were alerted that some lady claiming to be his only relative demanded for him to be released. By the time the doctor came in to let them know he couldn't be released they were gone."

"Come on Gretchen," Paisley whispered hinting she didn't want the authorities to follow us.

"Ok, well will you please call me if you hear anything? Here is my phone number." I wrote down my number quickly and followed Paisley back out to the car.

I started the car waiting for Paisley to give me directions. "Where are we going Paisley?"

"To Han's."

"Back to the café?"

"No." She looked at me as if I should have known what she was talking about. "To Han's house. Hannah's house. I call her Han."

"Oh, my Goodness!" I thought as it all clicked in my head. I remembered I didn't want Hannah to see Miles. I didn't have a choice now. I was going to have face reality and deal with it when we got there.

"Gretchen." Paisley looked at the clock in the car. "We only have thirty more minutes. We have to hurry."

I sped through town. I pulled up and we had twenty minutes left. I wasn't sure what would happen after twenty minutes but from what Paisley had told me so far it seemed like it was a life or death situation. "Wait here," Paisley instructed us.

Miles was in a trance staring at the door of the house. He did not even blink. I kept looking back and forth at the door and at the time. I was hoping Paisley would come out quickly. Three minutes had passed since Paisley entered the house and my nerves were getting bad. Miles started whispering but I couldn't hear what he was saying.

"What are you saying Miles?" I wanted to know what he was saying under his breath.

He kept whispering but I still couldn't make out what he was saying.

"Miles, talk louder so I can hear you."

He spoke a little louder and repeated over and over again, "The Cemetery. Let's go to The Cemetery. The Cemetery. Let's go to The Cemetery."

"Not right now," I patiently told Miles. "We have to take care of something else first." I looked at the time and Paisley had been in the house exactly four minutes. It felt much longer. The door opened and Paisley was running out of the house still holding the cup with the purple string. "Start the car," she yelled while she was running towards the car. I started the car and she jumped in and said, "We have to go to The Cemetery."

I looked back at Miles and he was staring at me with his large eyes. "What happened in there?" I was curious as to why Paisley took so long in the house and then came out alone.

"They were gone. I know he was there because Hannah left a note saying they would be at The Cemetery."

"How did she know you would find the note?"

"I don't know. She always does stuff like that. We have to hurry Gretchen. If we don't get this cup to Spencer in time, we will lose him forever."

"You keep saying that!" I raced through the streets still unsure about what she meant.

Paisley jumped out of the car first. Miles and I ran quickly behind her after I parked the car right in front of The Cemetery. She asked something to the receptionist who pointed to an open door down the hall. We rushed to enter the room hoping to see Langley and Hannah but they were not there. "We are out of time." Paisley was exhausted. She sat down in one of the chairs.

"What are you talking about Paisley?" The anger I was feeling inside splashed out with my words.

"Please sit down Ms. Gretchen." Miles tried to calm me down with a soft voice.

I sat in one of the chairs and the door closed. Some writing started showing across the panel.

"Han. Are you here?"

"Yes, I'm here. I have Spencer with me."

"Where are you?" Paisley asked.

"Not far."

"Is Spencer still alive?"

"Yes, but he can't talk right now. We are right down the hall in another room. Miles, these walls which you built have a healing mechanism. I knew you were special ever since you were born."

"Were you there when I was born?" Miles asked.

"I was baby. I am your real mother."

"My mother?"

"Yes. Susan and I had a chance to meet and talk with each other at the hospital the day you were born. Her and Chris had been trying for eight years to have a baby. I knew how important it was for her to have children. I used to be a nurse and I had seen a lot of women struggle to have babies. I know it's a lot for you to understand. We both went into labor at the same time and had baby boys. Her delivery was complicated so she wasn't able to see her baby right away. They kept him in the nursery until she recovered. When I went to visit you in the nursery, I checked on her baby too. He wasn't breathing. I looked for a nurse but I couldn't find one. I reached in his incubator and checked for a pulse. There was none. I thought about Susan and how much she had gone through already and I wanted to do something to help, so I simply switched you and her baby. I switched the name bracelets and everything. You were only a few hours old so no one could tell one baby from the next. I quietly went back to my room and waited for the doctors to come in and tell me my baby had passed away. I cried so hard. I cried because I thought I would never see you again but I also knew I had made the best decision. I couldn't afford to care for any more children. I knew Susan and Chris would love you and provide for you. I begged them to let me see the baby one more time. They took me to the nursery and they were preparing to take the baby away. Susan was there holding you. She was so proud. I gave her that bracelet to put on your arm as protection and I see she kept her promise."

Miles was rubbing his bracelet. "I knew you were around. I could feel you. I would dream about you."

My thoughts started flowing out, "Are you going to try to take Miles now?"

"It's all up to Miles, Gretchen. I gave him up once on my own before. I can't do that twice. What do you think Miles? Are you ready to come home with me?"

Miles looked at me and he could see the pain my heart felt with the thought of him not being in my life. The panel was blank for a minute and after a while Miles' thoughts came up, "I have to think about Zach. I want us to grow up together. I know you're my real mother and everything but I can still see you sometimes, right?"

"Of course you can."

"Great!" Miles expressed.

"When will we get to see Langley?" I asked.

"The process is almost over."

"What process?"

"The process of healing. It only takes seven minutes but it had to be done within a certain timeframe. If I would have brought him here too early, it would have made his condition worst. I had to bring him right when the timeframe started. I wasn't sure if Paisley would get to the hospital in time with the tea so I removed him from the hospital and brought him here. I know Spencer developed the tea to help control his condition but we all also have a special power within ourselves to prolong life."

"What do you mean?" I asked.

There was a long pause before the session ended. The doors opened and we left the room. It was one of the strangest sessions I had been in at The Cemetery. I held onto Miles' shoulder as we walked outside.

"Are you guys coming over to the café?" Paisley asked.

"Sure," I said still in a trance.

Paisley fixed us each a hot cocoa because the temperature had dropped outside. All three of us sat at a table in complete silence. The door to the café chimed and I couldn't believe my eyes.

"Hey baby." It was Langley. His voice was soft and pure without blemish.

I jumped up and ran into his arms crying. "I thought I had lost you."

"See," he teased. "I told you that you loved me."

I gave him a love tap on the chest. "So, you finally got to see Hannah huh?" I whispered.

"No." His expression changed into a man who seemed to have lost all hope. "I couldn't find her."

"But..." Paisley cleared her throat to get my attention and placed her index finger over her lips for me not to say anything. I looked back at Miles at the table but he wasn't there. I got scared and turned around to head towards the door but noticed he was standing right by the door looking outside and waving. "Who..." Paisley cleared her throat again so I wouldn't finish my question and   winked.

Chapter 19

My phone rings and it's my mother.

"Hi momma."

"Hi baby. How is everything going?"

"It's going fine momma. Are you ready for our trip?"

"No, the real question is are you ready?"

"What do you mean?"

"Well, from what I understand, there has been a slight change in plans."

"I didn't change the plans momma. What are you talking about?"

"I guess that's why nobody likes to tell me anything because I can't hold sweet water. Your loud mouth cousin, Tasha, came around here talking about you and that man are going elope. She even said you decided to use *our* trip as y'all honeymoon."

"What?" I asked in surprise. I tried to whisper to Langley who was sitting right next to me if he told anyone. He sat there laughing playing like he couldn't understand me.

"So is it a fib or the truth? Tasha is known for spreading gossip she doesn't know anything about."

"Well, this time I guess it's the truth," I strained to get my words out.

"I knew it. Why so fast sugar? Is there a 'lil pumpkin in the oven?"

"No momma," I laughed. "I'm not pregnant. We both felt the same way for each other and we didn't think it made sense to keep waiting."

"Well baby, as long as you're happy, I'm happy. He does know your momma is crazy, right?"

My laughter echoed in my phone, "So you're ok with him coming on the trip to Brazil?"

"Of course, I am," she said. "As long as you're ok with Chester coming on the trip too."

"Chester? Who is Chester?" I had an attitude.

"Oh honey, I might be old but I'm not dead."

"Momma stop. You have a boyfriend?"

"We don't call them boyfriends at my age. We call them benefits."

"Benefits?"

"Yes, child. When they get that social security benefit check they go all out for the cookie."

"Cookie? Momma what are you talking about?"

"Oh Lord girl. You have so much to learn. You will learn about your cookie one day, hopefully on your honeymoon. Mine is still moist too. Ain't no cookie crumbs around here."

"Oh no lady, that's way too much information."

"But seriously baby, you know you could have told momma you were getting married."

"I know. I was hoping to surprise you."

"I understand baby. Are you planning on giving me any grandbabies?"

"Well, speaking of grandbabies, you unexpectedly have two already?"

"What do you mean?"

"I was given sole custody over Miles and Zach after their parents died in the plane crash."

"Tasha said something about that too but I wasn't going to say anything. Listen, baby, taking in Miles and Zach is a good thing you are doing. You remind me of myself in so many ways. You have a beautiful heart. I would never want you to change that baby. I am truly happy for you and I am happy for those babies. Now let me think about what I want them to call me. What do they call you?"

"So far, they are still only calling me Ms. Gretchen. We haven't had any conversation about what they should call me. I don't want to push it, you know."

"I know baby. And don't push it. They will come up with their own name to call you in no time. You'll see." It made me feel special knowing my mother was being supportive and positive about the whole situation. "But as for me, I think I want them to call me Annie."

"Annie? Where did you get that from? Your name is not Annie."

"I know that child but I'm too hip for them to call me Grannie so they can call me Annie."

She was so funny. "Ok Annie. I like it. I'll make sure I let them know. Now, are you and... what's his name again?"

"Chester."

"Are you and Chester going to be ready for this trip?"

"We sure will be ready. Our clothes are already packed."

"Ok then. I will see you next week. We will have so much fun."

"Yes, we will baby. I love you."

"I love you too mom."

Langley and I went to the Justice of the Peace and got married. Carl and Paisley were our two witnesses. We all went out to eat at

Carmen's afterwards. We sat at the same table on the patio when Langley and I had our first date. Everything had come full circle.

"Surprise!" We heard a crowd of people shouting as they walked our way. It was the Koperneils. Gabi was carrying a beautiful two-tiered cake which she had baked and decorated herself.

"Congratulations baby!" Dad kissed me on the cheek.

They brought all the kids to help us celebrate including Miles and Zach. It was a beautiful moment.

"I guess all that mushy talk about getting you to walk me down the isle flew out the window like a fly escaping a fly swat, huh?" I joked with Dad.

"It's ok baby. When love can't wait, I do understand."

Everyone enjoyed their meals and we especially enjoyed the cake. Gab had practically outdone herself this time. I looked over at Miles and his face was filled with joy. The wind was warm for December. I heard the birds chirping just as before and when I looked down Miles' bracelet was getting brighter. I started to panic because I knew the last time this happened it was a nightmare. Paisley must have seen my expression, and she quietly came up to me and touched my arm. She signaled with her eyes for me to look outside the door of the restaurant. I saw the back of Ms. Hannah leaving from by the door. I looked back at Paisley and smiled. Miles' bracelet stopped glowing.

When it was time for us to leave for the trip to Brazil, Miles was terrified. He was afraid we wouldn't return and leave him like his parents. Langley overheard him and he came out to the living room to talk with Miles.

"Miles," he said gently. "You don't have anything to worry about. We will never leave you."

"I thought the same thing before." He lowered his head in despair.

"Well, this time you don't have to only think it. You can know it because you and Zach are coming with us." Langley pulled out two travel tickets from behind his back. Miles jumped in his arms with joy.

"Thank you. Thank you so much," Miles shouted. "Yes, we are going on vacation Zach," he cheered with his little brother. Zach started dancing as if he understood that he should feel excited.

"You are the best babe." I gave Langley a soft peck.

"And you are too." He had such a warm smile it made me want to love him even more.

"Hey," I reminded everyone. "Don't forget that we have the big office party to attend for New Year's Eve when we get back."

"What office party?" Miles asked. "I don't know anything about an office party."

"I know." I tapped Miles on his nose. "But you know now. And from what I hear, it will be at the community center so that kids can have their own section."

"Cool!" Miles jumped around and made a few silly dance moves.

"The party last year was star-studded," Langley added.

"So, it was just as fancy as Ms. Bernette said?

"I'm not sure what you heard, but Mr. Koperneil has connections in sports, music and the movie industry."

"Who showed up last year?"

"Everybody. It was crazy. I know for sure I saw Mary J, Adam Levine, Cam Newton, Chris Hemsworth, Scarlett Johansson, and Drew Brees."

"You have got to be kidding me." I was star struck just hearing the names.

"I'm dead serious. Some people just came to show their face so I didn't get to see everyone who went."

"Well, I can't wait for that party but right now I'm more excited about this cruise to Brazil!"

"Me too!" Miles was jumping around with his baby brother.

We arrived at the cruise port and there was a line that seemed to stretch out for miles. All of the attendants were full of energy so that helped move the process along quickly. Mom was standing there mighty close to this Chester guy who I didn't feel too comfortable with holding her by her waist. I know mom caught me eyeballing him a few times because she was looking at Langley the same way.

When the ship landed in Brazil we relaxed at the beach on the first day. Afterwards, we went on a day's worth of tours. I was awe struck by the massiveness of the Christ the Redeemer statue on top of the Corcovado Mountain. We did a lot of traveling to different areas. The tour guide brought us to an area that had houses stacked on top of each other. It looked like a place where people would just find some material and then piece it together so they could have some kind of enclosed walls to sleep in. It was a living work of art. Seeing the colorfully painted houses in Santa Marta reminded me of Ms. Hannah's house in Mintly. I wondered if my mother thought about the same thing. I knew she still couldn't figure out why Ms. Hannah's house changed colors and neither could I.

"Momma, look at all those colors."

"Child, I can't miss it. It's just like that house around the corner from yours out there in Mintly."

"I know. I was wondering if it made you think about the same thing."

"Yes, it sure did. Did you ever figure out what was going on in those pictures?"

"No, but I will try to figure it out when we get back."

"Ok baby. Don't worry about it too much. The main thing is to just avoid passing in front of there because something is definitely going on."

I just laughed off her comment because I knew in my heart that I wasn't going to listen. Langley was in the seat behind me on the tour bus. He was sitting right next to Miles. Zach was cuddled next to me eating snacks.

Experiencing the culture of Brazil during the Christmas season turned out to be a wise choice. Later that night, the kids enjoyed watching the fireworks and seeing the electric lights on the large Christmas trees. I could tell that Zach missed his parents but Miles made sure he gave him all the attention he needed. Before we left, my mother insisted on flying to Salvador in Bahia while we were in Brazil. We lucked up and found a flight from where we were in Rio de Janeiro. My mother's concentration during the flight was intense.

"Are you ok mom?"

"Yes baby," she said looking out of the window when we landed.

"It's just that I've been waiting my whole life to come to this place. My grandmother shared so many stories about her childhood here."

"Well, we made it momma."

The plane didn't pull into a raised gate at the airport. It was a small commuter plane. It parked in the middle of an oversized parking lot. We had to walk down about twelve steps when the door to the plane opened.

"I can feel the presence of my people," my mother announced holding her arms out and inhaling the air when she stepped off the plane.

I had to admit that the air was different and refreshing. We visited a few restaurants where the food had its own tasty flavor. The people were beautifully shaded with lovely accents. It almost felt like we were in a different time. I was so happy that my mother was enjoying the trip. In that moment, I felt like this is what life was all about.

After we returned back from the cruise, the New Year came and went faster than we could have imagined. It took a whole week for everything to get back to normal. Well, at least what was now my new normal. I had established a great work/family balance.

Ms. Bernette knocked on my office door and shut it quickly behind her after she came in.

"Hi Ms. Bernette." It was unusual for her to visit me in my office.

"Hey Gretchen." She seemed like she had some exciting news to share. She sat in one of the chairs at my desk. "I know you had a blast at the New Years party."

"Yes! I did. It was exactly the way you described. I met so many famous people all in one night. What's crazy is that some of them knew my name. They also knew all about The Cemetery. I still can't believe that happened."

"I'm glad you enjoyed yourself. Can you keep a secret?"

I wasn't ready for my year to start off like this. "Sure," I reluctantly answered.

"While we were at the party, my husband made me sneak off with him to a private room in the building. He really surprised me."

"Wait a minute Ms. Bernette. Are you telling me that you guys got buckwild at the party?"

Ms. Bernette slipped back into her Hollywood audition voice, "I guess you can say that. I'm not sure what buckwild means. But, if it means anything like having super crazy spontaneous sex, then yes. We got buckwild."

The thought of that even happening just tickled me. "Oh my Goodness! Well, I am just so happy for you."

"I knew you would be. I felt like you deserved to know since you already knew everything about my sex life from that day at The Cemetery." Satisfied that she shared her news with me, Ms. Bernette got up to go back to her desk. "Ok darling. Don't forget to keep this little secret between me and you."

"I promise," I assured her.

Each day got easier. Everyone was getting acclimated to all of life's changes. Langley and I were still fresh in love. Miles and Zach had a routine which included spending time with what I now knew as my siblings at the Koperneils. Everything was in order.

Before we knew it, the school year was over. Ms. Nancy asked if I wanted to send the kids but Miles insisted on staying and spending his summer at the center. We placed Zach in a kid's summer camp filled with activities for his age group. My mother was already planning another trip to Brazil. The first trip was the best. I learned so much about our culture and the places we visited were rich with knowledge. There was so much more to learn, so I did not have any objections on another trip there.

Funding barely came through for The Cemetery. The annual technology fair was coming up and there were groups registering to present their projects. I was surprised to see Miles was participating again. He kept his project a secret from me this time.

The day of the fair rolled around and I couldn't wait to see what Miles was going to present. I asked Langley if he knew anything about this project, and he said no. Just as before, Miles stood there waiting patiently for his turn. Mr. Koperniel was directing the crowd as usual with the three questions per project. Miles was the last presenter. He rolled his project cart to the center of the stage. Me, Langley and Carl waited in anticipation and the whole auditorium was quiet. No one knew what was about to happen, but people were at the edge of their seats. He removed the covering and there it was. A shiny key similar to the one from the year before. Miles removed the key from its clinched place, gripped it in his hand, rose it straight up in the air allowing the sun rays to shine directly through the center giving off a glisten identical to the stone in his bracelet and the same stone I remembered from the wind chime. "I present to you...The Clock."

www.ingramcontent.com/pod-product-compliance
Lightning Source LLC
Chambersburg PA
CBHW071146170626
46809CB00002B/797